ISSIE MAC

HEATHER WHITFORD ROCHE

THE RURAL PUBLISHING COMPANY

First published by The Rural Publishing Company 2023.

Print (Paperback): 978-1-923008-11-3
eBook: 978-1-923008-12-0

The story, all names, characters, and incidents portrayed in this production are fictitious.

Cover Design: The Rural Publishing Company
Layout and Typesetting: The Rural Publishing Company

The Rural Publishing Company
Email: hello@theruralpublishingcompany.com.au
Website: https://theruralpublishingcompany.com.au

For my sister, Kaye

Prologue

Melbourne 1935

They'd secretly feared this moment would never arrive and they would be forced to face the inevitable. Losing two children at childbirth has taken a toll only the two of them understand. They could not endure losing a third. This was their last chance to be a family, a real family. So much rested on the birth of this baby. He can barely believe they have a child, a live child.

The branches of the autumnal trees in the hospital grounds waver in the afternoon breeze; the light from the window flickers across the room. Late April promises shortened days, leaves thick on the ground and cosy nights. But today the world is on the outside and all that matters is in this room – a small miracle has arrived and changed everything.

Knill lifts the baby from her mother's arms as if she's a piece of delicate porcelain. He wraps his large hands around the small bundle. In the baby's perfect cherub face, inky blue eyes and mass of thick hair, he can foresee the future for the three of them.

'She's beautiful, Lily.'

'She will bring us happiness, Knill,' his wife says, her voice tired but exultant. 'But we need to choose a name, a strong name. We could call her Isabella.'

The faint smell of antiseptic wafts in the background and Knill's shoes squeak on the linoleum floor as he carries their newborn child to the window. The soft shawl trails across his trousers as he stares beyond the room, his thoughts far away.

He returns to Lily's bedside.

'Isabella is perfect. And she should carry the names of the women before her. Isabella Lily Eliza McMillan.'

A cautious look crosses Lily's face.

'Are you sure we are not passing on bad luck to our daughter? Remember, Knill, the women before her have suffered. My mother and baby sister died, and Eliza's child was taken from her.'

'What's all this about bad luck? You and my mother are strong women; Isabella is our good luck. You've said yourself she will bring us happiness.'

As he passes Isabella back to her, their hands clasp together over their precious bundle and their eyes lock in a fleeting moment of disquiet. The baby squirms beneath their touch as the afternoon shadows fall across the hospital grounds and the soft clatter of a tram in the distance is the only intrusion to the stillness of the room.

PART ONE

Melbourne

1956

Chapter One

Isabella

I board the tram in Elizabeth Street to the clanging of the catenaries and the din of paperboys calling '*The Sun*, get your paper.' Outside the window, the crowd weaves in every direction across the intersection. Where do these people go each day when they hop off the tram and vanish around corners and into laneways? Sometimes I'm tempted to disappear with them and join their mysterious and exciting lives. Instead, I simply sigh and let myself be carried to the university. I promise myself this year will be different.

The tram is airless and the heat already oppressive. It's when I reach over to open the nearest window, I see him sitting two seats back. He's immaculately dressed as usual, wearing a light, blue shirt, a navy-spotted tie, dark trousers with perfect pleats and his jacket looped across his arm. His blond curly hair is carefully combed from a part on the left. He catches my eye and raises his eyebrows in acknowledgement. I pray he gets off before me, but I know he won't. The tram grinds to a stop and the passengers begin to alight. He's behind me now as I'm blocked by a woman slowly collecting her bags.

'Isabella. I was hoping to see you.'

'Not sure why.'

'Can we talk?'

'I don't think so.'

The footpath is crowded with people scurrying by, but Alexander remains with me. We make our way shoulder to shoulder along the shaded path to the campus.

For a moment we are separated but he drops back and waits for me to catch up. Why is he pursuing me again? A hint of Old Spice aftershave wafts in the air between us and sweat beads appear on his forehead. There's something different about his demeanour this morning, an unfamiliar strain to his voice.

'Midday tomorrow?'

'We agreed it wasn't right and ...'

'Please, Isabella, it's important. I have something to tell you. Just this once. Tomorrow, at the Grattan Street entrance, the old oak tree near the Gatekeeper's Cottage.'

His hair glistens in the sun as he draws away toward the Old Arts Building with his tan briefcase swinging by his side. Dr Alexander Sadler attracts attention wherever he goes on campus. He's handsome and younger than most of the other lecturers. It's rumoured he has a big future in academia.

And now I'll have to make up some excuse to get out of work tomorrow without making Mother suspicious. My lack of resistance frustrates me. I'm so eager to meet him and hear what he has to say. It flies in the face of my resolution to end all association with him. Just one chance meeting and I'm agreeing to see him again. Alexander always has that effect on me. It's been the problem all along.

Chapter Two

Isabella

Last year I was lucky. I managed satisfactory end-of-year results, but I know my luck may not last. 'Knuckle down,' Father would say. He's a strong believer in the power of hard work in achieving success.

Father has always been the steady influence in our lives. It is clear to me, he has learnt to compromise in life, but if I'm to be honest, he gives in on matters too easily, especially to Mother. When I was growing up I would overhear her chastising him for being 'too soft' on me.

'She has to learn to manage tricky situations, Knill.'

'Being teased at school is more than tricky, it's unfair.'

'Knill, most people think Isabella looks like your side of the family. Yes, she has Chinese features, but she's lucky: she has the best of both worlds.'

'Well, I think it's hard for her. She's only a child.'

'When I was her age, I was picked on at school. I was the only Chinese kid in the grade. My father would say, "Too bad, just work harder and get good marks," and that's what I did. You're too soft on her, Knill. Isabella must learn to work hard: it's the most important thing.'

From an early age I was expected to be a high achiever at school. The family expectation was mainly unspoken but crystal clear: I was to get top marks and go to university, just like Mother. This goal was non-negotiable, and I didn't disagree; I enjoyed learning and became quite studious. But my parents never knew just how bad the bullying was at first. I was one of only a handful of Australian-Chinese at school and the fact I didn't look as Chinese as the others meant nothing. 'Hey, Isabella, what's in your lunch box? Dims sims and fried rice?'

I learnt to stand up for myself, though – it was that or be miserable.

I went on to make good friends and later in high school became quite outspoken, often standing up for the rights of others. This earned me popularity. The early days of being teased for being different quickly disappeared. And yet I always remembered overhearing Mother tell Father he was 'too soft' on me. I knew then it was my mother who set the rules and Father was the one to soften the edges. Regardless, I had a clear path set for me and here I was walking the path. To an outsider it may have appeared to be a life full of opportunities. But to me, my future was decided. I still feel the same way. There are no decisions left for me to make. In fact, making my own decisions is a life skill I've had no exposure to.

***

At the start of my second year at university I met Alexander. He stood out among a crowd, always smartly attired, well-mannered and always with a flashing smile at the ready. I would sit in the middle section of the tram so I could see him when he hopped on in the morning. Mostly we alighted at the same stop and walked the same shady path to the university grounds. I wasn't the only student to be noticed by him. Other students went out of their way to seek his company as well. I was no exception but for some reason, one morning, he came forward and singled me out.

'Did I see you at one of my lectures last week?' he asked.

'Yes, I sat in on a couple of arts lectures.'

'You're not doing arts?'

'I'm studying law, second year.'

He gave me a quizzical grin. I could feel my face heating under his playful scrutiny. His eyes sparkled as he noticed; seemingly I'd amused him.

'So, what's a second-year law student doing sneaking around the arts lectures?'

'I was curious.' We continued walking.

'Mm ... curiosity. That's exactly what I'd like some of my students to have more of. Is there not enough stimulation in the law faculty for you?'

I returned his smile. 'To be honest, you are exactly right. Sometimes law is too dry, too predictable – and yet it also has a way of exciting me, all the possibility around justice.'

His face became serious and he slowed his pace.

'I'm Alexander Sadler, by the way.'

'Isabella McMillan.' When I told him my name, he turned to me, his head tilted. It happens all the time. People think I should have a Chinese name. 'My mother is Chinese-Australian, my father is Australian, well, sort of.'

'A pleasing combination, I see.' We came to the end of the path; I could hardly keep walking with him as I needed to go in the opposite direction.

'I've got a class to go to.'

He looked at me quite sincerely. 'Good to meet you, Isabella.'

He strode off with purpose, but as he reached the Old Arts Building, he turned and looked back. I moved instantly, not wanting him to think I'd been watching him.

My lecture dragged on. Something about my encounter with Alexander left me feeling rattled and jumpy. My friend Louise found me sitting under the dappled shade of a lemon-scented gum tree in the Old Quad. Dropping her canvas bag and an armful of books, she sat cross-legged facing me.

'I saw you leave early. Are you sick?'

'I'm just over all this. Tired of pretending to like this place.'

Louise raised her eyebrows at me as if to say, 'here we go again'.

***

After the first meeting with Alexander, we sometimes struck up a conversation on the tram on our way to university. At first it all seemed perfectly innocent except I knew it wasn't. I watched out for him, slowing on the footpath for him to catch up. I was dizzy with anticipation; my thoughts were awash with a need to be close to him. My fascination with Alexander began to occupy almost all my thinking.

Our conversations on the way to and from campus became routine. I abandoned my university friends to fit in with Alexander's schedule, and although I attended my own lectures my thoughts were never far away from seeing him later in the day or the following morning. Our infatuation with each other moved up a notch when Alexander suggested we meet for lunch in Carlton. My thoughts were scattered all morning. Should students meet with lecturers outside the university?

The University Café in Lygon Street, a short walk from the university, was a place Alexander often frequented. We sat at a small timber table beside the stairs. Around us the sound of voices loomed large, lured to the café by authentic Italian fare. The regular café goers appeared to know people at the other tables and were clearly enjoying themselves, calling across the room and joking with the waiters. Alexander was comfortable, smiling; I was fidgety and on edge.

'So why law, Isabella?'

'I didn't have much choice really. My mother is a lawyer and so was her father and on it goes.'

'Following in their footsteps …'

'No. Well, yes. I suppose it looks like that. And I work for my mother as well.'

He grinned. 'A family practice waiting for you when you finish your degree?'

'I'm not too sure what I'll do. I might even change courses.'

'Sounds like the voice of discontent.'

'Just following my own intuition, maybe.'

'Do your family know about your ambivalence?'

'No, but it's not up to them.' I shifted in my chair and looked him straight in the eye. 'I have my own opinions, you know, and if I want to change my mind I'm perfectly entitled to do so.'

He raised his hands in front of him. 'I'm not saying you shouldn't do what you want, just wondering how difficult it would be for you. But I can see you have a mind of your own. That's always a good thing.'

A wide grin crossed his face and my indignation subsided. We laughed and relaxed back in our skinny bentwood chairs. One of the waiters placed two tumblers of red wine and a basket of crusty bread on the table. Two plates of spaghetti arrived soon after and the awkward liaison between us as student and lecturer shifted to one of friendship. But of course, it was something else altogether.

From then on, the relationship intensified. We sometimes met in the leafy surrounds of the Carlton Gardens and stole languid afternoons together. In the cooling shade of the giant white poplars with the warm summer breeze drifting across our skin, we discussed the law and my interpretation of what I was studying, and we talked about literature. Alexander's specialty was eighteenth-century literature, but he also had a fascination for the Augustan era. My own reading of literature was limited to seventeenth-century prose and poetry classics – Shakespeare, Benjamin Jonson, John Donne, Francis Bacon, and a few others. I was no match for the depth of Alexander's knowledge and yet he never tired of talking and explaining intriguing aspects of some of the texts. His face took on a glow when he talked about this unbridled love of his.

Our meetings in the gardens were the real beginning of our relationship and left me reeling in admiration for Alexander. I had no doubt I'd met the man I wanted to be with forever. He listened to me and took me seriously. For the first time in my life, I felt like an adult, an equal with a sense of confidence in my own ability well beyond anything I'd ever experienced. However, there was one sticking point between us, an issue we avoided on most of these intimate stolen occasions. Whenever it was raised it was like a sudden thunderstorm on a beautiful day.

'I've asked you to let me worry about my circumstances. It's my problem to deal with and I have it in hand.'

'But we have no future if you're married to someone else.'

'You know Helen and I are going to end our marriage.'

'I can't see how you can do that easily. On what grounds, Alexander?'

'We both agree the marriage is over. I'll stay here. Helen will go back to New South Wales. She's unhappy. She dislikes Melbourne and wants to be closer to her parents.'

'You can't get a divorce just because you're unhappy; it doesn't work that way. And what about the children?'

'The boys will go with their mother.' He straightens his shoulders and pulls his arm from my shoulder and picks at the blades of glass beneath us. 'Do we have to discuss this? It will ruin our day.'

'We do have to discuss it. There are only three reasons to get a divorce: cruelty, desertion, or adultery. Don't tell me you're going to involve me. My family would be mortified, and if I'm named as part of your adultery, it could ruin my chance of having a legal career.'

'A divorce will have to wait. Isabella my love, you're being dramatic – of course I wouldn't involve you.'

'What makes you think you'd have any choice? Helen could have you investigated. I know about this, Alexander. You forget I work in a legal practice and happen to be studying law.'

'Enough of this miserable talk. Your beautiful face is not supposed to look so serious. Smile, Isabella, everything is fine. I promise you.'

Over the months we met whenever we could. He was all I could think about from one meeting until the next. My half-year marks were poor. A couple of my lecturers asked me about my grades. I promised I would work harder in the second half of the year and make up some ground, which I believed I could do. I kept this to myself; I didn't want Alexander to know I was close to failing. And I certainly didn't want Mother or Father to know. Mother and I had not been getting on well at home or in the office. She was constantly questioning me, wanting to know my whereabouts, even suggesting I was hiding something from them. And I was, but I could hardly tell them I was having a relationship with a lecturer who happened to be married with children. During this tense time, Father, in his usual fashion, did his best to keep the peace between Mother and myself.

My relationship with Alexander intensified to the stage where we occasionally stayed in a hotel together. They were sneaky times, me lying to my parents, telling them I was staying with my friend Louise, and Alexander, I suspect, although he never told me, was also lying to Helen about where he was. In the hotel room, he would run his hands through my hair and tell me how when he first saw me, he knew we were destined to be together. Being with Alexander and hearing his soothing words was enough to convince me all would be well. In those moments, if he was happy, so was I. But I was constantly worried about becoming pregnant.

'Leave it to me, Isabella. I promise we'll be fine ...'

'I'm not so sure. Condoms are not foolproof ...'

I did in fact leave our contraception to Alexander but felt uneasy about it. Not when we were together, when the excitement of making love to each other engulfed us, but later when I thought about the consequences of having sex outside the confines of marriage. And yet I took the chance, anything to be with him. Alexander gave me a sense of well-being, of being loved in a way that gave me freedom to be who I wanted to be. We were in love and what else could matter?

Well, as it turned out there were other matters to be dealt with. Alexander's flippant dismissal of anything to do with his marriage hung heavily over our exciting times together. At first, I tried to forget about it. Alexander was right: it was his problem to deal with, not mine. And yet, I disliked knowing after being with me he was going home to his wife and family. It nagged at me and became a bigger problem between us as time went on.

'You told me months ago, the two of you were separating, but you're still living with Helen. When is this going to end, Alexander?'

'It's not so simple. Arrangements have to be made.'

'Then leave the family home and live somewhere else yourself!'

Alexander told me I was becoming possessive.

At the end of the year, Alexander and his wife were still living together. I had managed to sit my second-semester exams and hand in assignments, but I was waiting for my results with dread. Had I done enough to pass, or would I be kicked out of law?

I'd arranged to meet Alexander in Carlton. He was late and when he finally arrived, he stank of beer. Flopping down in a chair opposite me in the busy café, he seemed distracted and testy.

'I was just about to leave. You're half an hour late.'

He sighed heavily. 'I've been to my faculty Christmas break-up, Isabella.'

'Is something wrong? You're not yourself.'

'You're not going to start on me too, are you?'

I felt my confusion and anger rising. A voice in my head telling me this wasn't how it should be. Suddenly, I was on my feet. 'I'm beginning to feel taken for granted, Alexander. All year we've been sneaking time together, all the time pretending it didn't matter that you have a wife and children. You haven't ended your marriage. You cajole me into believing your separation from Helen is about to happen and you dare ask me not to start on you?'

Alexander pushed back his chair and stood in front of me. 'Calm down, Isabella, this is ridiculous – people are watching.'

'Let them watch. I'm past caring and I'm tired of your lies and pretence. We're finished, Alexander.'

Chapter Three

Isabella

The first time one of Mother's clients visited her office, they said, 'It's like stepping back in time.' And it is. At Sing, McMillan and Associates, faded Chinese paintings hang on the wall above the dark, lacquered chairs, lamps glow at each end of the polished cedar counter and a musty scent of years past wafts in the air. When I was a child, Mother would bring me in to visit and I would run behind the timber counter and climb on one of the large leather chairs. My grandfather would leave his office to gather me up, swing me joyfully toward the ceiling, 'Isabella, Isabella, Pa's beautiful girl'.

Mother's law firm now employs four people: Mother, Danny Gibbons, Lucy and me.

Danny joined the practice after university to complete his articles. He's twenty-three, quiet and unassuming with a confident nature and dry sense of humour. It's said he could get a job with any of the big firms in town but his loyalty to Mother keeps him here. I'm so grateful for his presence; he makes what could be a dull working day, bearable.

Mother is over-worked, and I have a lecture to attend and the meeting with Alexander. For so long now, we've tried to talk her into employing a legal secretary to cover the senior clerical duties. It's out of the question to even suggest she employ another lawyer to help her and Danny. Even getting her to employ Lucy – who makes the appointments, sorts the daily mail, and attends to the typing – was a battle. We are always running against the clock and there is a never-ending stack of files to action and appointments to keep. However, Mother insists we can manage. Her independence and stubbornness are a problem we all dance around. Since Pa Joseph died, Mother has managed the legal practice, often working late into the night to complete the day's work. Father and I think she drives herself hard in memory of her father, who worked tirelessly to build a successful legal practice and make a life for them in Australia. She has enormous respect for him.

Danny and I sometimes sneak out to the tiny yard at the back of the practice to have a cigarette. A habit certainly not sanctioned by Mother. We stand on the small square of concrete beside the metal rubbish bin, lighting up and waving the cigarette smoke away from the back door. The patch is devoid of plant life except for a spindly plumbago in the corner drooping forward in search of enough sun to survive. The trams in Collins Street clang in the background.

'You're a bit quieter these days, Isabella. Haven't seen you and Louise at the dances for weeks. Anything wrong?'

'You don't miss much, Danny. No, I'm fine. Study and work and …'

'And what?'

'Mother is always on my back. She doesn't understand I have a life outside the family and this practice.'

'She has high expectations of you, Isabella.'

'She always has. And it doesn't help when I have other complications to deal with, Danny.'

I drag heavily on my cigarette as Danny raises his eyebrows. For a split second I consider confiding in him about my secret meetings with Alexander. But somehow the moment passes.

'Complications? I'm always available for a chat, Isabella.'

'Thanks, Danny.'

He stubs his cigarette, shrugs. 'Well, there's work to do, I guess.' He picks up his cigarettes and heads inside but I notice the puzzled look he gives me as he holds the door open.

***

It's late morning when I flick on the radio. Mother is out of the office and the waiting room is empty. Lucy raises her eyebrows. Having the radio on in business hours is not approved of. But she's a music lover and begins to toe tap to 'Blue Suede Shoes'. Danny, who knows all the hit parade songs and goes to the Port Melbourne Town Hall rock n' roll dances at the weekends, turns up the volume and before we know it the three of us are jiving around the waiting room and singing at the top of our voices, that is, before the door swings open and Mother steps in. She stops dead, glares at us, then marches to her office without saying a word. Lucy scoots for the radio and turns it off in one swift action, leaving Danny and me still laughing at the look on Mother's face.

'It's no laughing matter, you two; I could lose my job over this,' says Lucy as she flees back to her desk in the reception area.

Danny tries to smother his laughter.

'Mother would never be so small minded, Lucy. It's me who will get the telling off.'

Danny winks at me. 'Judging by the smile that broke out on Mrs McMillan's face as she headed for her office, I don't think any of us have anything to worry about.'

Shortly after, Mother is back, laden with files to pass to Lucy. 'Isabella, don't make yourself late for lectures.' Today, her hair is pulled back tightly behind her ears and the grey streaks are more pronounced than ever.

'There's plenty of time. I'll finish these files first.'

'You need a clear head for class, Isabella. And less lipstick perhaps.'

I ignore the lipstick quip but she's right about needing a clear head. Third year promises to be more taxing than my first and second year. Sometimes I'm tempted to talk to Danny about my ambivalence, but I haven't yet. After all, he managed to get through university and his articles without doubts, with top marks. His parents were proud of him. And he achieved it all in the quiet way he is respected for.

As I'm walking toward the university, the day is hot and the north wind suppresses any hint of coolness in the air. Dust swirls from the nearby park and people on the footpath hold onto their hats and belongings. My thoughts are still on my parents as I quicken my own steps to escape the ghastly conditions. I compare them to Danny's, not that Danny's parents had it easy, but their circumstances were different. Danny's mother was demanding and difficult, but his father was quiet and unruffled; he lived his life and left Danny to do the same. I suspect Danny had the privilege of being male.

Like Danny's father, nothing rattles Father, in fact nothing rattles Mother, but the two of them respond to life in different ways. Father is relaxed and humorous and open to new ideas. His role as chief traffic manager at Victorian Railways is a big responsibility but he takes it in his stride. Sometimes, I think it was his country town upbringing with his older adoptive parents who allowed his generous nature to thrive. It makes me smile fondly when I think of him with his thick head of grey hair. When I tease him about it, he throws back his head and laughs. 'A sign of wisdom, Isabella. I've had to earn this grey privilege.'

Mother's seriousness, her need for everything to be precise, is more difficult to manage. People say how lucky I am to have them as parents. Well, I agree, but sometimes living up to Mother's high expectations and Father's adoration can be frustrating. Mother also has particularly strict ideas about how I, her only daughter, should be in the world. I know they love me and want the best for me, however, sometimes I feel I can't breathe or be myself. And one other thing – I think they love me too much.

Chapter Four

Lily

From the open door of her office, Lily watches her daughter at work with her thick black hair pulled high into a fashionable ponytail that swishes back and forth. Lily's aware of the admiring glances her clients give Isabella when they come into the office. She's taller by many inches than Lily – she gets her height from Knill and his mother, Eliza. Lily's proud Isabella is a confident young woman who people warm to. Lily at the same age was shy and unsure of how to behave. Her Chinese parents were reserved and humble and encouraged Lily to be the same. They came to Australia for a new start, full of hope and purpose. Lily's mother died giving birth to Lily's sister, who also died two days later. Lily had only been three years old when it happened, almost too young to remember the loss of her mother and the enormous toll the grief took on her father.

Lily's father's devotion to family manifested itself in how hard he worked to make a successful life for the two of them. He did it for Lily, to make up for losing her mother so young. With the help of family friends and a housekeeper, her father pursued his dream to establish a legal practice in Melbourne and to raise a dutiful daughter who went on to study law and work with him in his practice. And all these years later, she has a daughter of her own.

Mothering Isabella hasn't been easy for Lily. From the very start, even as a toddler, Isabella was strong-willed. As a child and as a teenager, she exerted a desire to do things her way. So, when she announced, or rather *agreed,* to study law, Lily was relieved. She was aware she and her daughter held different views but she expected

Isabella to honour family traditions, and when she entered university Lily was so proud of her. Knill wasn't as sure about Isabella's choice, she knew. He was concerned at some level Isabella was yielding to family pressure to conform on this crucial matter, was unable to say no. After all, Isabella knew how important it was for her mother.

Lily smiles as she thinks about finding the three of them dancing in the office when she returned from her doctor's appointment. Daniel, tall and handsome, singing along with whatever the crazy song was, Lucy with her red curls flying as she spun around in circles and Isabella laughing loudly, her hair shimmering across her back as she and Daniel danced together. Yes, it was totally unprofessional but a joyous moment to witness. Lily secretly wishes she'd had more fun as a young person, maybe been free to express herself in other forms. But her role in life was to be successful and respectable. These were the wishes of her father. She understood and accepted it.

Isabella doesn't quite have the same sense of needing to achieve and she's unaware her parents know about her average grades. Lily saw the letter from the university in Isabella's room and read her results. They waited for Isabella to tell them herself but when she didn't, Knill persuaded Lily to let the matter rest.

There are times when Lily feels cross with Nan Eliza, Knill's mother. She has too much influence. She puts money in Isabella's bank account each month and encourages Isabella to think broadly and to voice her views. Knill asks Lily to be tolerant of Eliza. Her life hasn't been an easy one, but she adores her granddaughter and wants the best for her.

But Lily is uneasy. There is something about Isabella's demeanour over the past year unsettling her. She's become secretive and irritable. Even Lucy and Daniel have noticed. Lily asked Knill to talk with his daughter, but Isabella brushed off his concerns, telling him there was nothing to worry about.

Knill never experienced family pressure to conform in the way Lily did when she was growing up. Knill's adoptive parents loved him, that's for sure, but their love was the sort that allowed him to follow his own interests. They supported him to take piano and violin lessons, learning skills they themselves hadn't been able to accomplish. He played cricket and football with his cousins and rode his bike around the town. It wasn't until Knill was a young man and discovered he was adopted that his life became turbulent.

What was the turbulence in Isabella's life? She had everything she needed. And why couldn't she manage it the way Lily had tried to teach her? What was wrong?

Chapter Five

Isabella

I walk down the shady footpath toward the Gatekeeper's Cottage entrance. Alexander is talking with a couple of students under the oak trees near the gate. The young women, with arms full of books, are chatting excitedly. Their voices rising above the hum of the traffic outside the gate. I assume they are students in the Arts Faculty. Not many females are doing law, but in arts there is no shortage. I envy them, their fascinating debates on obscure and mind-broadening subjects. Far removed from the practicalities of law.

Alexander sees me, ends his conversation, and picks up his briefcase from under the tree. I wait for the students to move on. They seem reluctant but eventually they sidle away, glancing at us over their shoulders.

'I wasn't sure you'd come, Isabella.'

'Tell me why I'm here?'

'Everything is about to change.'

'Again?'

In one word, we are back where we've always been.

'It's complicated, Isabella. Do you think a father just ups and leaves his kids?'

'Of course not. And isn't that why our friendship had to end?'

'A friendship! Is that all it meant to you, Isabella?'

'As it turned out, there was no way it could have been anything else.'

'But I need you, Isabella. I can't be without you.'

The fantasies of us being together as man and wife into the future return. Finishing my studies and practising with Mother, even taking over the practice one day. Alexander becoming a professor at the university. Maybe children, our own children. I know how happy Mother and Father would be about grandchildren. But I also know, given the circumstances of Alexander's marriage and children, they wouldn't approve of the relationship between us. And Alexander is twelve years older than me. No, they would be so disappointed in me. They must never know about Alexander. I can't do that to them.

'It could all be different now,' he says quietly.

'It doesn't sound like it, Alexander.'

'I'm going to England.' His words are sharp in the early-afternoon hue. I swing around to face him.

'England. When?'

'Straightaway … I've received a posting to Oxford University for two years.'

'And … and Helen, is she going with you?'

'No. She and the boys are staying in Australia.' He wipes away beads of perspiration on his forehead. His blond curls are falling over his brow. I can tell he's troubled. What should be a happy time, securing a position at Oxford, appears fraught with ambivalence. For someone who is about to embark on an overseas journey, he looks sad.

As we stand under the shade of the oak tree, the earlier hot north wind has subsided and a welcoming breeze is springing up from the south.

'You and Helen haven't parted ways?'

'Helen and the boys are moving to be closer to her parents outside of Sydney.'

'So, you won't see your children for two years?'

'It's what we've agreed.'

I don't know what Alexander wants from me. My feelings toward him are dangerously strong. As his arm brushes mine, I remember the night we talked for hours as we sat in the open window of our hotel room. He listened patiently and lovingly to me until the small hours of the morning. He understood just how I felt. I've never talked to anyone like that before, never.

But my memories of the hurt from last year are also fresh in my mind. I'm not blameless – I allowed myself to be part of a hopeless situation. And I made my decision last December. The relationship has no future.

'You know I love you, Isabella. No one has ever had a hold on me like you. It hasn't been easy for you, I know.'

'I'm sorry, Alexander, but I don't know what you expect me to say or do.'

He takes my arm. I pull away from his closeness, from the temptation. As I straighten from his touch, he takes a deep breath.

'Come to England with me.'

The southerly breeze has picked up, blowing the hair from my face, muffling the traffic and the conversations of the people on the path. Alexander's hand still gently rests on my arm. His expression, hard to interpret.

'Go ... go with you ... to England?'

'It will be a new start for us. The way it should have been last year. This is the turning point. You've talked of travelling and the chance to explore what you want to do with your own life. There's nothing to stop you. This is our opportunity.'

CHAPTER SIX

KNILL

Knill often feels he doesn't belong in this house. It's beautiful, but he can't quite understand why Lily wanted to live in such a grand home. Fondly, he thinks about the small single-fronted cottage in Moodie Street, Caulfield, thatthey moved into when they were first married. How hard he had worked to paint the walls and ceilings and how, bit by bit, they bought furniture for each room. Lily enjoyed choosing new wallpapers, bedspreads, curtains and passage rugs. The house sparkled with freshness and they both delighted in planting the garden out in annuals each year. In the back yard they had lemon and crab apple trees, which were well established before they moved in.

After her father's sudden death, Lily became the senior practitioner in the legal firm and they purchased the house in East Melbourne – 'to be closer to the practice', Lily reasoned. The Federation-era house is large, too large for the three of them – but Lily had loved it at first sight: its red brick bay windows, timber-lined passageways and a spacious dining room. In Knill's view, the house is too formal, unwelcoming even. Friends and family got lost on their first visit. When quests joked about getting lost and laughed, Knill joined in, but Lily couldn't see the joke. Knill thinks Lily feels the house is her way of having something for herself, something she's earned. He's tried to understand it, to see it from her point of view. And if living in a beautiful house, one where everyone gets lost, makes Lily happy, he can accept it.

This new house has a large garden, keeping Knill occupied. He enjoys his time tending the garden beds, cleaning the small pond and trimming the large peppercorn tree that trails its tangled branches across one corner of the garden. They often sit under its welcome shady canopy in summer.

Perhaps they should sit there tonight as they wait for Isabella. But Knill doesn't move.

Instead, he and Lily look at each other across the polished dining table. So much has changed since they met when Knill was twenty and Lily was eighteen. Years of trying to have a baby, two heartbreaking stillbirths: a boy and a tiny girl. And then the most healing of all life events, the birth of Isabella – how they adored their little girl. As did Knill's birth mother, Eliza, and Hattie, the daughter of Knill's adoptive mother.

'She didn't tell you anything about where she was going or why?' asks Knill.

'She had a lecture.' Lily looks at the clock on the mantelpiece for the tenth time in as many minutes. 'But she should have been home long before now.'

'And I've been thinking she's been more settled of late. Unlike last year's comings and goings.' Knill pushes his fork into the lemon pudding before sliding the plate away. 'Still, she's an adult now, not a child.'

'Daniel asked about her several times. He has his own worries at home about his mother being ill again. Between Isabella's absence and Daniel's distractedness, we didn't get much done today.'

'There's always tomorrow, Lily.'

'There is, but I won't tolerate another year of Isabella being secretive and scattered. It's time she showed a better attitude, and you must support me on this, Knill. I insist.'

Knill fears the situation between Lily and Isabella is about to become trickier than ever.

Chapter Seven

Issie

Mother and Father are waiting for me when I arrive home. They are still seated at the dining room table with the remnants of their evening meal in front of them. They look relieved to see me; they fuss around and ask if I would like my dinner.

'No, I'll fix something later.'

'You were expected back in the office,' says Mother.

'Yes, I'm sorry. I took longer than ... and I met Louise. For goodness' sake, I'm not a child.'

Father rises, his chair scraping on the polished floorboards. For a moment I see the anguish in his eyes as he hesitates and then steps toward me.

'Isabella, is something wrong?'

'No more than usual. I mean no, not really ...'

'No more than usual? Isabella, stop talking in riddles and tell us what's bothering you,' says Mother. Their eyes lock on me, Father standing in front of me, Mother still seated at the table.

'Stop insisting I tell you every detail of my life.'

'If you don't tell us, how are we supposed –'

'If you must know, I've been thinking of taking some time away from study and work. Maybe travelling for a while and –'

'Travel? The year has just begun and if you ...' Mother stops as Father turns to her and calmly places his hand on her shoulder, a gesture I've seen many times when she starts to become indignant. The clock on the dresser ticks its brassy seconds with annoying precision. Mother's lips remain pursed.

'What's all this about, Isabella?' Father asks. 'Travel and time away? It's a bit sudden – has something happened?'

I shouldn't have broached the subject, but I've gone too far now.

'Do I ever get a say in anything? I think not, it's always decided for me – when I work, what I study. I need a life too, you know. It was different for the two of you, you knew what you wanted, and you made your own choices.' Speaking out suddenly feels a relief.

'That's not true, Isabella. Your father and I had many challenges in our early life, challenges we hope you will not have. But it seems you don't appreciate that at all.'

The room is silent. Mother gets up and starts to clear the dishes from the dining table.

Father rubs his brow.

'And what is it you want to do?'

'I want to be free to make up my own mind for once.'

I know I've upset my parents. They are confused by my outburst, and I should have the courage to speak to them about what I'm contemplating. Alexander's request has thrown me into turmoil. Meeting him today reignited everything. I am ... dizzy with my feelings for him. My longing for him. I still love Alexander, but I also know I shouldn't.

'A fresh start so we can be together in our own right,' he rationalised. 'Not sneaking around in the shadows like naughty kids, feeling we are doing the wrong thing by everyone else.'

'There are just too many obstacles.'

'Obstacles can be managed, Isabella.' He was so sure, so convincing. 'England will free us to be independent. For the first time, you can make your own decisions and I can live with the person I love and not feel guilty.'

'It sounds simple but ... but it's not simple.'

'You're over-thinking the consequences and ignoring the benefits, Isabella. Don't you believe we are entitled to be happy?'

***

I'm never good with decisions but this one is the biggest and most unexpected choice I've ever been asked to make. Alexander must know by tomorrow morning. I do have a current passport, which I acquired when Mother and I travelled to China when her uncle was dying. There's nothing to stop me from going with him … he's made a commitment to me by asking me to go to England with him. Finally, he is ending his marriage to Helen.

The lamp beside my bed is comforting as I sink down into the familiar covers. Mother wanted everything to be perfect as usual, but I insisted on pale yellow and green bedroom furnishings. Tonight, this room seems so immature. My childhood dolls, all in pretty costumes lovingly made by Aunt Hattie, are lined up from smallest to largest along the white shelves painted by Father. The gold-framed embroideries, also meticulously stitched by Aunt Hattie, hang near the window. The wardrobe is full of clothes – I always had the prettiest clothes in school. Mother always liked me to be dressed well, and we often shopped at Myer for my beautiful dresses. For some reason they still hang here, a reminder of my fortunate childhood. My adult clothes and shoes are squashed to one end of the wardrobe.

All I know is here. My special cups sit on my dresser. I remember when Nan Eliza gave them to me for my thirteenth birthday. They were individually wrapped in purple tissue in a white box. The look on Mother's and Father's faces when I unwrapped the first cup – so fine, almost transparent and swirling with vibrant blue and green colours. Nan fended off my parents' protest – 'Isabella is old enough to look after them.' I knew they were precious.

All this luxury surrounding me, representing my life so far. All given to me with love. Given because they want me to have the life they didn't at my age. Sometimes,

I think my parents were the lucky ones. Sure, times were tough, things happened that shouldn't have, but they lived in their own shadows and ran their own races. They didn't have a chorus of barrackers and admirers watching their every move from the sidelines.

I did see Louise today. At least there was one thing I didn't lie to my parents about.

'England!' Louise's shock was so loud the word lifted above all the noise of the café for a moment. 'That's ridiculous. Surely ... surely, you're not considering going with him?' Louise put her glass on the table and leant forward, her eyes full of concern.

'I've never done anything that doesn't fit the blueprint my parents have for me. I always do the right thing for them, for Nan Eliza and even Aunt Hattie.'

'It costs money to go to England. What are you going to do?'

'Alexander will buy me a one-way ticket, and I have some money in my bank account.'

'But he's married!'

'Unhappily married. Soon he'll be separated, like he promised all along.'

'He's asking you to sacrifice everything for him and so suddenly. I can't believe you're even considering giving up your studies and throwing away your future to leave ... to leave on the whim of a man who already has a wife and children. It's so reckless.'

'It might be reckless, but it's not a whim. He loves me, Louise. And I love him ... I wish I didn't, but he's all I can think about.'

The hum of the café seemed far away. I barely registered the clatter of a cup and plate falling off a serving tray and the young waitress bending to scoop up the remnants of chocolate éclair among the broken china. I was lost in my thoughts and troubled by the enormity of the decision before me.

Chapter Eight

Lily

It's two days after their discussion with Isabella. Rain thrashes against the window-panes in the dining room as Knill, with shaking hands, rereads Isabella's letter. The standard lamp by the door flickers as the wind plays havoc with the power lines, but the weather outside is no comparison to the silent storm within the house tonight. Both he and Lily have read the letter several times since finding it on the hall stand late in the afternoon.

Dear Mother and Father,

When you read this, I will have sailed for England.

I know this will come as a shock to you both. I've struggled to make the decision, but I think it's something I must do to stand on my own two feet and become independent.

I'm intending to stay in Oxford and will write to you when I arrive. I will be gone for some time and may enrol in arts at Oxford University, if they will take me.

Please don't worry about me and try not to be too angry with me. I will keep you informed about my whereabouts, and I'll write to Nan Eliza and Aunt Hattie from Oxford.

I love you both.

Isabella

Lily is straight-backed at the table, still in the clothes she wore to the office. 'I can barely believe she's done this, Knill. This is simply unforgivable.' She glares at him, willing him to make sense of Isabella's actions. He places the letter back on the table and turns to her, his shoulders bowed.

'We know she's been unhappy. She told us she wanted a change, but to sneak off only leaving this ...' He taps the letter, gets up from the table. 'Something must be wrong.'

'Well, obviously! But England.'

Lily watches him as he paces between the table and the window, staring into his own abyss.

The sound of the thrashing rain escalates and the bulb in the flickering lamp finally gives out.

'Isabella has always been strongheaded but not foolish. This is out of character,' says Lily.

'Has she ever talked to you about going to England?'

'Never seriously – always into the future. After she completed university, perhaps.'

'What about her passport?'

'Gone from the dresser drawer.'

'What will she do for money? She doesn't have much money.'

'She has Eliza's money – your mother has a few things to answer for, Knill.'

The tension in the room heightens at the mention of Eliza's name. Lily and Eliza are respectful of each other and in some ways can acknowledge they have both experienced events in their lives that have strengthened them as women. But they are different personalities, and Lily particularly dislikes Eliza's tendency to express her views honestly and without fear. Lily knows Knill will defend his mother regardless and she also knows that Knill sometimes feels caught in the crossfire between them.

'The money Isabella receives from my mother is minimal – not enough to set sail to England and sustain herself there.' Knill frowns as he folds the letter and slides it into his coat pocket.

'Then how did she afford her ticket? We need to talk to Eliza first thing in the morning.' Lily places her cup back on its saucer.

'She will have no idea about any of this, but yes, we need to tell her about Isabella's departure.'

Lily brushes a crumb of madeira cake from the small lace cloth and taps her fingers on the table in front of her.

'If only Isabella had spoken to us.'

'She probably thought we would try to talk her out of going.'

'Well, of course we would have!' Lily refills her teacup and the sound of the tea hitting the bottom of the fine porcelain is louder than the rain hitting the windows.

CHAPTER NINE

ELIZA

Each afternoon at two o'clock, Eliza walks the short distance to the Fitzroy Gardens. Although it is sunny, there's a faint hint of autumn revealing itself. Soon the summer days will be ending and the leaves will begin to shrivel in readiness to fall. She walks the long path, past the kiosk and the fairy tree and then across to her favourite timber seat under the large bunya pine. She comes here often, it's her quiet space, a place for reflection. Today, she has a serious consideration on her mind. Eliza suspects Knill and Lily will be concerned when she tells them she is thinking of one last trip to China. They expect her, given her age, to be content to live a more settled existence at this stage of her life.

When her husband, Fong Choon, died twenty years ago in China, Knill and Lily insisted she come home. She hadn't resisted. Coming back to Australia had its blessings. Her granddaughter, Isabella, has given Eliza a purpose in life. There's something about the way she feels when she's with Isabella, an unspoken understanding between them. Isabella reminds her of herself at the same age, full of life and a spirit that can at times be disconcerting for those around her. When people say Isabella is just like her grandmother, it warms her within. But Eliza knows not to make too much of it, especially when Lily is present. It's true, despite her Chinese heritage, Isabella has a strong resemblance to her own family, the O'Dares, in looks and temperament.

When she returned to Australia after Fong Choon died, Eliza felt like a stranger in the land she had lived in for almost three decades. Bereft. Purposeless. It's different now. Her life is settled and in the shade of her favourite tree, her mind is clear. She will return for a visit to China while she still can. Eliza has a strong belief she must go back to China, a place she grew to love. To experience it in a different time, to see it in the fullness of the moment, not clouded in sorrow. She knows it's her last chance. The limitations of age will eventually hold her in Melbourne.

Now she has the unenviable task of breaking the news to Knill and Lily. The family will think she's behaving foolishly, except for Isabella – she'll understand.

A warm north wind fans her face and overhead the white clouds have darkened without her realising. The beauty of this place is not lost on Eliza. She is fortunate to live close to such serenity. But, she muses, 'It will still be here when I return.'

***

Eliza senses something's amiss as soon as she opens her front door to the two of them standing on her porch. Lily is pale and her hair is severely pulled back away from her forehead, a style she prefers lately, and Knill is kneading the brim of his hat. Eliza offers to make tea, but they refuse, filing into the sitting room behind her.

'Isabella's left for England,' says Knill, blurting out the words as if they are choking him.

'England!' Eliza sits in her armchair by the window. 'Whatever are you talking about?'

'She left us a letter.' Knill pulls it out of his pocket and waves it in the air. 'She sailed yesterday.'

'Without telling you?'

'She talked about wanting to travel, but we had no idea she was planning this.'

'Did she discuss her plans with you, Eliza?' asks Lily.

'I can't believe this. England! No ... no, of course not. Why would she tell me and not you?'

The three of them sit surrounded by exotic paintings and wall hangings. Many of the treasures collected in China and from other destinations Eliza has travelled to. Plump blue cushions, polished timber coffee tables, floral rugs and squat vases in vivid greens and indigo make the room inviting and lived in. Eliza loves this room, but it cannot work its charms today.

'Because you provided her with the means,' says Lily.

'The means?' asks Eliza, straightening herself in her chair.

'You put money in her bank account each month.'

'A small gesture, for personal spending while she studied. It would never finance an overseas trip.' Eliza turns to Knill, who takes a deep breath.

'I think Lily means –'

'Stop speaking for me, Knill. Eliza knows exactly what I mean. She has spoilt Isabella and encouraged her with notions of self-importance since she was a child. Now look what's happened.'

'That's not true, Lily.' Eliza rubs her fingers briskly along the arm of her chair. 'How could you for one minute assume I would encourage Isabella, my own grand-daughter, to flee without a word? I would never do that.'

'Perhaps not directly, Eliza.' Lily's hands are clasped tightly. 'But you've always talked about standing up for yourself and having a voice. Isabella's heard your views on life too often. We must earn the right to make decisions. Running away from family is dishonourable.'

Eliza looks to Knill, her face flushed. 'Surely you don't think I had anything to do with this; it's absurd.'

Knill looks to have aged since Eliza last saw him. She hates to see her son in pain. 'None of us are to blame. We don't know why Isabella left and the only person who can tell us isn't here.'

Eliza wisely puts off telling Knill and Lily she is about to sail to China. She must allow the shock of Isabella's departure to settle before dropping the next bombshell. Besides, she is still smarting from Lily's cutting words. It's not the first time Lily has accused her of interfering. Eliza always knew her granddaughter would eventually follow her own convictions. But why England? And why now? A sense Isabella's adventure may not end well nags at her. She knows from experience, running away changes everything.

The stony silence stretches out. Eliza folds her sinewy hands in her lap. Lily is perched on the edge of her chair. Out of the corner of her eye, Eliza can see Knill's fingers at the brim of his hat. Outside, the sun is breaking through the morning clouds. The faint sound of a car horn and the echoes of a tram, as it rattles and scrapes in the distance, can be heard through the front window. But today, her favourite room provides no comfort.

CHAPTER TEN

DANNY

Danny knows something is wrong when Lily calls him to her office as soon as he arrives. The two of them usually have an office meeting a couple of times a week but this is out of the ordinary. Lily is pale and distracted. He sits facing her, waiting for her to say something, but she's staring absentmindedly across the room. Lily has been a good and fair boss and Danny knows he can speak to her about most matters, but she is always highly professional and takes the lead. This lapse is different. He coughs, and she quickly returns to the moment.

'Isabella's gone to England, Daniel.' Lily's face is still, her eyes empty. 'She left a letter saying she'll write. She told us not to worry.'

Danny is silent, putting it all together in his mind. Her words rush through his body, but he suppresses his initial reaction. Lily doesn't need that right now. He studies her, taking note of every tiny detail showing how badly his boss's world has been impacted. Details that few people would notice.

'When did she leave?

'Two days ago.'

'Has anyone checked the shipping departures?'

'Knill investigated it at once. There was a ship called the *Fairsea*. It sailed two days ago. The officials refused to give Knill any details of the passengers aboard.' Lily's hands are trembling.

'She mentioned enrolling in an arts degree at Oxford. I guess we'll all know when she writes. Knill immediately wanted to follow her to England, but we know we just have to wait until she writes.'

'And her university friends, did Louise know about it?'

'We spoke to her yesterday. She was reluctant to say, but it seems Isabella did speak to her about going to England. However, Louise didn't believe she would do it.'

'We talked every day … if she'd been planning this, I thought I would have at least picked up a hint of it.'

'We can't fathom it either.'

Danny opens his mouth to speak, thinks better of it, shakes his head, and walks out of Lily's office. He passes Lucy and a client in the waiting room and closes the door of his office. The shadowy light from the window falls across an area of his desk, making it patchy and dark. Annoyed, he flicks on the desk light. How could Isabella have left? And right under his nose? He had been fond of her, well, more than fond. She was one of the reasons he worked for Mrs McMillan. Every day they talked, laughed at each other's jokes and shared forbidden cigarettes. He knew Isabella had not been herself last year, but this year had been better for her. Hadn't it?

Lucy taps on the door.

'Danny, you have a client waiting.'

***

Later in the day, he stands in the doorway of Lily's office, briefcase in hand, tie loosened. He needs a beer and a bit of time to think clearly.

'Do you mind if I have the rest of the day off?'

'Take a break while you can, Daniel.'

Danny nods, pretends not to notice Lily's reddened eyes. Unspoken between them is the extra pressure Isabella's departure will result in for the practice. But it is not something to raise. They both know there's nothing to be gained by further talk about Isabella today.

PART TWO

England

1956

Chapter Eleven

Isabella

Waking up in this new country, its different sounds and early-morning light is exciting. I can hardly believe I'm in England and there is land underfoot.

It is such a relief to be off the ship. Our cabin was small and stuffy and the ship overcrowded. The food varied in quality and choice. Chicken and vegetable broth, hors d' oeuvres of sardines, mixed pickles, cooked ham and olives, and mains of fish fillets, corned beef and boiled chicken accompanied by beans, French and white, with boiled potatoes. Sweets were usually puddings with sauces and ice cream. We heard others complaining to the waiters. But none of this mattered to us – we spent our days reading and gazing at the ocean into the ever-distant horizon. Often our time was spent in the lounges socialising with other travellers. Alexander relished singing around the piano with a drink in hand.

He was relaxed on board the ship and we talked for hours about the opportunities that would open to us in Oxford. Continental Europe at our doorstep, a new job for Alexander and a bold new start for us. There we were, with our lives stretching ahead of us. It felt wonderful. The breeze on our skin, birds wheeling across the sky. We rarely talked about home – Alexander's wife and family, my parents. But there were private moments, when the enormity of our actions threatened to overshadow our happiness. An awful day when we were halfway to our new lives. A day I barely spoke.

I'm not proud of my actions – slinking off while my parents thought I was at university. The short letter I left them. No one to see me off at the wharf. If only I could have told them. There was a moment of hesitation when I was rushing out of the house with my suitcase just after Mother and Father left for work. My feet stilled with the thought that I shouldn't be doing this. But I did not stop for long. Instead, I jumped into a waiting taxi and drove to Port Melbourne to meet Alexander.

I did consider talking to Father. I'm now sure he would have listened to me, maybe even understood the predicament I found myself in, maybe even given me his blessing. But it was too risky. I never considered telling Mother. She would have at once given rational and sound reasons against me leaving and I would have been back to doubting myself all over again.

And Danny – dear, kind Danny, whom I confided in often and love like the brother I never had. What must he think of me and our friendship now? I should have told him; he would have understood. A tiny thought creeps up unbidden. Would he really? This last little while Danny has been hinting he wants more from me than friendship. Right now, I bet he's not thinking too highly of me. He'll be hurt, I know that much. Oh, I have enough guilt to fill the ocean I've just crossed.

Writing to Mother and Father, Nan Eliza and Aunt Hattie was difficult. I was full of remorse when I wanted my letters to be brimming with joy and details of my new life. And yet I knew I owed them all some sort of explanation. I sent a card to Danny telling him I would write properly when I'm settled. For some reason there are no words to write to Danny right now.

Being with Alexander is so important for me and since he has written to Helen and told her their marriage is finally over, I feel hopeful for our future. But at the same time, I'm uneasy about the situation. I feel like I'm the one who's done the wrong thing to Helen and his children, not Alexander. It's as if by being here with him I've hastened his decision to end his marriage.

I can't bring myself to tell my family I'm with Alexander. I can only hope, when the time is right to explain in full, they will eventually be able to forgive me.

Chapter Twelve

Isabella

Oxford, with its sunny July days, is brimming with old-world charm and a sense of purpose. The pubs are small and quaint, and often overcrowded. Their low-slung doorways and ornate stained glass, lead light windows are characteristically English. Spending time in these establishments is a rite of passage and becomes part of everyday life for many students.

The university colleges are large and rambling with their own chapels and immaculate gardens, stately trees and sweeping green lawns. Oxford is steeped in history and is also elite in a sort of way I haven't encountered before. Certainly, more so than my experience in Melbourne. The colleges swarm with students. They can be seen crossing the lawns in groups, heading to their places of study. There is a higher proportion of male students here than at Melbourne University and the city has an aura of masculinity about it. Everyone looks as if they have somewhere important to be: lectures, tutorials, at the library or the pub.

The formality of life for academic staff is pervasive, especially among senior university dons. The wives endeavour to carve out some sort of existence for themselves while their husbands pursue their careers in academia or research. There is a certain scramble to be noticed. House dinners, college dinners, picnics, and theatres are important.

Alexander and I have been allocated a university residence for staff. Our first weeks are spent putting our touch on our semi-furnished apartment. We purchase a toaster to replace the broken one in the cupboard, new glasses and cups for the kitchen, and fluffy mauve towels for the bathroom. We throw out the old laundry mop and buy a new one, a bucket, linen tea towels and a red clock for Alexander's study. I hand-stitch check curtains for the kitchen window and make yellow and red floral cushion covers for the sitting room. Alexander praises my homemaking skills and I surprise myself by finding joy in some of the simplest of chores.

There we are, living as man and wife. Alexander lied on the housing application form, and because the university needed no proof of our status as man and wife, it was never questioned. I am now Isabella Sadler, Mrs Sadler. And there is a deep unease within me. The names don't fit. And there's already a Mrs Sadler and it's not me.

'I'm not so sure I should be using your name.'

'It makes it easier for now. Nothing to worry over.' Alexander turns back to the pile of papers he has scattered across the kitchen table where he sometimes prefers to work despite having a small study. He looks up and raises his eyebrows. 'Well, Isabella, what about that cup of tea you promised?'

'It's just ... yes, I'll put the kettle on.' I collect the new cups from the cupboard and place them on the bench in the stripe of afternoon light. For a moment I chastise myself for being difficult. Alexander looks up and gives me a forced smile.

'Soon you can get a job or apply for a small course. It's quite acceptable. After all, this is Oxford, not stuffy old Melbourne.'

That makes me laugh. Already, I'm learning that Oxford University is exactly that – stuffy. But Alexander doesn't see it. He returns his attention to his work, his brow scrunched into a frown.

'I wasn't counting on doing a small course –'

'Isabella, can't you see I've got work to do? I'm the one under pressure here, not you. Can you leave it be for now?'

'I understand you're nervous. It's a new job and strange –'

'How could you understand?' Alexander scoops up his papers and heads to his study.

***

Richard and Charlotte Smyth, originally from Canada, are housed in our apartment block. They have been so welcoming to us. Richard has a two-year appointment with the School of Geography. They've already been here for six months. Richard is loud and jovial; Charlotte seems content to spend most of her days in their apartment with occasional outings to the village shops.

She asks me to go with her one sunny afternoon and we meet at the front of the apartments. She's wearing a pink, floral dress pinched tight at the waist with a matching bolero. Her honey-coloured hair is pulled back into a tight roll at the back and her face is immaculately made up with rouge and light-pink lipstick. She obviously takes a great amount of time and care with her appearance. We walk along Cornmarket Street to Cadena Café, an Oxford landmark, I'm told. I follow Charlotte inside. The aroma of freshly roasted coffee beans wafts toward us as we make our way down the spiral staircase to the lower floor of the café. We choose a table in the middle of the room as Charlotte looks around for a waitress. My attention is taken by the ornate pressed-metal ceilings painted in gloss white and the display of historical photos lining the timber-panelled walls.

'And what did you do in Australia?'

'I was studying and working for my mother.'

'Studying?'

'I was in my third year of law.'

'I don't know any women who are lawyers.'

'Well, I'm not a lawyer yet. I haven't finished my degree.'

'Oh. Are you finishing it here?' Charlotte strains her neck to check on the waitress; she is keen to place our orders.

'I'm not sure. I might study arts or get a job.'

'That will be a bit unusual. I don't think any of the other wives work as well.'

'As well as what?'

'Oh ... as well as their husbands working, I guess.' She waves impatiently to a flustered waitress. 'Most of us are pleased to get out of boring jobs.'

A waitress wearing a white pinafore with piped white edges arrives and I order tea and a neenish tart. Charlotte orders coffee and a slice of Victoria sponge.

'I shouldn't indulge but I can't resist cream cakes. Anyway, what were we saying? I remember. Boring jobs. Anyway, once children arrive, there's just no time.'

'Oh, children?'

'We are trying.' She smiles coyly. 'How about you, any plans?'

Charlotte's coffee and my tea arrive, bringing the wonderful aroma of Earl Grey to fill the space between us. And I'm saved from an awkward conversation. Charlotte's ambitions in life certainly don't match my own.

Chapter Thirteen

Isabella

We've been in Oxford for two months when Alexander arrives home one evening
and announces we are going to a cocktail party at a colleague's house.

'You'll like James,' he says as we are getting ready. 'He's a good bloke – different
to some of the others.'

'How so?'

'They're a bit standoffish. But nothing to worry about. Let's enjoy tonight.'

I decide to wear one of my two best dresses I've brought from home and hope it's
appropriate for the occasion. My dress has a yellow floral pattern with a full flared
skirt, finished with a thin white belt. I pull my hair into a knot behind my ears and
clip on pearl earrings, a present from Mother and Father last Christmas. I slip into
my white high-heeled shoes and wrap a fine silky stole around my shoulders, and we
are ready to go.

'You'll be the best-looking woman there, Isabella,' Alexander says, hugging me
from behind, his strong arms around me, laughing as he caresses my neck.

I relish these times when Alexander is exuberant. It fills me with confidence to be
who I genuinely want to be; it is the reason I'm here with him.

'You look handsome too, Alexander. What time does this party start? And what
is our hostess's name?'

'Meredith. And the party starts when we get there, of course,' he says with a
cheeky grin. He's a good-looking man and when he's happy he can light up a room.
He must be a bit nervous, though, as we barely know any of these people.

The party is on the other side of the campus, our walk there filled with Alexander telling me about the difference between his workload here compared to Melbourne.

As we draw close to our host's house – a larger house than most – others are arriving, some in cars and some, like us, on foot from close by. A few of the women are wearing evening gowns and the men are in dinner jackets. I look at Alexander in his day suit and myself in my floral waisted swing dress and wonder if we stand out as underdressed. Alexander slows his pace momentarily, but then charges forward.

'Come on, Isabella. Fancy clothes can't deter us.'

The party is in full swing. The house has wide French doors opening out to an area under lights, where the lawns of Trinity College can be seen in the distance. Pots of yellow zinnias and white petunias are lined up along the edge of the patio, an immaculate border. A table with stemmed glasses and trays of finger food is set with glowing candles at each end. Our hosts, Meredith and James, usher us through the glass doors and introduce us to other guests who are milling with drinks in their hands. I find myself beside two men, while a few feet away, Alexander is in conversation with an older woman wearing a long satin gown. He keeps glancing at me and turning back to the conversation he's having.

'From Australia, you say,' says a gaunt man with a thin moustache. His eyes never quite meet mine.

'Yes, Melbourne.'

'Mm, and your parents? Where are they from?'

'Melbourne as well.'

'I see ...'

'You seem surprised ... and yourself, sir, where are you from?'

Alexander is looking my way again. Within seconds he is by my side and smiling at the man next to me.

'Isabella, this is the gentleman I was telling you about. Professor Robert Harrington-Jones. Robert is the Head of the English Department.' Alexander's hand is firm on my elbow. 'I see you've met my wife, sir.'

'And how are you finding Oxford, Albert?' says Harrington-Jones, turning from me.

'It's Alexander,' I say before either one of them has a chance to continue. 'And my name's Isabella.' I smile and take a tall glass of champagne from a hovering waiter.

'Yes, yes,' he says.

'I'm settling in well, sir. The environment is stimulating and –'

There is a movement next to us and Harrington-Jones turns to greet a fellow guest who has made a beeline for him. Next to me, Alexander tenses up. I swallow a rather large mouthful of the sweet liquid in my glass, and we start to retreat quietly. Harrington-Jones is now heavily engaged in the new conversation and Alexander's expression has turned surly. After a moment or two, I realise he's blaming me for the new head of his department shunning us.

The night limps on. We talk to the few others who can be bothered getting to know newcomers. Alexander drinks too much and monopolises James, the host of the party, for far too long. As eleven o'clock strikes, I persuade Alexander to leave. I know he'll regret his behaviour if we stay. He's in a bad mood and not good company. We walk in silence and arrive home much more subdued than when we left.

'Isabella.' Alexander turns to me in the hallway. 'You have to learn how to conduct yourself properly.'

'I need to learn – What do you mean?'

'You obviously upset Robert Harrington-Jones. Society here is not like home – you must know your place.'

'And what place is that?'

'I think you know exactly what I'm saying.' Alexander's face is reddening. 'You're here as my wife. I'm new, so you can't be outspoken. Asking Harrington-Jones where he was from. Why did you do that?'

'He rudely asked me about my parents' background. He was rude to us both. I refuse to be treated as if –'

'That's just the problem. You don't know your place.'

'I can't believe I'm hearing this from you.'

'Do you want to jeopardise my posting?'

'Of course not, but I can't see why I would. You've become very worried about these people who treat us as if we're not their equals, Alexander.' I take off my shoes. That's better. 'I understand what it's like to be treated with indifference and, frankly, I don't wish to bow down to it here or anywhere and neither should you. I'll make us some tea.'

From the kitchen, the sound of Alexander pacing the sitting room unsettles me. What got into him at the party? Surely, he doesn't expect us to be treated rudely and not react. I'm pouring hot water into the teapot when the front door slams and he's gone. I go to the window. He's striding across the lawn toward the colleges. His gait is alcohol-fuelled and his demeanour is one of anger.

Either the tea or my busy mind keep me awake. It's early morning when his key scratches at the door. The couch creaks and I realise he's sleeping in the sitting room.

Chapter Fourteen

Knill

There are times when Knill isn't carrying a weight on his shoulders, but these occasions are few and far between. He moves through each day more by habit than interest. He gets ready for work and he and Lily discuss what they will cook for dinner. He tries to continue as if they have purpose in life but at times purpose evades him. He knows it's the same for Lily. Ever since Isabella's departure there has been a gaping hole in the family's existence, a breach Knill works hard to step around each day.

On his way to the office, Knill catches a glimpse of a young women ahead of him, her heels clicking on the footpath. She's similar in age to Isabella, her long dark hair trailing down her back just like Isabella's. For just a few seconds he forgets his Isabella is in England, and then, as always, the reality of her absence once again stabs sharply in his chest.

On his desk is a letter from his old childhood friend Milton, who still lives in Castlemaine, the town Knill was raised in. Milton's letter is full of local news, and it triggers thoughts of home and his adoptive parents, Ted and Rhoda. His gentle dad and his doting mum who always supported him no matter what he did in life. He hopes he's been to Isabella what Ted and Rhoda were to him. Sometimes he's not sure. Milton ends the letter with an invitation, as always, for Knill and Lily to visit anytime.

Some years ago, Isabella, Lily and Knill had stayed with Milton for a couple of days. Knill had shown Isabella the landmarks of his childhood: the school, the cricket and football ground, the park where he learnt to ride his bike and finally his childhood home.

'I can't believe this is the house you grew up in, Father. Do you think anyone is home?'

Knill, peering through the rusted gate and the overgrown garden, also became curious. It had been many years since he had walked past the old house.

'It looks deserted to me.'

'Let's take a closer look.' Isabella pushed open the rusty cast-iron gate and beckoned her father to follow, which he did without hesitation. The enormous old liquidambar tree swayed its branches across the small front yard as the two of them paused on the path to gaze at the house.

'Which room was yours?' she asked as she rounded the corner of the house to peep through the windows. Following, Knill pointed to the second window, and instantly Isabella had her forehead against the grubby windowpane. He followed suit and soon they were moving excitedly from window to window with Knill describing what used to be in each room. Outside the window of his parents' room, emotion came over him. He told his daughter about when he'd found his adoption papers atop a wardrobe all those years before and the fallout with Rhoda and Ted. Isabella placed her hand on his arm as he managed a smile.

'Come on,' he said. 'We shouldn't be trespassing like this.'

With Milton's letter still in his hand, his attention returned to his office and the present, the pain in his chest. It seemed like yesterday his beautiful daughter was glowing with happiness and curiosity with him at the old house. He'd felt content within himself that he and Lily had provided her with the security of a family he had lost as a younger man when learning of his adoption. But that was then, this is now, and he has a mountain of paperwork to finish.

Chapter Fifteen

Isabella

My money is starting to run low. Before I left, I withdrew all my savings in Melbourne. I had been fortunate that Nan Eliza was giving me a small allowance each month and I'd accumulated almost a hundred pounds. When I came to Oxford, I opened a new account and deposited it here. With setting up the apartment and contributing to our day-to-day living costs, it's going to run out soon. Alexander has become evasive about his finances. I suspect his wages are not covering our expenses. Whisky is expensive and he buys two or three bottles each week.

There's an autumn chill in the air and the trees are beginning to shed their golden leaves. The days are shortening, and a tone of grey is nestling across Oxford and its many history-laden landmarks. The grand Sheldonian Theatre is one of my favourite places, with its grey sombre exterior and its view of the exquisite Bridge of Sighs. I dawdle past it, until I'm jostled into hurrying by a group of students passing me. I follow their laughter and banter on the narrow footpath until I'm past the Bodleian Library in Bond Street. This is another exquisite building, with an enormous arched doorway depicting the different colleges' coats of arms and ancient stone engravings atop the footings. I've yet to work up the courage to enter.

A walk to the village helps to alleviate boredom. It's late September, we've been here four months and I'm at a loss to fill my time. In the window of the shop next to the bakery, an advertisement for a bookkeeper catches my eye – it's three days a week in a village called Iffley, about a fifteen-minute bus ride from Oxford. It pays two pounds a week. Eagerly, I copy down the details. If I hurry, I can have a letter in the mail before Alexander comes home. No reason to mention it to him.

At Patty's Bakery, a bell above the glass-panelled door chimes, or rather clangs, as each customer enters. It's a tiny shop with a glass counter full of iced cakes lined in trays and delicious-smelling bread stacked in square cane baskets. I buy a loaf of rye bread with a dusting of flour across the top, the sort Alexander prefers, and two currant buns. The young woman behind the counter recognises me from my frequent visits. It's only a small gesture but somehow it reduces the totality of my loneliness.

It's been several weeks since the party incident and Alexander has rejected all my attempts to discuss it. It took days for him to recover after his unsettled mood; I am growing to understand he resolves things by himself. That is, when he's ready to move on, somehow magically I should be ready to do the same. Still, I'm relieved he's in a good frame of mind again. His lectures keep him engaged and learning the ropes in a new institution is challenging him. After all, it's why he came in the first place.

My days have been less than stimulating. When I broach the subject of resuming study, Alexander is unenthusiastic.

'Can't you see how difficult it would be?'

'In what way?'

'You would have to apply for your University of Melbourne results to be transferred to Oxford for application. Your results are in your name ... well, not in your current name.'

'That can be easily explained. Anyway, you said it doesn't matter, Alexander.'

'It's too risky. I don't want any problems with my appointment.'

'So, given I'm supposedly married to you, I can't study because someone might realise I'm not? And it might cause you trouble.'

'You never know. Come on, Isabella, you know how important this job is for me. I've worked hard for it, and I don't want your whim to study to get in the way.'

'My whim? My *whim*?'

'You're being silly about this.'

'We discussed this on the ship. You agreed I should take advantage of the time to explore more study and now you say it's too risky.'

Alexander huffs loudly and pushes back his chair, accidentally knocking his cup from its saucer. He leaves it where it tumbles and walks to the front door, collecting his jacket from the coat stand. Without another word, he is gone.

***

It seems my naïve idea of studying in Oxford was just that: naïve. My thoughts lately are of home. Laughing and joking with Danny, Mother's serious face as she scurries around the office, always burdened by the stack of files on her desk. I think of Father and his calm disposition and an ear for everyone – how I wish I could talk to him right now. I even miss Aunt Hattie's letters from Maryborough with her attention to every little detail of her life. And Nan Eliza, my wise grandmother, what must she be thinking of me? Running off without a word to anyone, frightened they would talk me out of going, instead acting like a spoilt child by running away.

When Alexander's at work, I read my way through his English texts. I raise snippets of these readings with him, but mostly he's too tired or had too much to drink to carry on a conversation to any level and in any depth to my satisfaction. Harrington-Jones is difficult to work under and I'm getting the impression that Alexander is under more pressure than he bargained for in his new role. He spends long days at the college and when he comes home, he's not always good company.

Late in the day, I push my job application letter into the bright red mailbox at the corner of the street. It feels like ... something.

Chapter Sixteen

Isabella

One week later a letter arrives in the mail requesting me to attend an interview for the assistant's job at the accountant's office in Iffley. Again, I don't tell Alexander. There is no point until I know if I have the job; even then I'm not sure how he's going to respond to the idea of me working. I put his demeanour down to work pressure and finances and find myself not being as open with him as I should be. If I get the job, it will ease the money situation and surely ease the tension for both of us.

The bus journey to Iffley lightens my mood. The road narrows and we pass green fields and country houses. The Thames River comes into view, winding its way through the lush countryside. Today, although it's cold, the sky is blue and the river is glistening with a silver sheen.

The village of Iffley is a cluster of old cottages, many with thatched roofs and ivy creeping across the walls, their gardens well-tended. As I make my way past a row of charming row houses, I imagine their sitting rooms with English furniture, floral cushions and decorative porcelain cups and plates. There are also newer buildings and it's among these I find James and Kendle Accountants. It's a light, airy building with large front windows. The firm seems well established. As I push open the frosted glass door, a young woman looks up from her polished desk.

'Isabella McMillan?' she asks.

'Yes, I'm here for an interview –'

'They're expecting you.'

A woman, with auburn hair tied neatly behind her ears, wearing a smart grey skirt and matching jacket, comes out of the office area. She stops when she sees me at the desk, hesitates then smiles reservedly.

'Neva, this is Isabella McMillan,' says the receptionist.

She invites me to come with her and leads the way down a well-lit corridor, opening the door to yet another light-filled room. Inside, an older man half stands and nods to me. He is as old-fashioned as the office is modern and well laid out. I can't imagine he had anything to do with its design.

'Mr James, this is Isabella McMillan, she's here for the interview. You have her letter.'

He shuffles the papers on his desk, peers at me over the top of his glasses and throws a look toward Neva.

'Yes, yes, Neva. Sit down ... Isabella.' Neva remains standing. 'I notice in your resume you studied law in Australia, University of Melbourne?'

'That's right, I was in my third year.'

'And before Melbourne?'

'Before Melbourne, sir?'

'Where are you from originally?'

'Melbourne: I was born there, sir.'

'Well then. Mm, I met your Prime Minister once, Mr Robert Menzies ... a forthright chap. So, what brings you to England without completing your degree and articles?'

'I'm having a year or so away, just a change really.'

I can't tell him I'm here with Alexander. And I can't lie and pretend I'm married, as it would jeopardise my chances of being employed. I know my explanation sounds feeble but I'm hoping they'll give me a chance to prove I'm worth employing. There is silence from Angus James; he looks across to Neva, who remains poker-faced. She will not help him out. I realise she's a woman who doesn't hold out for her employer's approval. He checks my application again.

'Three days, two pounds a week. Let's have a trial of one month. I'm sure you have all the necessary skills, but that's how we'll do it. You can start tomorrow.'

I see a flicker of what I take to be relief fall across Neva's face.

'Thank you, Mr James. I look forward to working for you.'

Neva is already by the door. When we are in the passageway and out of earshot of her boss, she rubs her hands together in what might be a gesture of victory.

'Well, Isabella. That went well. Angus James is not always obliging but you handled yourself well, considering he's not fond of confident women!'

'Thanks, Neva. Tomorrow at nine.'

Neva walks to the front door with me. Her earlier reserved smile has vanished; in its place is a warm and inviting expression as she tells me a little about the tasks expected of me. I like this woman and already I know the decision to apply for the job was right for me.

A sense of achievement travels with me on the bus back to Oxford where I buy two pork pies, the ones Alexander loves, and a small box of raspberry tarts. I will tell him about the job over a special meal this evening. This will be the turning point for us. With both of us working we will have enough money to enjoy our time here and I'll have my own sense of purpose.

A letter from Mother and Father arrived this morning. Recently I sent them a short note with my address. My hands shake as I open the thin air-mail envelope in Mother's familiar handwriting.

Dear Isabella,

It was wonderful and such a relief to receive your letter. We have been worried about you but put our trust in your ability as an adult to manage your life.

We hear Oxford is a wonderful city, steeped in history and tradition. We trust you are making many new friends.

All is well for us, except for missing you of course. The practice is managing well enough. Daniel has stepped up to take on many of the senior practitioner roles. He has been our 'rock' and never complains when the place gets busy as it has a way of doing. You will remember those times, Isabella.

There is one matter we need to raise. Money. Are you in need of assistance or do you have employment?

Father and I are well, and hope this letter finds you the same, Isabella.

Please write again soon.

With much love from

Mother and Father

I read the letter through again and again. They are trying to accept my absence. But underneath I know they're hurt. I didn't speak of Alexander in my short letter to them. In fact, I was vague to the point of being ridiculous about my circumstances. But having a job now means I will have something to tell them. I take out my pen. I will write while I wait for Alexander.

***

It's nine-thirty when Alexander comes through the door. He's cursing under his breath.

'You would think no-one else knows anything about teaching. The old bastard had a go at me in front of the students today.' Alexander grabs a glass from the tray and pours a neat whisky. He's been at The Eagle and The Child – one of his drinking holes – with a couple of other disgruntled staff members.

'Come and have dinner. It's pork pies, the ones you love.' I have no appetite myself but if we eat Alexander might become less distraught. I try to coax him to the dining table but he flings himself into the large armchair in the lounge room.

I sit opposite him, hoping he'll settle. Instead, he refills his glass.

'Do you want your dinner, Alexander?'

'Is that all you can come up with? *Do you want your dinner, Alexander?* I'm not a child, Isabella.' His voice is loud and mocking.

'No, I don't want my bloody dinner.' He glares across the room. 'Have you any idea the lengths he takes to humiliate me? The pompous bastard is out to get me, wants to see me ruined, doesn't like Australians. Colonists, he calls us.'

'Alexander, if –'

'How could you understand? Never had to do it hard, brought up like a princess, the idol of your parents' eyes. Ha, you've fallen from grace now ... running away with a two-bit English lecturer who can't make it in Oxford because he doesn't have the right connections.'

'My parents don't know I ran off with someone,' I say feebly.

Alexander stands abruptly. Unsteadily, he crosses the room to the whisky tray and reaches for the neck of the bottle. It slips from his hand and thumps onto the floor. I jump up to pick up the bottle, but he turns on me.

'Leave it, leave the bloody thing where it is.'

I freeze. What's left of the whisky is pooling across the lounge room mat. Then suddenly, Alexander's energy seems to drain from his body and his shoulders slump. Without looking at me, he turns and staggers out of the room. I hear him at the front door, his heavy breathing close to sobbing. The door slams and he's gone.

Chapter Seventeen

Isabella

He still hasn't arrived home when I wake in the soft dawn light. Do I wait for him, miss my bus to Iffley and give up my job before it even begins? Or leave for work regardless? I scribble a note, put it on the table, collect my bag and hurry to the bus stop. It's hardly a good start to a new job.

The bus ride to Iffley allows me to relax a little. I'm hoping being with others might take away the isolation of being alone in Oxford. I lay awake for much of the night, trying to make sense of what is happening to me, to us, to Alexander. He's not the person he was in Melbourne. Back home, he was so sure of himself, loving and personable. Other than his marriage, everything he had set out to do had worked for him. He was one who navigated change and planned for his future. Now his confidence is sliding and whatever personal crisis he's in, he refuses to share it with me.

Lashing out at me about my background and family ... this is a new level of bitterness. His own family background is a subject that's off-limits. He has no contact with his two brothers or mother. He is the youngest of his siblings and, apart from knowing his father died when he was fourteen, I have no sense of his early years at all. In fact, he treats his childhood and adolescence as if they didn't exist. Any attempts to discuss his family, even in passing, is met with a sharp retort or a wall of silence.

James and Kendle Accountants. I arrive ten minutes early, take a deep breath and open the door to my new job. I leave my worries outside. I must concentrate on making a good impression.

'Good morning, Margaret,' I say to the receptionist, who seems surprised I remember her name.

'Hello, Isabella. Neva will be so pleased to see you. We're snowed under.' She ushers me down the passageway.

'Neva's office is the one at the end.'

'Welcome and good morning, Isabella. Come in, you'll be sharing an office with me. We're a bit short of space since last month when two new accountants started with the firm.'

Neva is the office manager for the firm. Her desk is neat but has a large pile of files stacked to one side. A teacup sits on a small mat beside her typewriter. On the other side of the workspace are two wire baskets: *Inward* and *Outward*. My desk is across the room from hers and smaller. I hang my coat and handbag on the stand near the door.

'I'll show you around, introduce you to the others and then we'll get down to business. Today, we'll be working on monthly accounts.'

Neva doesn't waste time on frivolous talk and niceties but she's someone I like already. Her serious face is softened by a smattering of freckles across her nose and a couple of recalcitrant red curls at her temples. She is capable and organised. She gives me a good introduction to the tasks and hands me a large pile of files. The morning passes quickly; my mind is engaged with bringing each file up to date, marking them for attention and letters. The work isn't taxing, but it occupies me in a way that feels productive. At some stage during the morning I realise how much I've missed work. Neva occasionally glances across at me, half smiles and busies herself again.

The afternoon is similar. I get through all the allocated files and accounts and Neva offers a wide smile when I hand them over to Margaret for filing.

'Not bad for your first day, Isabella,' Neva says as we get ready to close the office.

'I enjoyed it. It's good to be active again. See you tomorrow morning.'

***

I arrive home in good time to prepare dinner. I put the key in the door but find it's already unlocked. Alexander is in the lounge room. There is a glass of whisky on the small table beside him.

'I didn't expect you to be home yet.'

'I've been home all afternoon.' Alexander gets to his feet. To my relief he's not drunk – he's calmer, more like his old self.

'Did you read my note?'

'Yes.'

'I'll make us some dinner.'

'Wait, I have something to say.' He takes my bag from my hand and places it on the floor. 'I should never have carried on the way I did last night. I was under pressure at work and probably had too much to drink … I'm sorry. It will never happen again.'

'We don't have to stay, Alexander. You can leave the university any time you want … I have a job and we could find another flat and –'

He pulls me close to him and his body heaves. He sobs uncontrollably for what seems too long and then stops quite suddenly. After dinner, as we sit on the sofa together, much of the tension from the day before has evaporated.

'I'm so sorry, Isabella. I'll make it up to you. And now that you have a job, it will make our living costs manageable.'

'There is something we need to talk about, Alexander.' I press his hand with mine. 'Your drinking has become a problem.'

'It only happens when Harrington-Jones –'

'But that's the point: you have to find a way around it.'

'He makes me so angry, Isabella.' His hand tenses beneath mine.

'But you barely know him.'

'He makes my blood boil. You just don't understand what it's like. The constant humiliation.'

'Alexander, I don't know what to say, but we all get angry. Maybe if you walk away, calm yourself down? After all, Robert Harrington-Jones is in a powerful position ... I'm sure he gives others a hard time as well. Finding a way to manage it is all you can do.'

'I tell myself to ignore it, but when it happens, when he makes his snide remarks and belittles me, I can't bear it. Isabella, he's just like ... he's like my bloody father!'

Momentarily I'm taken aback. 'Tell me about your father?'

'He's not worth talking about. Not now, not ever.'

Chapter Eighteen

Lily

Dear Isabella,

We hope you are continuing to find Oxford the experience you want it to be.

Father and I are pleased you are working but surprised to hear that it's for a firm of accountants. Still, many of the bookkeeping skills and processes are similar, I suspect. I have missed your thorough and precise work.

Daniel also says it's not the same without you. Poor Daniel, his mother continues to be unwell and he's constantly at her beck and call. Sometimes, I think he is too kind and generous for his own good. Then again, I don't think he ever thinks of putting his own needs ahead of others'. Although, it seems Daniel has some relief from his worries at home – he has a girlfriend. He hasn't exactly said as much but Father and I saw him after work, meeting with an attractive young lady.

One small piece of office news. I have employed a woman to fill the gap left by you. She worked as a legal secretary for a firm of solicitors

*in Sydney for several years before coming to Melbourne. Her name is
Audrey Robertson and she has already made a big difference to the
office. Lucy gets on well with her and she's an enormous help to me.*

*And the biggest piece of news. Your Nan Eliza is leaving for a visit to
China. She sails in two weeks and plans to be away for several months.
We were shocked when she first told us, and now we worry that such a
journey will not be good for her. But you know Nan Eliza, once she has
decided to do something there is no way she will be persuaded out of it.
It seems this characteristic might run in our family, Isabella.*

I trust you are in good health. Your father and I send our love as always,

Mother

Lily sits back in her chair contemplating her words to her daughter. It's taken her several attempts to write a letter that neither encourages Isabella to stay in England nor asks her to return. Coming to a position of acceptance rather than anger and hurt has been difficult and painful for Lily. She has always believed that a good daughter or son considers their parents in all decisions. Never would she have contemplated doing what Isabella has – putting her own needs first, leaving without permission, without discussing it with family. Still, she and Knill agreed they had to somehow live with Isabella's choice. They cannot reject her. They will not lose her. After all, she will be home sometime, surely. Lily secretly hopes it will be sooner rather than later. That their lives will return to the old ways. In the meantime, they will act as if everything is normal. When Lily wakes, sometime in the predawn light, her heart sore, she hopes she can keep it up.

CHAPTER NINETEEN

ISABELLA

Over the weeks, Neva and I form a close friendship as well as an efficient working relationship. She's a serious person but once she trusts people, her real personality appears. I love coming to work and Neva is a big part of why I enjoy the job so much. We sometimes take our lunch break together and, when it's sunny, we sit by the river at the end of the street. She knows I left Australia and my life there to be with Alexander.

'You must be smitten with him to make such a risky decision, Isabella. Leaving your studies and family.'

'Ha, I know that now more than ever. Still, you know the old saying – you make your bed, you have to lie in it.'

Neva gives me a quizzical look as the sun dances off the ripples on the water.

'Exactly what my poor old mother used to say, not sure it was much help for her though. You see things you shouldn't. There was even a time when I resented Mum for putting up with all ... with all that abusive rubbish. I now know she had no choice, no choice at all.'

'And you went to London to get away?'

'Bermondsey, it's an area south of the Thames, not far from Tower Bridge. Some would laugh at that, not exactly an improvement on Iffley but I didn't care at the time, I needed to skedaddle from here.'

Neva gazes across the river and for a few moments it's as if I'm not there – I begin to realise how tough her earlier life was.

'You took a risk as well?'

'Not as gigantic as yours. I suppose it could have been worse, but I was so lonely at first. I knew no-one except my cousin Victor, who's older, his wife Nancy, and a few boarders at Ester House.'

'And you went to secretarial school at night?'

'Except during the war years. Then we all did our bit for the country.' She smiles, tucks a red curl behind her ear. 'We kept calm and carried on.'

'I can't imagine what it was like living in London during the bombings.'

'We were all under the same hardships. We were lucky – Ester House was miraculously unaffected. Some streets close by were reduced to rubble. People suffered enormously. Still, thank God, it's over now.'

'So why come back to Iffley?'

'Because I was born and bred here. I think eventually we all want to be where we belong. I guess I wanted to prove I could be somebody. Kids from poor circumstances often feel that way.'

'Poor circumstances?'

'There were others worse off, I suppose. Still, I always knew I had to stand up for myself and not expect too much from anyone, especially men.'

Neva's eyes are lowered as if she's scrutinising something in front of her on the riverbank, but she's deep in thought again. She does it whenever our talk becomes serious. She goes to someplace where she can't be reached, then when she realises, she smiles a little awkwardly as if she's been caught out.

'Where were we?'

'Men ...'

'Ah, yes, men. My dad and brothers would turn anyone off men. Dad ruled the house, spent his wages at the pub and left Mum to manage as best she could. He'd come home drunk every Friday night and things escalated after that. My sister and I used to run to our neighbour ... oh, why am I telling you all this? Sorry.'

'Don't be sorry. It sounds horrible. I understand why you left for London.'

'Well, my choices weren't great. Marry and end up like my mother or make a different life for myself. My sister married her boyfriend and I skedaddled the hell out of here. Funny though, the whole time I was in London, I felt like I should have been home here, looking after Mum. Torn between survival and responsibility, I guess, but living with my cousin and his wife in Bermondsey wasn't always fun either.' Neva laughs. 'There were some strange people at that boarding house. Anyway, eventually I came back when Mum took sick.'

'And you've worked for James and Kendle ever since?'

'Nine years. They should give me a medal, Isabella.' She nudges my arm and we laugh together.

We sit for longer than we should with the sun glistening on the Thames, watching the boats languidly moving upstream. I'm reminded of story books about England, the ones Nan Eliza gave me when I was a child. She would take me to a little bookshop in the Royal Arcade in Melbourne. I always chose books about England with its green fields and gentle rivers. And I also loved the English Christmas books brimming with white snow scenes, people wearing fur-lined coats and woollen gloves, snowmen with carrot noses.

We jump up when we realise the time. Giggling like schoolgirls, we hurry back to the office, arriving flushed and out of breath. I think we are both surprised by our developing friendship. We've found a connection that's more than just the work we're doing. Despite our different family backgrounds, we identify with something fundamental in each other. A need to be independent.

Chapter Twenty

Isabella

He's late again and our meal is ruined. Outside the window, the bleak night shadows fall heavily across the path to the university. He hasn't been this late in weeks, though over the past days, his temper has soured again, and the whisky has reappeared. He complains constantly about his head of department. My attempts to talk about it have once again been rejected.

I'm about to leave the window when I see him in the distance. He's with two other people. Rugged up in hats and scarves against the cold, they're laughing and talking. Even from a distance and in the dark, I can tell Alexander's been drinking, enough to make him unsteady on his feet. I wait in the kitchen. The door springs open and the three of them are suddenly in the hallway.

'Isabella. Come and meet my friends. Thomas and Barbara, students from Cornwall.'

The boy, perhaps a couple of years younger than me, looks sheepish to be here. Barbara is oblivious. 'I'm from Wales,' she teases Alexander. Alexander shrugs as if to say, does it matter, and Barbara laughs at him. He drags his overcoat off, misses the coat hook and leaves it crumpled on the floor. 'Drinks?' he mumbles to his companions. They look at me for permission, hang their scarves and coats and follow Alexander to the lounge room. I look to Alexander for some sort of explanation but he's in one of his silly, cantankerous moods. He pushes drinks into their hands and looks sideways at me.

'Isabella, have a drink to celebrate.' He thrusts a glass of whisky at me despite knowing I never drink whisky. I take it rather than cause a fuss.

'What are we celebrating?'

'Peace. There will be peace. He's gone. Away on sabbatical for three months.'

'Harrington-Jones?'

'Who else would I be talking about? Yes, Mr Harrington bloody Jones has gone. Not that the old bastard deserves a sabbatical to France, but at least it gets him out of my hair.'

It's embarrassing hearing Alexander speaking belligerently about the head of department in front of the students. And why are they here, why has he brought them to our home? Barbara seems suddenly to ask herself the same question.

'I see,' I say.

A pause. His voice turns nasty. 'Is that all you can say, Isabella?' The students recoil from him and I know things will get worse from here on.

He waves his glass at me in a mocking gesture. Barbara and Thomas are passing confused glances to each other. Alexander seems to have forgotten they're here.

'I would have expected a bit of bloody support.' He spills his drink, turns back to the liquor trolley and refills his glass. He falls heavily into an armchair and puts his head in his hands.

The students quietly place their glasses on the trolley and back away. They glance over their shoulders at Alexander who hasn't moved. Collecting their coats, they leave without a word. Back in the lounge room, he turns to me.

'You're an arrogant, self-righteous bitch.'

I stare at the man sitting in front of me. I don't know him anymore.

'Don't speak to me like that.'

As I turn to leave the room, he lunges at my skirt. It rips in his hand before he lets it go. He gets to his feet, no longer unsteady. Without warning he raises his arm and hits me across the face with the back of his hand. I stumble back and fall against the door frame. He comes toward me again. I back up against the wall and slip to the floor, raising my hands to shield my face. He hovers over me.

'Stop it!'

He steps back, jerkily. A moment later, in another sweep of his arm, he strikes at the tray of glasses and bottles on the liquor trolley. They crash and splinter across the room. He stands very still as he scans the damage and then his attention is back to me.

'Stay there,' he says in a voice I've never heard before. 'It's where you belong.'

CHAPTER TWENTY-ONE

ELIZA

Dear Isabella,

When you receive this letter, I will be on my way to China. Despite my age, I have an urge to visit my friends and my husband's family. I spent too much time in their land to accept I'll never see them or Shanghai again. I expect you already know your parents were not happy with my decision, and I understand why. After all, they say, haven't I lived a full and exotic life? Should I not slow down, be close to home and be content? But contentment only comes when the heart is settled, Isabella, and I have a need to go to China one more time.

Are you content, Isabella? Content with your move to England. Oxford, I believe, is a thriving university city with history on every corner. I can imagine you there among the old buildings and beautiful gardens and colleges. My only wish is that you might be tempted to finish your studies, or indeed, start a different course of study. Don't waste your talents, Isabella.

England is a special place and many of us have our roots there. My father, your great-grandfather, was born and lived in London until he was a young man. He never stopped talking about his childhood, his four siblings and the antics they got up to beside the Thames. I have a longing to visit London one day also.

I received a letter from Hattie recently telling me how much she misses you. She's all alone except for you and your parents and I worry about her health. Of course, she always says she is fine but she's not the woman she used to be. She looks forward to Knill and Lily's visits to Maryborough.

My love follows you, Isabella.

Nan Eliza

Eliza seals the letter and places it on the sideboard. She'll ask Knill to post it when he arrives to take her to Port Melbourne later today. Her bags and case stand near the front door in readiness for her departure. A familiar sensation is building within her, a sense of freedom that reminds her of her earlier years. She has missed the thrill of adventure.

Chapter Twenty-Two

Isabella

Alexander can go for weeks without touching the whisky bottle and then, without warning, he will embark on a drinking binge with whoever is available. Sometimes it's other disgruntled staff members; at times, again, it's his students. He has been given a warning about fraternising with students, but he hasn't heeded it. With Harrington-Jones on sabbatical, the acting head of the department has asked to speak with him on several occasions. Alexander has now taken a dislike to him as well and accuses him also of discriminating against Australian academics.

There is no reasoning with him. He oscillates between being intensely angry and threatening, and then sad and remorseful about his situation at the university and how he treats me. He has not raised a hand to me again, but I find myself expecting it.

I'm not proud to admit to this, but a few days ago I searched Alexander's briefcase and found a letter from Australia, sent on to him by the University of Melbourne. Helen's name and address were on the back of the envelope. I had enough self-restraint to leave the letter sealed but why hasn't he opened it himself? And why would Helen send a letter to Alexander via the University of Melbourne?

'Will you send the children Christmas presents?' I ask before we leave for a village concert in the afternoon. It's early November and if we post them soon, they'll arrive in time for Christmas.

'I'll think about it. Come on, we'll be late.'

We pile on our coats and gloves and leave in the clear chill of the day. It is invigorating and bracing. I love the cold. It reminds me of childhood memories of the England I envisaged from my picture book. Alexander is the opposite. Since the weather has turned, he has been surly, complaining about the cold as well as his job. But this afternoon he's in better spirits. It's the reason I broached the subject of his boys; I'm sure he must miss them. I can understand Alexander's reluctance to discuss Helen and his correspondence with her regarding ending their marriage, however, I will never understand how he can ignore the existence of his own sons back home.

Once at the tea rooms in the village, a couple with two children takes the table next to us. Alexander would not move an inch to allow the older child to squeeze past us. He suggests we take our tea to a spare window seat. Does being around other children remind him of the responsibilities he's not fulfilling? Is that what it is?

I put it out of my mind. Today is a good day. And it's days like this when flashes of our earlier relationship appear. On these days, Alexander is warm and affectionate, the man I fell for when I first saw him on the tram. He jokes, we walk arm in arm and talk about our trip to Scotland – Alexander wants us to go to Edinburgh for Christmas. Not that we can really afford a holiday, but he thinks we can, and it will do him good to get out of Oxford. James and Kendle close for the Christmas period and I have the week off. So, the train tickets and a room in a small hotel in the centre of Edinburgh are booked.

Making holiday plans and Alexander's enthusiasm for Edinburgh gives me hope that the difficult times are behind us. People *can* change and sometimes it takes time to recover. I want to support Alexander. If he stays away from the drink, I'm again hopeful about our life together.

The voice is small at the back of my mind, but it is nagging, insistent. It tells me not to let my guard down; it's too painful to be shattered all over again. I try to take the good times as breathers, pleasant breaks in what's turned out to be a confusing and difficult relationship. It's funny, though, how the voice in my head keeps me watching for signs of trouble. At times it frustrates me. It's almost as if, in my own mind, I'm willing something to happen to justify my lack of confidence in Alexander.

Sometimes, I do think about leaving. I want to stick it out – I love the real Alexander. But I'm starting to wonder where the real Alexander is. When he becomes troubled, when he leaps between craziness and anger, he's not someone I understand anymore. I'm not sleeping well. And when he's not here I start to feel shaky. There are times when he's been legitimately held up and walks through the door in a perfectly fine mood, but until I know, I can't relax.

But, leaving is such a final and complicated choice. I haven't enough money to return home to Australia and renting a flat here on my own is out of the question for now. I know I could write for help from Mother and Father, but I can't bring myself to do that. I made the decision to be here, giving up my family and life in Australia to live 'in sin' with an 'unstable' man. But how am I going to make this situation work?

Neva's friendship has become my only anchor and I've found myself telling her more about my problems with Alexander. The arguments and his unpredictability.

'I don't want you to think poorly of Alexander. He's a good person. It's only when he drinks. Alcohol changes him.'

'And if he continues to drink?'

'He was so upset after the last big outburst. He promised never to let it happen again. He knows it's not normal. I want to believe him; I have to believe him.'

Neva doesn't know about Alexander hitting me. I can't believe it myself and revealing it to someone else is out of the question. It's as if I'm somehow to blame – perhaps if I hadn't been so challenging maybe it wouldn't have happened. I tell myself it's my fault, but the little voice insists it's not right either.

'You're really saying you can't trust him, Isabella.'

'I can't trust him when he's drinking.'

'It's taking a toll on you. You're as thin as a stick, your clothes are hanging off you.'

'Oh, I've lost a bit of weight but –'

'But nothing, Isabella. You're looking worn out. Living this way is exhausting. You said as much yourself.'

'The break to Edinburgh will do us both good and Alexander has been good for weeks now.'

'Yes ... well, it's not for me to say but ...'

When Neva's voice joins the one in my head, I become more unsettled. She's not one to make comments lightly. And she's right, I have lost weight. Sometimes I can't eat in the evening because of the anxious feeling in my body. Neva makes me promise to leave the apartment if Alexander starts to drink heavily. She gives me her address and tells me to get a taxi or a bus anytime, night or day.

Chapter Twenty-Three

Isabella

It's the first time I've been away from home and family at Christmas. In November, I sent cards and small presents to Mother and Father, Nan Eliza, and Aunt Hattie. I also sent a card to Danny, a scene of an English pub. Two days before we left for Scotland a parcel arrived with letters and Aunt Hattie's traditional fruit cake. Mother and Father sent a money order tucked inside their lovely card and a beautiful pair of tan leather gloves. The money was a lifesaver. I quickly deposited the order into my bank account and drew out some of it to cover our expenses in Edinburgh. They sent photographs taken with Father's new Brownie camera. Seeing their faces smiling at me was too much. That night in the kitchen I cried.

'Isabella, there is no point in upsetting yourself.' Alexander's voice is carefully neutral.

'It's Christmas. I miss them.' I turn on the gas under the kettle and wipe my eyes. My voice turns hard. 'Surely you miss being home with your children?'

As soon as the words are out of my mouth, I regret them. Alexander takes a deep breath and spreads his hands on the table.

'Pull yourself together, Isabella.'

'I'm sorry. I just feel a bit homesick.'

'It's no good crying over spilt milk ... you made the choice to come to Oxford.'

'I'll be fine when we get to Scotland.'

In the bathroom, I splash cold water on my face and try to push all thoughts of home out of my mind. Christmas will be over soon enough; it will be New Year and then I'll be back at work where Neva will cheer me up.

***

It's a sleet-filled day with thunderous skies when we arrive in Edinburgh. We find our hotel and take our bags to a room three flights up rickety stairs. The place smells musty and I wonder why we are spending our money to stay in a dump like this when we could have stayed in Oxford, cooked a lovely Christmas meal, and watched the snow fall gently across the university grounds. Alexander is quiet and I suspect he is having similar thoughts.

Christmas Day dawns and we are both subdued. Christmas lunch in the pokey hotel dining room turns out to be an ordinary affair – heavy beef with roast vegetables, a large Yorkshire pudding, horseradish sauce and gluggy brown gravy. The Christmas pudding is equally unspectacular. It's a miserable time and I hold back tears most of the morning and throughout lunch. Alexander drinks two brandies but stops when offered more.

In the afternoon we pull on our coats and gloves and wander the streets. It's then I see, for the first time, the amazing panoramas and historical sites that Edinburgh has to offer. The spectacular view from Calton Hill, weathered stone buildings lining the pavement, cobbled streets leading to narrow laneways with front doors opening directly onto the street. In shop windows, Christmas lights flicker in the still afternoon. My spirits are lifted when we hear singing in a nearby church. The old carols are so familiar. My family always attended church on special days and always at Christmas. I convince Alexander to come into the church. He's relaxed after the brandies at lunch. Indulging me, he takes my arm and we pull open the heavy wooden door to step inside.

We slide into a pew near the back. The church is old, its stained-glass windows reaching the domed ceiling. The choir sings 'Silent Night' and the congregation joins in. I love the melody of this hymn, but I don't trust myself to sing for fear of crying again.

The next few days pass quickly. We walk all over Edinburgh and have lunch in small tea rooms. At night, tired from sightseeing, we eat in the small dining room of the hotel. For the first time in what seems like an age, we talk honestly with each other. It is like those precious stolen hours in Melbourne when we were first together. Finally, we discuss Alexander's work situation. It's been almost seven months since we arrived in Oxford. It seems longer.

'You can choose to leave.'

'You know that's impossible. What would I do? I can't go back to the University of Melbourne after resigning to come to England.'

'Somewhere else?'

'If I leave this job without good references, I'll find it hard to get a position anywhere.'

'Can some of the other colleagues give you a reference?'

'No ... that puts them in a difficult position. It's the head of department's reference I need and they're both against me.'

'But it can't continue the way it's been.'

'I know it's been unfair on you, but I'll fix it, Isabella. Leave it to me.'

Chapter Twenty-Four

Isabella

Back in Oxford I sense a rise in tension and mood. Alexander is due back lecturing next week and already he's distracted and testy. Attempts to talk the way we did in Edinburgh fall on deaf ears; he's not responsive. Quickly he's forgotten his plans to fix our problems as he spirals back into frustration. Large amounts of each day are spent preparing for lectures and pacing the apartment. He's starting to doubt himself and his ability to deliver the content of his lectures, the subject he knows so well, even before he goes back to work. Harrington-Jones is set to return and I'm sure Alexander is expecting more trouble ahead. And he takes any suggestions I offer as criticism.

The bus ride to Iffley is my cue to relax. The clouds are low and getting darker; I wish I'd remembered to bring my umbrella. Arriving at James and Kendle, I find Neva already at her desk looking as if she's been there for some time. I can't remember a morning when she's not already been in the office working when I arrive. She looks up, her face bright.

'How was Edinburgh?'

'Better than expected,' I say as I hang my coat and scarf on the stand in the corner. 'It was freezing but we managed to see quite a bit of the old city.'

A look passes between us, and I know Neva's question is really about Alexander.

'It was fine, really it was, Neva.' I'm pleased when she leaves the conversation there. We get to work. Focusing on the backlog of files that require attention is a settling feeling. Hard work and a few cups of tea with Neva and I'm laughing at the story about her nephew and the Christmas pudding. I am enjoying myself in the office again.

***

The next couple of nights, Alexander paces the flat, trying to settle on the lectures he'll give next week when he returns to teaching. Harrington-Jones's imminent return has elevated his anxiety.

'You know your subject as well as you know your own face,' I say. But he is too distracted to respond, back to doubting himself and his own expertise.

A week passes. Then one evening, he's late. I take over his habit of pacing the apartment and watch the window for a sign of him across the grounds. It's one in the morning when the door creaks open. I pretend to be asleep. I hear him knocking into furniture and swearing loudly, then he's in the kitchen opening the cupboards. There's a crashing sound and more swearing. It's quiet again until the bottles on the glass-topped drinks trolley rattle. I assume he's pouring himself a whisky. Pulling on my dressing gown, I creep to the lounge.

'What do you want?' he says without looking up. He's slumped in the armchair with a cigarette in one hand and a glass on a precarious angle in the other.

'Have you eaten anything?'

'Leave me alone. Stay away from me!' He takes a swift drag on his cigarette, partially spilling the contents of his glass over the padded arm of the chair. As I move toward him, he holds his hand up. His face is lined and sallow; his shoulders droop in a way that makes his suit jacket ride up on his neck.

'Just leave me alone!'

Back in the bedroom, his deep breathing and heavy sighs are audible through the walls. He mumbles and shuffles across the room to the drinks trolley. He swears and I imagine he's spilt more whisky on the floor. I feel heavy, heavier than I have before, and so very tired.

Eventually I doze but I wake to find him standing over me. The stench of alcohol reaches me. The light in the hallway is on and the room semi-lit. What time is it? The edges around the blind are blackened still.

'You lie in bed … and … ignore me.' Slurring, 'Just like them … the bastards think they're better than me … I'll show them, the bloody lot of them. And you, you're just like them.' His face distorts and a loud sob escapes him. He stumbles to the bed and holds his head between splayed fingers.

'Alexander, I'll get up –'

'Stop treating me like I'm stupid.'

As I pull back the blankets, he lunges at me and grabs my arm. He drags me toward him, twisting my wrist as he does.

'Let me go, you're hurting me.' I shove against his chest; he flinches as my hands push against his tense body.

He staggers back, surprised, then seems to calm. He goes to leave the room but doesn't make it further than the door. He turns back, grinding his teeth and his face contorted.

'Can't you just bloody well listen to me?' He grabs hold of my wrist again and grips my shoulder with his other hand. He's shaking me.

'Stop this!'

Pleading with him to stop has no effect. He doesn't appear to hear me.

The door, I want to get to the door, but I can't move. He is holding me too tight.

'So prim and proper, what would you know?' His breathing is now a rapid pant.

He releases my wrist but unexpectantly grabs the back of my hair. It jolts my head back. He's focused and staring hard into my face, but it's as if he's not seeing me at all.

'Just like him. You're all like him.'

His face is only inches from mine and his spittle is spraying in my eyes. Pinned hard on the bed, I push against him again as his chest heaves under my hands. Momentarily, he lessens his grip and I pull away, but I can't move from under him.

'Please stop this, we can talk –'

'Talk, talk … is that all you can bloody well come up with?'

'Get off me. Please, Alexander. Stop.'

'It's always my fault, never them, never you … always me.' He raises his free hand and hits me hard across the face. My head smacks against the bedhead under the force of his strike.

'Stop, Alexander. Please.'

He hits me harder.

He hits me again.

I stop trying to get off the bed. Instead I huddle while he continues to yell at me. There is blood on the bed. My arm is pinned beneath me. Is he trying to kill me? Am I going to die? My heart is pounding, deafening me. I can't make out what he's saying now. My face is turned toward the wall away from him and I'm willing myself to stay silent.

Someone is hammering on our front door.

'What's going on in there?' a man's voice calls. Then more loud knocking.

At once, Alexander lets go of me. He glances toward the passageway and falls away from me across the foot of the bed as if stunned. He's sobbing now and whimpering like a child. The knocking and calling stops. Whoever was at the door must have left. I lay frozen to the spot, for fear of Alexander starting up again. After what seems to be an unbearable length of time, he finally drags himself away from the bed. He groans, covers his face. I don't move a muscle. I don't look at him. I don't utter a sound. He staggers out of the bedroom. I can hear the tap running in the bathroom, then there's movement in the sitting room.

Sometime later, the front door opens.

Not sure if he's really gone, I pull myself to the side of the bed. In the darkness, I feel my face. There is a raised lump on my forehead, my left eye is swollen and closed. As I place my feet on the floor, my head spins. Has he left or is he still in the house? With my good arm I push myself off the bed and stand for a few moments. The pounding I hear is my heart thumping hard within my chest. I take short, silent breaths and make my way to the lounge room. I peer around the door frame. It's too dark to see but the room feels empty. Flicking on the light, I stand breathless, facing the remnants of the night. Empty bottles, glasses on the floor and the contents of Alexander's briefcase scattered across the couch and floor.

I check the kitchen, the hallway, bathroom and study. He's gone. I breathe out for what feels like the first time since Alexander left the bedroom. Sliding the lock across the front door, I will myself to move quickly. The clock in the sitting room says it's five to five. I wipe clean the blood from my face using my left hand as best I can. Waves of nausea slow me. I have a rest after each effort. I dress slowly. My right arm is already stiff and painful and putting on my clothes is agony. All the time I'm listening for Alexander to return. Finally dressed, I collect my handbag and stuff my passport, diary and bankbook inside it. With one hand I button my coat, then step into the darkness.

Chapter Twenty-Five

Isabella

It's pitch-black on the narrow path on the far side of the apartments. I could have gone the quicker route, but Alexander is more likely to use the main path if he's returning home. At the bus stop, I edge under the bus shelter and slump into the seat. There are two other people waiting: a middle-aged woman huddled in the shelter wearing a tartan coat and a felt hat, and a younger man with a large, battered suitcase. Pulling my collar higher against the icy night air, I settle in to wait for the next bus. The dizziness has stopped but my arm and eye are throbbing.

'The night buses come hourly, dearie, but you don't look so good.' The woman frowns as she looks at me.

'I'll be all right, thanks.' I just want to get on the bus and then begin to sort out what to do next.

'They never stop once they start, you know.'

The welcome sight of the bus lights come into view. It turns at the intersection before pulling in close to the kerb. This thankfully ends the conversation – I'm taken aback by what she said. I creep onto the bus behind the woman, my body hurting with every step.

I ask the driver if the bus goes to Wittingly Street, Iffley, and he tells me it does.

'I'll call you when we get close. You look like you need to go to the hospital though.'

'No. Just Wittingly Street. Thank you.'

He watches me in his mirror as he pulls away. I know what he's thinking. A woman on her own in the early hours, injured and going somewhere other than home. My arm throbs as the bus stops and starts along its route and we move out of streetlights. The darkness is a blessing as I huddle in my seat. Across the aisle, the young man is already sound asleep.

'Wittingly Street, next stop.'

Turning left into Wittingly Street, I begin searching for number twenty-two on the letter boxes. I'm on the wrong side of the road. As I cross, a man wearing a long flapping coat appears behind me and pushes his bike onto the footpath. My heartbeat quickens. He gives me a look, slows as if he's going to say something, then keeps going. I don't want any trouble. I just want to find the right number. A dog barks incessantly inside a house nearby. Then a pale light from a nearby lamppost reassures me. The house numbers are in the right sequence now.

There are eight letterboxes out the front of 22 Wittingly Street. It's a large house and 22B is on ground level. It's still dark and I wait on the footpath, hesitating for several minutes until I see a light go on inside.

The sound of my knocking echoes in the stillness of the early morning. Another light flicks on in the hallway.

'Who is it?'

'Neva, it's me. Isabella. I need your help.'

The latch chain rattles, and the door springs open. Neva peers at me from behind her screen door. She's still in her dressing gown.

'What's happened – oh no.'

'Sorry, I had nowhere else …'

She gently ushers me inside. Nestled into the soft fabric of her sofa, I cry and cry. Neva makes tea and watches me from the kitchenette but doesn't say anything.

'Here, drink this, you look half-frozen.'

The tea warms me as Neva packs another cushion behind my back.

'I'm sorry to … to just turn up. I didn't know what else to do.'

'Exactly what I told you to do, remember?'

'I never thought I would have to ...'

The relief of being somewhere safe washes over me. Unfiltered sobs wrack my body and Neva takes my teacup and places it on a side table.

'We need to get you to a doctor. I'll get ready and we'll go to the hospital. That eye looks nasty and your arm, well, it could be broken, Isabella. It'll take me just a few minutes to get ready.'

Neva brings a pillow and blanket and settles me like a child. I burrow into the soft pillow and close my eyes.

Neva's gentle tapping on my shoulder startles me and I pull away from her touch, my heart racing.

'Isabella, it's all right. It's me, Neva. You're going to be fine. I've called for a taxicab. It'll be here in ten minutes to take us to the hospital.'

Chapter Twenty-Six

Lily

The hot January days seem endless, stretching on with lazy monotony. Lily thinks of Knill and his dislike of summer, how he's always relieved at the first sign of autumn. Even as a small child, he was bothered by hot weather and north winds. They bring with them a sense of dread, he tells her. Today, he promised Lily to leave work early so the two of them can visit Daniel in South Melbourne. Daniel's mother died suddenly yesterday after one of her bouts of illness.

Lily is at her desk when Knill arrives – she hears him go to the kitchen and turn on the tap. It would be good if he were making a cup of tea. She needs one. Since Isabella's departure, work has been frenetic. Both she and Daniel are under mounting pressure.

'There's just so much work, Daniel.' A conversation from earlier in the day. 'We just clear our deadlines each week, only to start the following week in the same manner. Audrey's sudden return to Sydney hasn't helped.'

'Have you heard how her father is?'

'No, but such a serious fall. Poor Audrey might not be back for some time.'

'Maybe we could reduce the amount of incoming work until Audrey returns.'

'What do you mean?'

'Mrs McMillan, we are working long hours and still we are behind. Perhaps we should not take on new clients for now. Give us time to catch up and find a way to manage the work in the future.' Daniel, Lily knows, is as concerned about managing the business of the practice as he is about the work itself.

'We could never do that. In all the years my father ran this legal practice, he never once refused to take on new work. People expect us to act promptly, they rely on us. If they can't, they'll go elsewhere. There are so many loyal clients. No, it's out of the question. We will cope.'

'Just a suggestion.' Daniel's face was serious. 'Since Isabella left, it's become clear just how much work she did.'

Lily was sure Daniel would see the small shadow cross her face at the mention of Isabella. Pretending to reach for a file, she turned away and missed the concern and kindness in Daniel's eyes as he returned to his desk.

Lily refuses to talk about Isabella and when clients ask, the stock standard answer is: 'Isabella's in England, taking some time off from her studies to see the world.'

Today she's feeling the full impact of the past months. Worrying about Isabella and waiting and hoping to hear from her soon. Working harder than ever, often with her heart not in it, and pretending that all's well, when underneath the surface nothing is as it should be. There are some days when it all becomes too much; today is one of those days. Lily knows her eyes are red and doesn't want Knill to see her upset. At the door he coughs lightly and comes in, empty handed.

'Sorry, I thought you were in the kitchen. I won't be long, Knill.'

'You're upset.' He sits down in the chair beside her desk.

'I'll be fine. It was just a busy day and ...'

'I think we need to talk about your busy days, Lily.'

'Another time.'

Lily knows she can't address this now. She looks to her kind and gentle husband, always there for her, and feels like weeping again, but she won't. As Knill places his hand over hers, she allows herself to slump a little in her chair.

'It's all becoming too difficult, Lily.'

'Do you think you might be over-reacting, Knill?'

'Not if I'm reading the signs right. Long hours, you're looking pale and tired, but still you push on.'

It is well understood between them that Knill thinks she's too wedded to the memory of her father's practice. She also knows in the past it's worked well for their family. Until Isabella left, that is. Obviously, it wasn't working well for Isabella. Perhaps, Lily ponders for the umpteenth time, Isabella thought her future in the shadow of her mother and grandfather's legacy was too daunting.

Lily wipes her moist eyes and smiles at Knill.

'Something has to change, Lily.'

'You're the second person to say that today.'

'I'm worried about you.'

'Oh, come on. There's nothing to worry about. Besides, we need to get to South Melbourne. Daniel needs our support right now.'

Chapter Twenty-Seven

Isabella

It's three days since I arrived at Neva's house. She arrives home from work, her face flushed.

'You had better sit down to hear this,' she says as she drops her handbag near the door and sinks into the nearest chair. 'He's been to the office – walked in as bold as brass and demanded to see you.'

Neva's eyes are flashing. It's not often Neva is this animated. I know it's bad.

'He frightened the heck out of Margaret, started yelling at her when she told him you weren't there. I heard the commotion and went out at the same time as Mr James.'

'No!'

'Yep, and it gets worse. Mr James told Alexander to leave or the police would be called. I didn't think Mr James had it in him.'

'And – did he?'

'Not before having a swing at a vase and leaflet stand on the front counter. Water and flowers went everywhere. "You know where she is. You're hiding her from me." He told Mr James to tell you to come home. He slammed the front door so hard one of the glass panels cracked.'

'I'm so sorry, Neva. He's never behaved like that in public.'

'You don't have to be sorry. Remember, that's why you're here. It's not safe to be around him anymore.'

'It's alcohol. When he drinks, he ...'

'You can't keep making excuses for him, Isabella. What we saw today was bloody scary. And you've been through more than that.'

'I don't know what to say, I'm sorry …'

'Mr James hauled me into his office and forced me to explain what I knew.' Neva's eyes are full of sympathy. 'He doesn't want you back in the office, Isabella. He's worried Alexander will keep coming in and cause more trouble.'

'That doesn't surprise me, Neva. It's not fair you had to explain for me or for Alexander for that matter.'

'I'm used to Mr James's reactions, but Margaret was so upset she's now refusing to work in the reception area on her own and Mr James is re-configuring the front office as a result.' A grimace crosses Neva's face. 'Oh Isabella, it's not just that Alexander might come looking for you again. He's worked out you two were unmarried and living together.'

'Is that against the law in England?'

'Ha, only his moral law, but there are many who would think the same, Isabella. You know that already.'

It's dusk outside. I now have no job and no income. It settles over me the way the night replaces the daylight – softly at first, then fully dark, fully black. I have no job. Everything hurts still. My arm is in a sling. A nasty sprain, the doctor at the hospital said. There are stitches in the back of my head. I cannot bear to look at my face in the mirror.

'But that has nothing to do with my work.'

'No, but that's through our eyes, not his. He told me your situation doesn't align with the good standards and reputation of James and Kendle.'

'And he won't change his mind, will he?'

'I've tried. I told him you're the best bookkeeper we've had in years. He acknowledges that but he's stubborn. He never goes back on a decision once he's made up his mind.'

I draw in a breath. 'Well now, I don't want to *taint the reputation* of James and Kendle.'

We both scoff but it's half-hearted at best.

'Mind you, he's an old hypocrite,' Neva goes on. 'We all know why the female staff avoid him. Wandering hands! He's a dirty old sod and gets away with too much. But when it comes to others, he makes all the judgements in the world.'

The two of us fall silent, both lost in our private thoughts in her pretty lounge. It's totally dark now and getting cold. We avoid the obvious but we both know I can't stay with her forever, sleeping on a stretcher bed in the corner of the room. Soon I'll have some serious decisions to make.

Chapter Twenty-Eight

Isabella

It's four weeks since I came to Wittingly Street. Neva insisted I stay until I recover. And true to form, she's given me the time to come to terms with what's ahead. I'm wearing her clothes, eating the good food she's insisted on, and resting. The sling is no longer necessary and the ugly bruise on the left side of my face has disappeared except for a yellowish shadow across my cheek. The swelling around my eye has receded and the stitches in the back of my head have been removed.

The days are beginning to lengthen as spring gets closer. Neva is trying to persuade me to think about my future, at least the next step.

'There are other jobs, you know. You could work full-time, get back on your feet – that is if you want to stay.'

'I'm in such a mess, Neva. I still can't believe what Alexander did. A job would help but …'

'No one would blame you for going home to Australia. In fact, it might be the safest place for you,' she says in her quiet voice. 'We all make mistakes, Isabella. Owning up to them is always the hardest part. You're not the first woman to fall for a rotter. Your family will surely understand.'

Of all the things I've considered these last few weeks, going home isn't one of them.

'No. I made the decision to come to England. I can't just run back home to my parents whenever something goes wrong. How would I explain what's happened?

That I fled to England with a married man who turned out to be a drunk and beat me up? I can't do that to them.'

'That's just your pride speaking. What about your future, your studies, for instance? You really should finish your degree.'

'Forget studying. I've messed that up. Oh, how I wish …'

'No good wishing, Isabella. If wishes were horses, beggars would ride. Promise me you'll think it over.'

'I will. Oh, Neva, how can I ever thank you?'

Tears flicker at the edge of my eyes as I try to ignore the queasiness washing over me. This has been happening a bit lately. Neva waves away my gratefulness in a no-nonsense manner and I know better than to make too much out of it. Neva doesn't like it when I become emotional; she deals in the practical. That's what I admire about her.

Even before Mr James told Neva I couldn't return to my job, I knew I would never work there again. These past weeks have given me time to reflect, to clear some of the confusion in my head.

My parents would send money at once for my fare home if I asked them to. But I can't bring myself to do that. I'm responsible for the mistakes I've made, including the consequences.

In a way, I owe Alexander a chance to make good on the way he behaved. I also owe it to myself. After all, we invested heavily in our relationship. We also sacrificed our previous lives for it. There's a good reason for both of us to try to make it work.

He'll be remorseful, I know. He always is. He can apologise to Mr James and pay for the damage he did in the office. And he can seek help with his drinking. Maybe talk with the college doctor; he's not the first academic to struggle with alcohol.

We can develop new hobbies, change our lifestyle, have more fun. In the coming weeks, the weather will become warmer. Spring in England is a beautiful time of year. The warm weather will lift Alexander's mood.

And if all fails, I might even be able to convince him to return to Australia. He has a return ticket – it was part of his contract with the university. We'll have to scrape up my fare together but I'm sure we can find a way. Once there, we can set ourselves up, he can sort out his divorce and hopefully even return to the University of Melbourne.

***

'You can't be serious, Isabella,' Neva says when I tell her my plan. She's just arrived home after work. Her red curls are darker. She forgot her umbrella today and it's been raining.

'I've thought it through. He'll be mortified at what he's done. He's not all bad – he can be such a good and clever person when he's himself.'

'And, when he's not himself?'

'Well, that's the point, Neva. I know he'll be remorseful. He needs to get help.'

Neva goes to the little kitchen and lights the gas. She fills the kettle and returns it to the gas ring. She sets a tray with her matching Ainsley cups and saucers, sugar bowl and milk jug. The teapot comes next; she rattles the lid as she removes it in readiness for the boiling water. It's then she turns to me.

'You know he could have killed you, Isabella.'

'I know it wasn't right but –'

'No, really, he could have killed you. You heard what the doctor said. The blows to your head could have been fatal.'

Neva carries the tray to the dining table, pours the tea and sits down next to me.

'I saw you when you arrived here, bloodied, swollen and barely able to stand. Someone who loves you doesn't treat you like that, Isabella.'

'At some level I can understand how it appears, but he does love me. That's the bit I can't make sense of myself.'

For the rest of the night, Neva can barely speak to me. Her face is ashen. The only thing she asks of me is to delay my decision to see Alexander for another week.

Despite my promise to Neva and worried what she will think of me, the next day I catch the bus to Oxford. I will wait for Alexander to come home to the apartment after his morning lectures so we can talk.

It's a cold morning, brisk and clear. The colleges of Oxford appear in the distance. This, I tell myself, could be the start of a new beginning for us. It's Tuesday and Alexander won't be lecturing this afternoon. It was the only day he used to come home early except when he ... No. I must not go there in my mind. Thinking about the past is not helpful.

I take the familiar path to the apartments. Mothers with prams and little children rugged up in coats and Wellington boots cluster around the playground on the edge of the lawn area. A squirrel runs across my path and scampers up a nearby tree. A strange sensation floods through my body – these surroundings that were familiar just four weeks ago, now represent something in the past. I'm queasy again.

I cross the lush lawn. There's a small truck parked outside the entrance to our apartment with a University Construction and Maintenance sign on it. I pull my key from my handbag but hesitate when I see the front door wide open. Men are talking inside, their conversation blurred by the sound of hammering. I poke my head nervously in the door.

'Hello.'

A man in overalls and a thick work jacket appears.

'What's going on?' I ask.

'Do you live in the apartments?' he asks.

'Yes, I –'

'Sorry, we might be making a bit of a din. The chap who was in here smashed it up proper. We're cleaning it out and fixing it up. Needs a lot of work, a few days at least.'

While he's talking, I peer down the passageway, where our clothes are strewn across the floor. Another man is sweeping up broken glass and crockery and throwing it in boxes. He picks up one of my white high-heeled shoes and drops it on top of the other rubbish. I glance sideways and see our books, torn and littered, in the sitting room doorway.

'The man who did this ...?'

Around me, the apartment slowly starts to spin.

The workman is looking at me closely. 'You all right, lady?' He puts his arm out to steady me. 'He's not here – don't worry, he won't be bothering anyone around here anymore.'

'Not here?'

'The boss says he's gone back to Australia. We have instructions to change the locks.'

He lets go of my arm and I can feel his eyes on me as I shakily make my way to the footpath. Nausea rises in my throat. I clutch my handbag to my stomach and breathe deeply to stop myself from being ill. Behind me is the shattered kitchen window, the checked curtains torn and snagged on the jagged glass still in the window and our scattered belongings on full display for anyone who pokes their head in the door.

***

I collapse on a seat in the park. The children are playing, and I am utterly, utterly numb. Someone is calling my name. It's Charlotte Smyth, wearing a flame-red coat and scarf and a look of pity. I make a feeble attempt to collect myself, but I know I look terrible.

'Isabella, what are you doing here?' I haven't seen you in weeks and then with all the fuss over ...' She pauses. Leans down to put her hand on my arm. 'We heard you left him.'

I pull away. 'I don't want to talk about it.'

She steps back, her pity intensifying. But I want to know about Alexander and she will have the details.

'What happened … after I left?'

She looks surprised, but then quickly takes advantage of my vulnerability and sits beside me.

'He was drinking heavily and there were reports of him being seen drunk and passed out on a bench in the park. Richard tried to talk to him, but nothing worked.'

Which bench? I wonder. The one we are sitting on? The one closer to the children playing?

Charlotte's face is close to mine, too close, and my body is shivering but I must know more.

'And then –' Is she enjoying this? She seems to be '– Richard said Alexander's contract was cancelled several weeks ago. He'd stopped turning up to lectures.'

'And the apartment?'

'One night, two weeks ago. Everyone heard it. Richard went over and tried to calm him but someone had already called for the police. There was hell to pay that night, people everywhere. He was arrested and taken to the police station.'

'And is it true, has he really gone back to Australia?'

'Yes. Last week.'

I manage to stand up. 'I have to go.'

'Isabella, you don't look so good. Come back to my place and have a cup of tea.'

'No, I need to go. Thank you.'

Surely the only good thing in this moment is that I never have to drink tea with *this* woman again.

I stumble down the path toward the bus stop, leaving behind the play of the children and the torn curtains I had so lovingly sewed. But my humiliation? That, I take with me.

Chapter Twenty-Nine

Isabella

The bus trip back to Iffley is a blur. I must have paid for a ticket but I have no memory of it. My head's full of the details so eagerly shared by my former neighbour but I can't quite believe what she told me. And yet, I saw the state of the apartment, it's cemented in my mind. Had he gone completely mad? Was it my fault for leaving?

'You look like you've seen a ghost,' Neva says as she takes off her coat.

'Just the remnants of my shattered life in Oxford.'

'You went to Oxford?'

She loosens her hair and sits down opposite me.

'I had to talk with him. I needed to be sure he would be open to my suggestion of getting help. Well, that was the plan anyway.'

'And he didn't agree to your terms?' There is an edge of frustration in Neva's voice.

'It's worse than that.'

I tell her about the workman and the state of the apartment. Neva's now leaning forward in her chair.

'He didn't follow you here?' she asks.

'No chance. He's gone back to Australia.' I tough it out and hold back the tears.

From Neva's point of view – it's a good thing. Her expression has lightened, her shoulders relaxed. But I feel, how do I feel? Discarded. Discarded and abandoned. Even if I left Alexander first.

'Well, it's one decision you don't have to think about, it's all settled.'

'What's settled?'

'Well, he's out of your life now and you can make your own plans. You can find work here or write to your parents and ask for the fare home.'

'No.'

'Isn't that what you want?'

'Yes and no. But I can't go home, not now.'

'Why ever not? Your family will be over the moon. You can go back to university. You're too clever to work as an assistant in an office, Isabella.'

'I cannot return to Australia. Neva ... I'm, I'm expecting a baby.'

Chapter Thirty

Isabella

With Neva's instructions in hand, I arrive at the corner of Tolley Street in Bermondsey. It is long and curved with narrow double-storey red-brick terrace houses lining each side. Many are identical, with rows of chimney stacks along the roof tops. Some have small front gardens but most open directly onto the narrow footpath. Tall gas lights, some with broken glass panels, are dotted along the footpath and add a sense of charm to the gloomy feel of the place.

It's Sunday and the street's swarming with children, running and shouting. A group of older girls are playing hopscotch in the middle of the road as the smaller ones watch on with envy. The coloured chalk squares of the game I played as a child are closely guarded by the noisy group. They look up as I pass with my small bag of possessions. Neva has put together a small wardrobe for me to get by with. It's nothing glamorous but at least I have a change of blouses and skirts. I pull my blue woollen coat around me and glance at the girls who have now stopped hopping and are watching me.

'You lookin' for someone, missus?' says an older girl wearing a green knitted cardigan with missing buttons.

'Yes. Number seventy-eight.'

'That's Ester House, missus. Up the end.'

Under the watchful eye of the locals, I find the dark two-storey house that Neva has prepared me for. 'It's not fancy but it will do for now, until you get back on your feet,' she said as we discussed my plans for the next few months.

I fold the piece of paper with the address on it and slide it back into my coat pocket. There's a brass knocker on the door that has seen better days – it's rusted into place and unusable, so I knock instead.

'You must be the Australian?'

I swing around to the street, to a woman standing on the footpath with her hands on her hips. She seems to match the house.

'Yes, I'm Isabella McMillan. Are you Nancy?'

'That's me. You'd better come in, luv. I'll show you where your room is.'

Nancy, who is in her fifties, is married to Neva's cousin Victor. She opens the door with a firm push of her shoulder; we step inside. The entry is a pokey space with large brass hooks over-loaded with hats and coats. Shoes, umbrellas, a tartan shopping jeep and a bike with turned up handles line the narrow hallway. The odour of sour food lingers, a telling sign that the doors and windows don't get opened too often. I follow Nancy up the narrow flight of stairs to the first floor. She puffs and heaves ahead of me, then motions to a door at the end of the passageway.

'This one's yours.'

I squeeze past her with my bag and open the door.

The room is small and dark. A narrow window facing the alleyway provides the only natural light. A grey blind is pulled down below the window ledge. I can already tell the spring is broken. Two mismatched eiderdowns are folded on the single bed along with a couple of flattened pillows. A small dressing table with a cracked mirror is squeezed into the corner, next to a single timber wardrobe missing its handle.

Nancy hovers in the doorway.

'The bathroom is across the hall. You put three pennies in the slot to have a bath.'

'Thank you, Nancy. It's good of you to take me in.'

'And how's she doing, our Neva?'

'Neva sends her regards and she's fine. She's been a wonderful friend to me.'

Reaching into my handbag I pull out an envelope with a month's rent inside it. Nancy's face breaks into a smile for the first time as she takes it from me.

'Thanks, luv. Don't often get rent in advance. I can tell you're going to do the right thing. Supper's at six, down the stairs in the room at the back.'

I hesitate to ask about the work. Neva has negotiated with Nancy for me to do three hours' housework a day in exchange for reduced rent with meals included. I can make my money spin out for a few months this way. Then I'll have to come up with a plan.

Nancy's about to go but pauses.

'So, how far along are you, luv?'

'Umm ... four months.' I can feel the flush rising in my cheeks.

'Try to hide it as long as you can, luv You know how some people can be.' Nancy crosses her arms and continues. 'And there's no need to tell the other boarders you're on your own and all. The least said the better. I've had other girls here, same problem. You're not the first and won't be the last. You can get on with your life when it's all over.'

'Thank you.' I look away as she watches me. I wish she would go.

'See you at supper then.' She pulls the door after her. I hear her humming as she descends the stairs and then she breaks into song, *All things bright and beautiful, all creatures, great and small.*

I'm taken aback by Nancy's directness. Neva had told me that she doesn't waste time on niceties, what you see is what you get. However, I'm a little apprehensive about meeting Victor. According to Neva, he's grumpy and impatient but he's a bit of a softy underneath.

When Neva heard about the baby, she wanted me to stay. But her flat is tiny, and she'd already done so much. She then tried to talk me into going home to Australia. Eventually, she came around to accepting my decision to stay in England for now.

'But what about Alexander?' she said one night. 'He gets off scot-free. Behaves appallingly, then takes himself back to Australia, leaving you to pick up the pieces and deal with ... to cope alone with a pregnancy.'

'He didn't know I was having a baby.'

'On his record it probably wouldn't have mattered. He's more than likely gone home to his wife.'

Neva was echoing my own thoughts. Has he gone back to Helen and the boys?

'I don't want to think about him anymore. I need to get through this time. Staying with your cousins in Bermondsey would be an ideal situation. Are you sure they can put me up?'

'Yes. It's not a fancy set-up, but you'll be safe and looked after. And Nancy will be pleased to have someone to help her out around the house.'

I twist the thin gold band on my left hand that Alexander insisted I wear in Oxford.

'It makes things simpler if you wear a wedding ring. Stops people asking too many questions,' he said at the time. And here I am about to extend the lie yet again. Neva suggested I tell people in Bermondsey my husband is working in Scotland until the end of the year.

'No good giving the local sticky-beaks more to gossip about,' she said in her matter-of-fact way.

I wish she were here with me.

After unpacking my few clothes, I try to get the blind up. Finally, it moves half-way up the window frame, but now hangs crooked. The dank alleyway has been used as a dumping ground for anything unwanted. Old bedframes, dirty mattresses, broken bicycles, old baby prams, sodden boxes of newspapers and piles of other indistinguishable damp and scattered rubbish. The afternoon light is already fading.

Turning away from the window, I investigate the scant room. It could not be more different than my lovely room at home in Melbourne or, for that matter, the apartment in Oxford or Neva's beautifully cared for and spotlessly clean flat in Iffley. Without warning, exhaustion overtakes me and tears dance in the corners of my eyes, but feeling sorry for myself is not an option. I'm craving a cup of tea; I consider asking Nancy if I can make one when voices in the hallway distract me. The tea idea is abandoned.

'Hello, Nance, coming to the local tonight?' calls a man with a strong accent unlike Nancy's or the Oxford accents I've become accustomed to.

'I'll see what his majesty wants to do,' says Nancy. 'We'll have to mind our manners, Jack, we have a new lodger ...'

'Right on, Nancy.'

The voices grow faint and I assume they are whispering so I can't hear what they say. Then a few hoots of laughter and a key being turned in the door next to mine. After checking my door is locked, I lie on the bed, pull my coat across my feet and close my eyes. And then it happens, a fleeting movement in my tummy. I lie still with my hand across my stomach. It happens again, a faint stirring reminding me why I'm here.

***

Gentle knocking wakes me.

'Are you coming down for supper, luv?' says Nancy.

'Just a moment.'

I need to use the bathroom and look both ways down the hall before stepping out. The bathroom is cold and damp. Everything is painted moss green and could do with a good clean. After using the lavatory and quickly washing my hands and face, I scuttle back to my room. There's a threadbare towel hanging behind my door that I use to wipe my face dry. Taking out a brush from my handbag, I quickly pull it through my tangled hair.

Downstairs, the floor creaks under my feet as I make my way to the laughter and loud noises coming from the room at the back. When I enter, there's a few seconds of stark silence. Everyone has turned in unison to stare. I look at the room, rather than the people. A heavy timber table in the middle of the space dwarfs all else around it; a few pictures, mainly country scenes and one of a large bunch of roses, hang on the dull walls. At the far end of the room, the lone window is covered by a heavy tapestry curtain. Nancy gets up and points me to the spare place next to her.

'This is Issie,' Nancy says to the room at large, 'our new lodger.'

'Hello, pleased to meet you all, but my name is Isabella. Isabella McMillan.' I nod, trying to sound friendly. In fact, I wish I were anywhere but in this room with people I don't know.

'Yes, luv, Issie's short for Isabella. Friendlier, not such a big mouthful and all. Anyway, this is Victor, Jack, Nessa, and Janet.'

'Hello,' says Jack. I recognise the accent from the voices earlier. Janet and Nessa watch me across the table. Janet, with her fair hair falling across her cherub face plied heavily with make-up and Nessa, big eyed and curious. Both smile but neither speaks. Victor too is silent as Nancy places a plate in front of me. They've all started their meal.

'I'm sorry for being late.' It's twenty past six. 'I must have dozed off.'

'That's all right, Issie. You've had a big day.' Nancy looks to the rest of them. 'She's never been out this way before, had to find her way on the buses, didn't you, luv?'

'Yes. Still, I'm here now …'

'So, Issie Mac,' Victor says. 'How do you know Neva?'

Sitting at the end of the table, Victor hardly gives the impression of being head of the house. A well-worn brown cardigan hangs from his shoulders and a thick growth of greying whiskers hides his chin. But his eyes are kind and non-judgemental. I can see why Neva said his bark was worse than his bite.

'I worked with her in Iffley.' I ignore the shortening of my name as no one else takes much notice.

Nancy grins at me.

'Don't mind Victor, he has his own little names for everyone.'

Victor nods and cuts a sausage, spearing a piece on his fork, which he waves at me.

'Bermondsey is a far cry from Iffley, mind you. No airs and graces here.'

Janet and Nessa snigger loudly; Nancy gives them a cold stare. Victor resumes eating his dinner and the others sneak glances in my direction.

'Well, it's good to have you here,' says Janet. 'You have a funny way of talking though. Where are you from?'

'Australia.'

'You don't look Australian.'

'My mother is Chinese-Australian if that's what you're asking.'

'Oh. That explains your dark hair. How long are you staying, Issie?'

I'm often asked about my nationality, but here at Ester House it seems a matter of course and not at all demeaning. Janet is simply curious.

'I'm not sure. A few months ... while my husband's in Scotland.'

'I'd rather be in Scotland than here,' she says. 'Whereabouts is he anyway?'

'Ah, he's ... he's in Edinburgh.'

'Don't worry about Janet,' Jack says. 'She has to know everything, don't you, Janet?'

Janet pokes her tongue at him and the others laugh. The tension falls away and the chatter begins again. It becomes clear that Jack, who is in his thirties, is held in high regard. Janet and Nessa are nineteen and full of energy and fun. It's not long before I'm entertained by their light and easy manner and, for an hour, I forget my worries.

Victor watches everyone, laughs at their jokes occasionally but mostly he acts like he's not overly interested in anything they're saying. But I can tell he is. Nancy is clearly the one who keeps the place running. She seems to be responsible for everything. Her cooking is old-fashioned and not at all fancy. Mashed potato, which Jack referred to as *teddies*, peas, sausages browned crisply and drowned in brown gravy. For dessert, apple crumble with a strong taste of cloves, covered with thick yellow custard. After the dessert bowls are cleared, and much to my relief, there is finally a cup of tea.

As soon as they finish their tea, Nessa and Janet spring to their feet and announce they are going down to the local. Victor stays in his place and Nancy starts to clear the table. Jack pushes his chair in and looks over to me.

'What about you, Issie? The Marygold is at the end of the block.'

The thought of drinking any sort of alcohol, especially beer, turns my stomach. My pregnancy is changing everything, including the way things taste. Does he know why I'm here? Have Nancy and Victor told him?

'Not tonight,' I say and am reassured by the kindness in his eyes.

Chapter Thirty-One

Issie

Although fatigued from finding my way to Bermondsey and meeting everyone, I sleep poorly. A soft light in the hallway shines under my door and I hear every noise in the house. The others coming back home from the pub, doors being opened and closed, Nessa and Janet giggling at the top of the stairs.

I envy the freedom of the others in the house, laughing between themselves and knowing what the days and weeks ahead hold for them. I long for the days back home, working at the practice, hurriedly getting ready to go to university lectures, jokes with Danny, the rattle of the trams, my friends in the law faculty and Mother and Father discussing the day's events. I'm surprised how much I mourn my old, simple life. And yet when I was living it, I wanted more. So much more than the routine, the eyes of adoring parents, the expectations placed on me. And now, all these things are gone. Replaced with a life laced with more apprehension and dread than I could ever have imagined.

I doze, but in what feels like just a moment later, doors open and close and there are voices in the hallway again. The alleyway is grubby in the early-morning light. I have to leave. Flee. Who are the people in this house and this neighbourhood? I don't belong here. But there is no leaving.

Downstairs, Nancy is waiting for me.

'Morning, luv, did you sleep all right?'

'Good morning, Nancy. Yes, not so bad.'

'Have breakfast, then when we clean up here, you and I are going up to the shops. We need milk and today is pie day.'

I quickly finish my cup of tea and toast while Nancy refills her cup and fiddles with her purse and string bag. We wash the breakfast dishes and then make our way out. After the tea and toast, I'm feeling slightly recovered from my sleepless night.

'Every Monday, luv, I go down to the pie shop to get the pies for our tea. Victor loves them and I do too, mainly because it saves me cooking.' She jiggles her shoulders as she pulls the front door shut behind us.

I laugh along with her but I'm guessing buying pies for Monday night's tea is probably going to be one of my tasks from now on.

'Everyone knows Manze's pie shop. It's been in Tower Bridge Road forever. Best pies in London.'

Nancy swings her basket, lined with lilac and blue rose wrapping paper, as we amble along the narrow footpath. Her feet are encased in solid black lace-up shoes and strike the footpath firmly. The morning is cool but the sun is peeping through the clouds, giving the houses, trees and gardens a light silky sheen. The dark, enclosed streetscape of yesterday is gone. Nancy is easy to be with. I have a strange sense of her protecting me, as if she has me under her wing. She's a straight-forward soul and I'm about to discover she's honest, 'honest as the day is long' as Father used to say about someone he trusted. She speaks to people in the street, some passing us and others leaning over their low picket fences. Most of them she calls by name. We turn the corner into Tower Bridge Road, with its array of fruit and vegetable shops, newsagent, butcher shop, a dressmaker and hairdressing parlour.

Even before we arrive at Manze's, a single-fronted building with a queue stretching out the front door, the enticing aroma of fresh baked pastry greets us. The woman at the end of the line turns around as we take our place. She nods to Nancy and stares at me.

'Morning, Shirl,' says Nancy.

'Morning,' she says to Nancy without looking at her. Meanwhile, Shirl is eyeing me up and down for longer than I'm comfortable with. Her eyes rest firmly on my thick stomach, despite my coat being buttoned up. She purses her lips.

'This is Issie,' says Nancy. 'She's staying with us for a while.'

Shirl keeps looking over her glasses at me with a face like she's sucked a sour lemon.

'Must be money in boarders, that's all I can say. Don't know how you do it. Where do you get them from?'

'I've always had boarders, Shirl. And no, there's not much of a quid in it but Victor and I don't worry too much about money.' Nancy winks at me.

The other shoppers in the queue are listening and I wish I could run but I stand next to Nancy and tug at my coat.

'So where are you from, lass?'

'Australia.'

'Australia? Well, I'll be!' Then it's her turn at the counter, but I hear her say from the corner of her mouth, 'More likely China if you ask me.'

Nancy pulls a face and lets her voice carry.

'Don't take any notice of her, Issie. She's always sticking her nose in where it's not wanted.' Nancy sniffs and looks ahead. A couple of people laugh. Nancy is clearly pleased she's had her say. We step up to the counter as Shirl leaves, throwing a sideways glance at me as she does.

Nancy orders six meat pies and a jar of potted eel. The women behind the counter are quick to place the pies in Nancy's basket and scoop half a pint of brown gravy into Nancy's billy can.

'Got caught up with old Shirl, Nance?' The older woman behind the counter laughs. 'One of these days someone's going to give her a clout and tell her to mind her own blinkin' business. She's always having a Darby and Joan about someone.'

Nancy throws back her head and laughs with the shop attendants. I'm struggling to follow the conversation as I take Nancy's basket from the counter.

'This is Issie, our new boarder.'

'Pleased to meet you, Issie. And don't worry about Shirl, she's a cranky old bitch at the best of times. See you next week.'

On the way home, Nancy is still riled up.

'Don't let the likes of Shirl worry you, Issie. Best to ignore her. She's had a hard life herself and should know better, but she doesn't. She's a gossip and thrives on other folks' misfortune.'

'I can stand up for myself, Nancy.'

'She'll already be talking to others about you. And making assumptions about your condition.'

'I suppose I should expect that. Can't say I feel proud about it though.'

'Too late for those sentiments now, luv.'

Chapter Thirty-Two

Issie

It's been a month since I arrived at Ester House. Each morning, from nine to twelve, I help Nancy with the chores. She's slow to get moving and most of the cleaning has already become my task.

Each day I start with the upstairs bathroom and lavatory. Twice a week I vacuum the frayed rugs in the hallway and the guest rooms, that is if they remember to leave their doors open. Jack never leaves his open and says he cleans his own room. Janet and Nessa are overjoyed to have someone picking up after them. Their rooms are untidy and cluttered, but I quickly pick up their shoes and stack them in the wardrobe and hang up the discarded clothes left draped over their messy beds. Then a quick wipe of the window ledges and a sweep of the linoleum floors before heading downstairs for another round. I've realised Nancy has only been doing the bare minimum in the house for a long time.

We stop for morning tea each day. Sometimes Victor joins us in the cluttered kitchen with its blue floral wallpaper and tea cannisters lined up along the mantelpiece. I'm beginning to like Victor. At first he was reserved, but I suspect he's been biding his time, deciding if I'm someone he'll be bothered with. Well, he must have settled the question because recently he's been up for a chat about Australia. A friend of his left Bermondsey a few years ago and now lives in Sydney.

'Ten pounds, that's all he had to pay. With conditions, of course, couldn't come back for two years. But he's stayed there, loves your country, Issie Mac. Has a job in a butcher shop and he's just bought a house over there. Guess he'll never be back now.'

One morning, feeling more tired than usual, I gratefully flop into one of the wooden kitchen chairs and let out an audible sigh.

'I need this cuppa, Nancy.'

'You need a rest, Issie. You don't have to work so hard, you know. The house has never been so clean.'

'Being busy keeps my mind off … off what's ahead, I guess.'

'Been meaning to talk to you about that, luv.' Nancy shifts in her chair and leans across the wooden table toward me. 'Have you thought what you will do when your time comes?'

'I think about it all the time. I've been wanting to ask you how I make the arrangements for the birth. I don't know who to go to. Neva told me that most women have home births and the midwife comes to the house. Is that what happens, Nancy?'

'Yes. But we'll have to get you booked in with one of the nurses first and she can make the other arrangements as well.'

'Other arrangements?'

'About the baby.'

'I haven't made my mind up about what to do about the baby.'

'You haven't? Adoption is the only option, isn't it, luv? It's your business, of course, but the other girls, well, they put it behind them and get on with their lives.'

The room becomes silent, interrupted only by the lid of the kettle rattling with the steam of the boiling water. Nancy is frowning and it's clear she's surprised I'm hesitating about giving up my baby. The general assumption is I will adopt my baby out; Neva thought so as well. The truth is I am confused, almost to the stage of being immobilised by my situation. Panic within tells me I need to take action. The sooner the better.

'I need to make arrangements for the birth.'

'I'll talk to Mary Rundle … She knows and her daughter's a midwife. Leave it to me, luv.' Nancy gets to her feet, placing a hand on my arm. Her hands are thin and weathered, but her touch is light and soft.

****

The next morning the routine is as usual. We finish the chores, or rather I finish the chores, by cleaning the kitchen benches. Well, cleaning is perhaps an exaggeration – it's near impossible to get a clear go at Nancy's bench tops. She has every imaginable knick-knack covering almost every inch of bench space in the kitchen. Cups, little jugs, containers, stacks of plates that won't fit in the cupboard, bowls and ornaments sitting on doilies and trays of various sizes standing behind anything that will hold them up. Yes, cleaning Nancy's kitchen takes considerable imagination. Victor often knocks over and sometimes breaks one of her treasures; it's the only time I see Nancy annoyed. On these occasions, Victor knows he's in trouble and flees as quickly as he can, calling profuse apologies over his shoulder.

Once Victor was trying to fix a shelf in the back room that displayed Nancy's special ornaments and precious crystal vase. He was singing and tapping away when Nancy came in to see the shelf sagging at one end and the contents above wobbling precariously.

'My mother's vase, oh my God.'

Nancy grabbed it just in time to save it from toppling over the edge. A couple of other items fell and scattered at her feet but miraculously stayed in one piece.

'Sorry, Nance, should have been more careful.' Victor was sheepish.

'I would never have forgiven you, Victor!'

As I carry a cup of tea to my room, which has become my special treat each day after the chores are finished, I catch my reflection in the hallway mirror. My pregnancy is well and truly showing. My skirt is too tight and my swollen belly pushes the waistline higher each day. In fact, my body bears no resemblance to its former shape. How can a body possibly return to its normal shape after this? And in twelve weeks, this baby will be ready. Will I be ready? What if something goes wrong? I have no idea how to look after a baby. Nancy has already told me she won't be much help. She and Victor were unable to have children. 'And I'm not too keen on kids anyway, luv.'

I'm about to climb the stairs when Nancy calls after me.

'Issie, your midwife is all sorted. Mary took no time at all in speaking to her daughter, she'll be here this arvo.'

'She's coming today? Oh, what do I need to do?'

'Don't be worried, luv. She's real smart. Knows everything there is to know about pregnant women and babies. You go and have a rest and I'll send her up when she gets here.'

At once the loneliness of it all takes over. I've been trying hard to hide my condition under loose clothes, though this is becoming less and less effective. Now it's as if I really am having a baby. And the thought of someone looking at my pregnant stomach and asking tricky questions unsettles me. For the first time since being in England, I wish I had my mother with me. She would know what to do. She would take charge. But she's not here, I'm on my own and it's all my doing. I just need to stay calm. This will all be over in a few months.

A little while later there are voices in the downstairs hallway and light footsteps heading up the stairs. Then a gentle knocking on my door.

'Come in,' I say as a head appears around the door.

'Hello, I'm Esme. I'm one of the district midwives here in Bermondsey.'

Esme is a petite woman of about thirty. Her hair is fair and pulled back in a ponytail and when she smiles, her eyes wrinkle. I like her immediately.

'Thanks for coming, Esme. I'm Isabella ... Issie McMillan.'

She glances at the wedding ring on my finger.

'I hear you're a long way from home, Issie.'

'Yes, I'm Australian.' I sense Esme already knows where I'm from, but she nods politely. I'm sitting on the edge of the bed as she sits on the rickety chair opposite and opens her bag, pulling out papers and chatting at the same time.

'Now, I'll need a few details about you, then have a look to see how you and your little one are faring. Nancy tells me you are well and robust. That's always a good sign.'

'I hope so.'

Esme asks about my health and any concerns I have. I want to tell her I'm petrified but I've promised myself I'll remain dignified throughout all of this. I tell Esme about my mother's stillbirths before I was born, but she doesn't appear concerned. She tells me to lie down and then examines my stomach.

'Can you feel bub moving about, Issie?'

'Yes, especially at night or when I'm resting.'

'Good.'

She's smiling as she rubs her firm hands over my stomach. I can tell she knows what she's doing, and I'm surprised how comforted I am by her being here.

'How many months do you have your pregnancy at, Issie?'

'Six.'

'Mm ... that seems about right. You're a fine candidate for a home birth. Young, healthy and sensible.' She smiles across the bed at me and the wrinkles at the sides of her eyes close into one another. 'Everything seems perfect.'

'So, what happens when the labour starts?'

'Let's talk about the next twelve weeks first. We have a day clinic you can attend every fortnight until your baby is due. It's in the afternoon and we'll give you a check-up to see that all's going well. Can you come along to the clinic, Issie?'

'Where is it?'

'Just a few doors down from St Mary Magdalen Church. I'm leaving this envelope with you. It contains all the information you need.'

I put my trust in Esme at once. All this baby and birth talk is like being thrown into a foreign world and far removed from my former life. I am so much more naïve than I'd realised. With Esme here prodding my stomach and talking about my confinement, I'm forced to think about the baby I'm carrying inside me. I'm starting to feel less capable physically and getting tired easily. I'm scared and sometimes I am angry. But there is nothing to be done until this baby arrives except to get through the moments of worry between now and then.

'Issie, do you have a friend or someone who is able to help you when your time comes? Will your ... will your husband be here? I'll come for the delivery but sometimes there is a time leading up to the actual birth that can be a bit drawn out. A relative or friend nearby is what we recommend.'

'No, my ... my husband won't be here. I don't have anyone. I can manage as long as I know you'll be here for the birth.'

Esme tilts her head and looks at me, her face full of concern that I'll be alone. I'm feeling the same way. When I discovered my pregnancy and learnt that Alexander had returned to Australia, I'd convinced myself I could manage this alone, but I'm not so sure anymore.

Esme hesitates, then smiles as she pats the back of my hand.

'We can work that out as we go along.' She hands me the large brown envelope.

'Here is a list of requirements for you and the baby after the birth.' She picks up her bag. 'See you at the clinic in two weeks, Issie. We can talk more then – there are some decisions you need to make.'

As the door closes behind her, the emptiness of the room envelops me. Now it's just me alone with a problem bigger than I could ever have imagined. I'm trembling as the afternoon light shines through the small window and the dust motes float in the air.

Having a baby was never part of the plan. I don't know if I can do this.

CHAPTER THIRTY-THREE

ISSIE

Ester House is an endless buzz of chatter, cups of tea and an unchallenged belief the world revolves around 78 Tolley Street. One day after my chores are finished, I have a sudden urge to get away, to be alone and to put some distance between my daily routine and my afternoon.

'Take a brolly, it looks like rain today,' says Nancy.

I'm not sure where I'm going as I pull on my coat, although I hardly need it today and will soon have to abandon my 'hide all' camouflage – it's getting warmer.

There's an unpleasant odour in the air around Bermondsey – a sickly sugary, chemical smell. When the wind is blowing it clears but on a sunny day void of breeze, it hangs low over the streets and houses. The factory chimneys pump out smoke and steam day and night. These brick stacks rise high above the buildings and dominate the skyline; children play on footpaths sometimes just a short distance from them. Nancy looked surprised when I mentioned the acrid smell to her.

'It's just the biscuit factories, smells like burnt sugar some days, luv. You get used to it. I hardly notice it.'

It's easy to put my problems out of mind when the household is bustling with Jack, Nessa and Janet coming and going, Victor fixing things and Nancy's running commentary on all things domestic. It diverts my attention, and the distraction serves me well in some ways, but I can't ignore the fact I'm about to have a child and my money is running out. It's time I faced what lies ahead.

How good it feels to be out of the house. I find myself in front of St Mary Magdalen's, an old Anglican church with its distinctive white rendering. The rear section is damaged and fenced off. The war left very few streets intact, and even though more than a decade has passed since those unforgiving bombing raids, areas of London are still badly affected. Funny though, the locals go about their daily business without fuss. I guess the war-damaged buildings are simply part of the landscape now. I'm reminded of how quickly we adjust to our circumstances when there is no alternative. I guess that's what the people of London did during and after the war: they adjusted.

The large elms in the church grounds have an abundance of spring buds bursting into flower. Two women sit on a bench with prams drawn up. Mothers engaging in talk, simple talk about babies and motherhood. It looks so easy for them, so natural. Could it ever be this way for me? They look toward me in a friendly way as I draw level with them. But personal talk about babies and motherhood is something I can't handle right now. In fact, these women with their appearance of normal and acceptable lives highlight that my life is anything but normal or acceptable right now.

I'm at the end of the path now, past the old gravestones and damaged statues, being lured toward the church entrance. Maybe it's the sense of seclusion, the restfulness of the church grounds that draw me here. There's no distraction other than for the two women behind me in the park, whose eyes I can feel on me as I push open the heavy door.

St Mary Magdalene. The name is written over the doorway. The irony brings a smile to my face – she's known as the patron saint of wayward women, although originally she was cast as a sinner and a fallen woman. I leave my sinner thoughts at the door and step inside, shoving my hands into my coat pockets as I move further into the foyer. It's dank and bleak inside along with a faint musty odour that's almost lost in the chill of the place. The faded green carpet in the aisle leads me to the steps of the marble altar.

I have no idea why I'm here. Perhaps it's for the sense of calm that washes over me as I slide into the second front pew. The prayer stools are upholstered with worn tapestry, each one different. I ponder the women who stitched them. Aunt Hattie comes to mind, her constant need to be knitting or stitching. Women like my aunt are the backbone of churches like this.

To the right of the main altar stands a life-sized statue of Mary Magdalene draped in a pale-blue robe with a crimson stole across her shoulders. She carries a white urn. Her head is tilted skyward, but her eyes look down as if she's watching me. They are kind eyes and for a few lingering moments I take in the comfort she has to offer.

It's been over a year since I left home. What must Mother and Father be going through? What will their reaction be if I tell them about the baby? Will I be welcome home? No, I will bide my time. Everything depends on me waiting until after the birth. Although not overly religious, I say a small prayer to the Virgin Mary and the small baby Jesus staring down at me from the stained-glass windows. 'God, let me make the right decision,' I whisper.

I'm about to leave when there is a presence behind me. I swing around to find a man wearing a clerical collar just a few feet away.

'I didn't mean to startle you,' he says, rubbing his hands together. 'Please stay as long as you wish, but it's chilly in here.'

'I'm just going.' I move across the aisle toward him.

'I'm Monty Downing, the assistant vicar here at St Mary Magdalen. I haven't seen you in the church before. Are you new to the area?'

'Yes. I'm Issie McMillan. I'm staying in Tolley Street for a while.'

'Good to meet you, Issie. Is there something I can help you with?' He notices my hesitation. 'Maybe we could talk in the supper room; it's warmer there,' he says as he leads off, expecting me to follow him.

I follow behind Vicar Downing to a side room, wondering if I really want to talk to him. His clothes – a checked jacket over his clerical shirt and collar – doesn't strike me as common attire for a man of the church. And he seems too young to be a vicar. Perhaps only a few years older than me. He opens the door to the red glow of a heater and a comforting warmth. The room is small compared with the vastness of the church. There are boxes of Bibles and hymn books on a nearby bench and folded trestle tables leaning against a wall. Folding chairs are stacked in piles underneath a window and, at the end of the room, there's a small kitchenette with urns and crockery lined up on a blue laminate bench top. Several tables sit in the middle of the room. He pulls up another chair alongside the small table near the glowing heater. There are papers and books sprawled on the table. He's been working here in the warmth.

'Would you like a cup of tea, Issie? The water's boiled – I was just about to make one when I noticed you in the church. It's a cold church, you see, there's no heating during the week, only on Sundays. Anyway, spring has arrived and the warmer days should help.' He smiles in a way that is matter of fact. I accept the offer of tea.

Within seconds, two cups of steaming hot tea appear, along with a little jug of milk. I wrap my hands around my cup and take several sips before looking at the vicar across the table. It's quite warm in the room but I leave my coat buttoned up.

'Sorry, I'm out of biscuits,' he says.

'This is perfect, thank you, Vicar. I'm sorry if I've interrupted your work. I'm not even sure why I came here. I just needed some time to think.'

'Please, call me Monty. I'm newly ordained and I'm not used to being called *Vicar*. I've only been here a few months and I'm still finding my way around and meeting the parishioners.'

'I am not a parishioner. I'm Church of England though. Well, if being Church of England in Australia counts?'

Monty grins.

'They didn't cover that in theology school. But I suspect if you're an Anglican in one country, you remain so in another.'

I like this man with his intense green eyes and wavy auburn hair. I like the way his body relaxes as he speaks, giving me a sense he's got as much time as needed. He has a way of making me feel I've known him for a long time. He sips his tea then finds a clear spot to put his cup on the paper-laden table.

'You're a long way from home. What brings you to Bermondsey, Issie?'

'It's quite a story. And not a happy one at that.'

'An unhappy story?'

'Not at first but ... I made a foolish choice and now I'm facing the consequences.'

'Sometimes the wrong choice can lead us to the right places, eventually. Are you sure you're not being a bit tough on yourself?'

'No.' I look around the room again and question why I'm talking about my predicament with this stranger. But I don't stop. 'I have decisions to make.'

'Are the decisions you have to make urgent?'

'I'm pregnant and I'm unmarried.' The words fly out. A challenge almost. Will he stiffen and turn against me? Will he judge me as others will and probably do already?

Monty's green eyes don't leave mine. The stillness of the room hangs over us as we sit by the messy table beside the glowing heater.

'The decisions are about your pregnancy?'

As I begin to tell him about my dilemma, I'm caressed by a strange sense of floating calm. I like it here, sitting in the warmth, sipping hot tea with church paraphernalia all around us. It's the quiet I need.

I leave out the really bad bits, the violence that I can barely bring myself to think about let alone speak of. It's a relief to throw my life onto Monty's table with the church papers and empty teacups. All the time he watches me, nodding at times but never interrupting. Finally, I fall silent. Monty rests his chin on his hand and for a few moments, I think I've shocked him. After all, why should this young cleric have any understanding of the things I've just told him?

I straighten in my chair as he asks, 'And when is your baby due to be born?'

'In eleven weeks.'

'And you can't decide if you should keep your child or adopt it out?'

'It's assumed I will give my child up, but I'm not sure.'

'Can you afford to raise a child on your own?'

'Not at the moment. But ...'

'But later?'

'Yes. I want to keep my baby, but I know it might be better to let him or her have a real family. Life can be cruel and being illegitimate is shunned. Can you see my dilemma?'

Monty looks uncomfortable for the first time. He lets out a deep breath and stares at the ceiling. It's as if there's a private dialogue going on in his head. He slowly turns back to me.

'I think I understand. You want to keep your baby but are frightened about the way your child might be treated. And yourself perhaps.'

'My father was given up for adoption at birth. And although, as an adult, he was reunited with his mother, it wasn't easy for them. He felt abandoned and cheated and my grandmother felt remorseful all her life – she still does.'

'And you don't want to repeat history.'

'No. But the stigma of not having a father. Isn't that just as bad?'

'Maybe, maybe not. Adoption masks the problem but only on the surface. I understand exactly what you're concerned about, more than you think.'

'What do you mean?'

Monty hesitates, glances at his shoes before looking me in the eye. I'm hot now, becoming uncomfortable. I unbutton my coat. Monty's neck is flushed. He uncrosses his legs and places his hands on his knees.

'Illegitimacy isn't a disease. There are some people who might call it a sin, but God forgives sins, Issie. My mother was only seventeen when she gave birth to me. I was raised by my grandparents. So, there you have it, Issie. I was born illegitimate. I was fortunate though; I always knew who my family were.'

'I'm so sorry, I ...'

'There's no need to be sorry. I just felt it would be dishonest not to tell you. I hope my story allows you to see you have the possibility of more than one choice.'

I hold back a sudden rush of tears. 'I appreciate you telling me, Monty.'

As I'm leaving, Monty tells me to return anytime. I nod and hurry away. I can't keep the tears at bay much longer and I don't want Monty to see them. His kind voice and honesty have undone me.

Outside, I lean on the wall of the church. I've been so confused about what's ahead of me and the baby. Putting off thinking about it, making a decision. For the first time I allow myself to be honest – I want to keep my baby. How I'm going to manage I don't know, but I will. I take a deep breath of the spring air before buttoning my coat. The two women are still sitting on the seat with their babies as I pass.

'You all right, luv?' one of them asks.

I wave to the women and walk back to Tolley Street with Monty's words ringing in my ears. 'I always knew who my family were.'

Chapter Thirty-Four

Issie

Nancy's screams pierce the silence. Her voice is shrill. Calling for help. It's still dark outside as I bolt for the door. In the hallway, Jack is ahead of me, flying down the stairs. Nancy, in her old red dressing gown with the buttons undone, grabs his arm as he reaches the bottom.

'He woke with pains. He's turning blue, can't breathe. I've been telling him, telling him for years he smokes too much ...'

'Nancy. Stop. We might need an ambulance.' Jack vanishes into Nancy and Victor's bedroom. Nancy backs away as I edge in after him. The dressing table is jammed up against one wall and a chair piled high with clothes is beside it. There is barely enough space for the two of us by the bed where Victor is slumped. Nancy hovers outside the doorway.

'He should be sitting up a bit, Jack? I'm not sure lying flat is helping him get enough air into his lungs.'

Jack nods and we gently ease Victor up onto the pillows. He moans, his eyes barely open.

'Issie Mac,' a rasping voice, 'help me ...' Victor's lips are blue and he's dragging in small gasps of air. Each breath sounds like it could be his last.

'I'll go to the phone box and ring for the ambulance.' Jack is gone.

Nancy is crying and wringing her hands by the door.

'Come over to the bed, Nancy,' but she backs further into the hallway.

Nan Eliza used to say, 'A person who stays calm makes a difference.' Janet and Nessa are on the stairway now, asking what's happened.

'Nancy, go to the kitchen and get a damp towel.'

She returns in no time with a tea towel dampened from the sink tap. She hands it to me and backs out of the room again as I wipe Victor's forehead. He's hot and clammy but opens his eyes. He's still gasping for air. The raspy sound of his fragile grip on life fills the room and spills out into the stuffy hallway.

We're all relieved when the front door opens and Jack comes in, out of breath.

'Ambulance on the way.'

'Hear that, Victor? Won't be long and we'll have you sorted.'

Victor squeezes my hand.

Nancy's sobbing has eased; she's talking to Janet and Nessa, who are hanging over the banister in their night clothes.

'I've been telling him for years the smokes will kill him. Begged him to stop but he never listens, never listens – look now!'

'Nancy, it might be an idea to get dressed. So you can go to the hospital with Victor.'

Nancy shrinks into herself. 'Not the hospital, I can't go to the hospital.'

Jack raises his eyebrows at me and shrugs.

Five minutes pass, then there is a commotion outside the window. In the half-darkened street, two men leap from an ambulance. Some of the neighbours, in an array of coats and night attire, are out on the footpath.

Jack ushers the men inside and we wait in the hallway as they tend to Victor. They bring in an oxygen cylinder and place a mask on Victor's face. He resists, becoming agitated, but then settles enough for them to get him on the trolley and wheel him to the waiting ambulance. Nancy watches from a distance with her hands to her face but doesn't make any attempt to go to Victor or even to say goodbye.

We're a bedraggled lot in the open doorway, watching the ambulance. Me with my long messy hair, Jack in his trousers and coat pulled over his blue striped pyjamas, Nancy in her well-worn dressing gown half-hanging off her shoulders, Janet with a blanket wrapped around her shoulders, and Nessa on the stairs, shivering in a nightdress.

'I'll put the kettle on.'

'Yes, Issie. I need a strong one.' Nancy has stopped crying and mutters something like, 'I have to pull myself together.' She follows me to the kitchen.

Jack winks at me.

'Pleased you were here, Issie McMillan. You're a cool head when it counts.'

'You didn't do such a bad job yourself, Jack Tremayne.'

Chapter Thirty-Five

Issie

Once Nancy knew Victor wasn't dying, she quickly rallied, and life returned to some sense of normality at Ester House. We all knew, though, that Victor wasn't going to settle back into his old habits when he arrived home, not if Nancy had anything to do with it. The flowers the neighbours gave her have wilted in her mother's vase while Victor recovered in hospital. Collecting the dead stems, I drop them into the bin on my way out. Nancy has given me a couple of smocks to wear when I'm doing the daily cleaning, but when I leave the house, I squeeze back into my own clothes. I've let out the waistline of the skirts and changed the buttons on the blouses. Everything is still too tight. I button my coat in a futile attempt to cover my bulging stomach.

Today is my appointment at the antenatal clinic. It is housed in a drab brick building with steps and a pram ramp leading to double doors. A serious-looking woman with wire glasses sits at a desk inside the entrance. She barely looks at me as I enter.

'Do you have your book?'

'No, I'm new. Esme told me to come.'

She sighs, leans forward with pen poised. 'I'll need some details then.'

The noise of the children playing in the waiting area makes it hard for her to hear me. Still, she's louder than necessary as she asks about my husband. I repeat the fanciful story about him working in Scotland. I only wish it was the truth. Sometimes I let myself imagine I really do have a husband in Edinburgh. When

I'm feeling strong and confident, I'm tempted to stop the charade about the absent husband. But would I be entitled to this service if it were known I wasn't married? I don't know. The woman hands me a small book with my name on the front and tells me to wait my turn.

The waiting room is cavernous; the echoes of the scraping of chairs and the conversations of the other expectant mothers reverberate around the room. Prams are parked at odd angles and grubby children run about and crawl across the timber floor. Some cry. I slide into a vacant chair. The woman sitting across from me is wearing a green cabled cardigan that has seen better days, monotonously rocking a cane pram back and forth with one hand, stifling a yawn with the other.

'Been up all night with this one. Had colic since he was born, never shuts up all day, all night. They say they grow out of it, he'd better hurry. I'm at my wits' end. First baby for you, luv?'

'Um, yes.' I don't know what to say to her, but it turns out she's just as happy to tell me her own troubles.

'This one's my fourth. The other three were easy, put them in the pram, a few rocks and they were asleep. But this one, he has a mind of his own, colic or no colic.'

What can I say that sounds sympathetic? It doesn't matter, she's already distracted by the bellowing coming from the pram. She scoops up the baby, unbuttons her blouse and smacks him against her chest. The baby nuzzles her ample breast and the loud crying stops.

'Mrs McMillan.' Esme is standing at the edge of the room. She smiles when she sees me, her eyes twinkling in a familiar way. Relief washes over me.

'Issie.' She takes my arm. 'You found us.'

Chapter Thirty-Six

Issie

It's been a week since Victor's return from hospital. Apart from being slower and a little unsteady on his feet, he's resumed his daily routine. In the morning he sits in his favourite chair in the front room and, when he thinks Nancy's out of sight, sneaks out the door for a cigarette. He goes to the Marygold each afternoon for a pint. Nancy's on tenterhooks and watches him closely for any signs of another heart attack.

Since the night Victor went to hospital, Nancy's been quiet and teary at times. She spends much of her day sitting at the table in the kitchen – the only house task she attends to now is cooking the evening meal. My workload has increased and I'm feeling heavy and tired most of the time. I'm also counting the weeks.

'You should rest more, luv,' Nancy says as she pours what seems like an endless stream of tea into her favourite pink rose cup. 'You're getting closer to your time.'

'I'll be fine, Nancy, it's you who's not yourself.'

'Is it that noticeable, luv?'

I sit down with her. 'Are you worried about Victor?'

'Oh, Issie, I can't go through that again. Him nearly dying on us.'

'He's recovering, Nancy.'

'But you never know with hearts.'

'But he takes his pills, and his doctor assures you he's doing well.'

Nancy's not comforted by my logic. She's not one to consider fact or reason if she feels otherwise. She can't seem to stop herself tapping her fingers on the stained linen tablecloth.

'There's no assurance for anyone in this world, Issie.' Nancy's glasses are low on her nose, her eyes tired. 'If you'd been here when they dropped the bombs you would understand. We never knew whose house was going to be next. Who was going to be killed or maimed, lives ruined forever. Always nervous, lived on the edge for ages, we did. Then felt guilty when we were safe and someone else's family wasn't.'

'They were terrible times, Nancy.'

'We had each other and that counted in those days. But me, well, I've never been any good when someone is sick. I go to water. It wasn't just the war, it goes back to when I was a little one.'

Nancy stirs the sugar in her tea, the spoon hits the sides of the cup in a slow rhythm; seemingly she's thinking about those terrible times. The clock ticks on the cluttered mantelpiece. Comforting. I count the seconds until she speaks again.

'My own dad died sudden as anything in the backyard, when I was about six, I reckon. I'll never forget it. The look on his face as he lay on the brick path. And all the time my mum was up the street at the butchers, buying chops for our tea.'

'You were alone with him?'

'Yes, I didn't know what to do.' Nancy looks as if she's about to cry but refills her cup instead. 'It happened a long time ago, but when Victor took sick it's all I could think of. It came back to me in an instant, as if it was just the other day.'

Nancy is occupied with her own thoughts, she's miles away and in another era. Her face is blotched and puffy and her hair hangs in thin strands around her neck. Her favourite knitted yellow cardigan droops from her shoulders.

And then she pulls herself up straight and takes a deep breath. She stands abruptly, picks up her cup and saucer and goes to the sink.

'Enough of my idle chatting. Sorry, Issie. I don't know what gets into me sometimes, feeling sorry for myself, acting all sooky. Go and have a rest for a while. You work too hard, go on, have a rest.'

***

It's less than seven weeks before the baby is due and I'm obsessing over the birth. Esme's told me about the first signs of labour. The plan is, I will ring or get someone else to ring Esme when my pains start. She says she will come early enough to help me through.

I've managed to buy the necessary baby things. Nancy, despite a self-confessed lack of interest in children, has knitted a white layette with jacket, bonnet and booties. One day she came home with a pram. Nancy said she was given it by a friend whose daughter didn't need it anymore. I don't question this, mainly because I suspect there is plenty of talk about me and my circumstances. Sometimes it's best not to know. At least I have a pram and baby clothes, which I'm feeling grateful for. Mother and Father would be appalled to know I am accepting charity from people who probably can't afford it, but I try not to think about my family too much.

Concentrating on the next six weeks and not beyond – this is a strategy I learnt from Mother. 'When the pressure is on, just focus on the task in front of you. There is nothing to be gained by worrying about what might happen.'

Nessa and Janet are friendly and funny to be around. They work together at the Lipton factory but after work their talk mainly consists of music, rock n' roll dancing, young men and clothes. They have an uncanny way of ignoring my predicament, at least in my presence. My situation is a secret that everybody knows about. I know they don't believe I'm married with a husband in Scotland, but they play along with the story. It is decent of them.

Sometimes in the evenings after our meal, when Janet and Nessa have gone to their rooms or to the Marygold, and when Nancy and Victor have retired to the front room, Jack and I clear up the stacked dishes. We chat as we wash and dry and wipe down the table. Sometimes we make another cup of tea and sit for a while before heading to our rooms. We can hear Victor and Nancy's new television; static has driven the rest of us away from trying to watch it. Nancy says Victor's mate is coming to fix it but, in the meantime, the two of them tolerate the snowy picture and somehow seem to enjoy it.

'It's a strange situation for you to be in, Issie.'

'You mean here alone without a husband?'

'Yes and no. What I mean is, you wouldn't normally stay at a place like this. You've clearly lived a different life to the one we're living here.'

'I'm grateful to be here. I don't know what I would have done otherwise, Jack.' He looks at me in his questioning way. 'You're right, though. I did have a different life in Australia. I was lucky, too lucky. I had everything until I came to England to be with a man I didn't really know. I'm so embarrassed. Jack, there's no husband in Scotland. Just me in a muddle because I made a bad choice.'

'Sometimes things go wrong.'

'I can't believe I was so gullible.' I feel tears well up but take a deep breath. 'And now, I'm living with my mistake.'

Jack puts sugar in his tea. He stirs for longer than is needed before looking up, his dark hair falling across his forehead.

'Events happen in life that change us forever, Issie. I learnt that during the war.' He turns away and for a moment and I think he's going to get up from the table. 'My wife and son were killed in the Blitz. It's over ten years ago now, but sometimes it seems like yesterday.'

The drone of the television in the front room seems a mile away as we sit in silence. I reach for Jack. He flinches but doesn't move. I feel the warmth of his arm under his cotton shirtsleeve. He nods and then the tension falls away.

'I had no idea ... I'm sorry, Jack.'

'I was in the army, in France, and hadn't seen them for two months. It was three days before I found out they'd been killed in an air raid.'

'Were you able to come home?'

'Yes, but home wasn't here, it was Redruth in Cornwall. But that was a long time ago, and as they say, life must go on. But it took a few years before I came to terms with losing them. Sometimes I'm not sure I have. It should never have happened.'

'What did happen, Jack?'

'It was here in Bermondsey. They were staying with Delia's mother who was sick at the time; that's why they were here and not in Cornwall. My son, Will, was only two years old, not much more than a baby. Full of life, he was. Could talk and sing. They say he looked like me, but you can never see it yourself.' Jack shifts in his chair and I remove my hand from his arm. 'Anyway, they were asleep when it happened, in the back bedroom. Earlier in the afternoon the sirens went off, they sat it out in the Anderson shelter for hours until the all-clear sounded. Then they went back to the house. The next attack came without warning. Delia's mother got out, but Delia and Will had no chance.'

'Oh, Jack.'

'Sometimes, I think it's just a dream … but it's no use trying to fool myself. Life goes on, Issie. It has to.'

Chapter Thirty-Seven

Issie

The queue at Manze's pie shop snakes down the street. It's a warm morning and I feel foolish in my overcoat. The two women at the end of the line are talking and laughing as I take my place behind them. One of them asks after Nancy. Says she's glad to hear Victor's on the mend. Then I see her. Old Shirl is three spots ahead of me in the queue and looking in my direction.

'Where's Nancy?' she calls out. I pretend not to hear her until the woman who'd asked after Nancy taps me on the arm and nods in Shirl's direction.

'Is she home with Victor? Poor man, he nearly died by all accounts.'

'Yes. Nancy's home with Victor.' I turn from her and curse the wait; the line is barely moving. My back aches and I'm hot in my stupid coat. I twist Nancy's shopping bag in my hand and check my watch.

'She's lucky to have you doing her errands. Still, she's doing you a big favour, I suppose. Although by the look of you it won't be for much longer. How long to go?'

I can feel the eyes of the other women watching me. Everyone falls silent. I pretend I haven't heard Shirl.

'High and mighty, aren't you? Do you think yourself too good for the likes of us? Mm, seems it can happen to the best of us.'

'It's none of your darn business,' I say to Shirl.

She tucks in her chin and sniffs. A couple of women giggle as the line shuffles forward.

I want to leave, to be away from the curious stares, and yet I know I have to collect the bloody pies or there'll be nothing for tea.

'Types like you never learn,' she snarls.

The woman in front of me huffs loudly and lets her voice carry. 'That's enough, Shirl. You can see the girl's upset. No need to make a fuss.'

'It's not me being rude. You heard her, she told me to mind my own business. No manners and no morals, that's the problem.'

I'm about to leave without the wretched pies when one of the girls behind the counter beckons me over. No one says a word as she packs two bags of pies and potted eel in Nancy's shopping bag. Fumbling in Nancy's brown plastic purse, the one she insists we use for housekeeping, I hand over a pound note rather than count out coins; my hands are shaking too much. Tears are running everywhere, but my back is to the sea of women in the shop and the only people who can see my face are the shop assistants behind the counter. As the girl hands back my change, she squeezes my hand.

'Go home and have a hot cuppa, luv. Everyone knows what an old cow Shirl is.'

***

The mail arrives and I notice a large envelope in Neva's writing. I take it to the privacy of my room to open it. Surprisingly, there are two letters inside. I read Neva's first.

Dear Isabella,

I finally have another assistant, your replacement left after an altercation with Margaret and Mr James. Did I tell you already? Harold Broome is slower with his work than you were but he is quiet and well-mannered. He plays the organ for one of the local churches. He's asked me to go out to the local dance with him but I told him mixing work and social activities is not a good idea. I like him, he is a very decent chap.

Issie, the accompanying letter came for you at work. It has an Australian postmark. Margaret had the good sense to bring it to me right away, instead of giving it to Mr James.

Please write soon with news of your situation. Have you thought about what to do after the baby arrives?

Your dearest friend, Neva

With shaking hands, I open the other letter in Father's handwriting. How did he know about Iffley? The only address my parents have for me is Oxford.

Miss Isabella McMillan,
C/O James and Kendle Accountants,
Iffley. UK.

Dear Isabella,

We have written to you several times over the last few months but have not heard back from you. We can only assume you are no longer at Oxford. Your mother and I are concerned and need to know you are well.

Recently we had an unexpected visit from a gentleman we believe you know. A Dr Alexander Sadler. He told us he was an acquaintance of yours in Oxford and hinted you'd spent time together when he was there.

He told us he is moving to Sydney with his wife and family to take up a lecturing position at the University of Sydney. Your mother and I both thought he seemed concerned for you and he wanted to know if we had heard from you. He seemed to be reluctant to talk about Oxford much at all but was able to give us your work address.

Your mother has not been herself since you left. At times I consider coming to England to find you but leaving your mother to cope on her own is out of the question. And as you know, Nan Eliza left for China adding to our sense that everyone we love is halfway around the world! I'm sorry if I seem a little dramatic, Isabella. We just need you to contact us. When this letter reaches you, please write back or send a telegram.

I have included a money order in the hope you might consider booking a passage back to Australia.

We miss you, Isabella.

Your loving Father

Father's letter is wet with tears as I fold it back into its envelope. Oh, how much I want to write and let them know where I am and to tell them I'm sorry. They shouldn't have to worry about me, it's not fair. How am I going to tell them about the baby? They'll be so ashamed of me.

How dare Alexander go to my parents masquerading as a fine, upstanding man concerned for their wayward daughter. And to think he's back in Australia with

Helen and his children and moving to Sydney. If only they knew what he did to me – the lies, the scheming, the drinking, the anger, the beatings. But who is going to believe me, an unmarried woman about to give birth to an illegitimate baby in a rundown boarding house in Bermondsey?

There are footsteps on the stairs. Jack is home from work at the brewery. He calls my name through the closed door. Earlier I pretended not to hear Nancy and now she's sent Jack to try again. They are keeping an eye on me and I'm so grateful to them for caring, but I need my space right now, at least until I settle myself.

'Issie, you in there?'

'I'll be down soon.'

'Everything all right?'

I can't fool Jack. I dab my reddened eyes and stand up from the bed. My back and head ache and a sense of deep dread has lingered all day. What I would do for this nightmare to be over. I open the door. Jack is leaning on the banister, head on the side.

'Nancy's in a fuss about you. She's worried it might be your time coming a couple of weeks early. Are you sick, Issie?'

'I'm having a strange day, but I'll be down soon. I would love a cuppa if you're making one, Jack.'

'Right away.'

Jack smiles at me. He's trying to jolly me up as he heads down the stairs. When I enter the back room, Nancy, Jack, and Victor are deep in conversation. The chatter stops abruptly.

'Issie, sit here.' Nancy pulls out a chair as Jack pours the tea.

Their concerned and kind faces looking at me bring comfort, then the tears again, running down my cheeks.

'We know you're miserable. Been in your room all afternoon,' says Nancy with a gentleness I've not heard before. 'Do you think the baby's coming, Issie?'

'I had a letter from home today and it's made me homesick and guilty. My parents are worried and they have no idea what's going on for me here.'

'You never talk about home, luv.'

'I'm trying to get through all of this before I can think about them.'

Victor and Nancy are sitting either side of me and Jack is opposite. Victor pats my arm, which surprises us all. But since the night of his heart attack, he's gone out of his way to have little conversations with me whenever we are in the same room. Nancy is fiddling with the plate of arrowroot biscuits.

'Issie, let's not get ahead of ourselves here,' Jack says. 'Surely it can't hurt to send your folks a telegram telling them you're fine and will send a letter in a few weeks. That way you'll all feel better.'

I smile at Jack, always so sensible and thoughtful. He's right. I can't remain silent anymore. My parents need to know I'm at least alive and hopefully the promise of a letter will ease their worry. Victor nods and Nancy reaches for the teapot.

'There you go then,' says Nancy. 'I always say there's a solution waiting for every problem.'

***

Sleep, despite my tiredness is hard to find. My mind is tangled with thoughts of Mother and Father at home. I toss from side to side until eventually I doze.

The front gate sticks against the rusted steel frame. It finally grinds open enough to allow me to squeeze through with my case. The garden is overgrown, the lawn uncut. The roses are unpruned, their leaves sparse and brown, and the box hedge is sprouting at odd angles with long weeds piercing its once immaculate shape. A patch of daffodils poke their heads along the path edge, fighting for some resemblance of normality.

Lugging my suitcase up the three front steps I place it beside the two large clay pots that once held colourful pansies, Mother's favourites. They're empty except for lumps of caked, brown soil.

The doorbell is missing so I knock on the wooden timber door.

'Mother, Father.'

Peering in through the glass panels beside the door, I see sheets covering the furniture along the walls.

I knock louder.

The gate scrapes behind me, breaking the silence. 'You came at last.'

I swing around and squint into the sun. A woman is silhouetted on the path before me. She steps into my view. She's wearing a green tweed overcoat with a black velvet collar buttoned high under her chin. Her hands are on her hips.

'Aunt Hattie?'

'It's no good knocking again, there're gone.'

'Gone!'

'They couldn't bear it anymore.'

'What are you saying?

'Your parents. The shame of it all, too much … too much … too much!'

Jolting upright in the bed, I wait for my breathing to slow. My face is wet as I fumble for the cord to turn on the light. My watch says it's four o'clock in the morning. Oh, what have I done?

Chapter Thirty-Eight

Issie

Monty smiles as I open the door to the supper room. 'Biscuits today, Issie.'

'What sort?'

'Custard creams and garibaldis.'

'The best of the best.'

Monty makes the tea and places a plate on the table. This is the fourth time I've visited him since our first meeting. Four conversations where he's turned from a stranger to a trusted friend. A lifeline thrown when I need it most. He is the antidote to my middle-of-the-night panics. With him in the full light of day, I find my strength again.

'How's your week been, Issie?'

'I've sent my parents a telegram telling them where I am. But I can't stop thinking how much I've put them through and the bombshell I'm about to drop.'

'A good decision to contact them, I would think.'

'About time I made a good decision.'

The sun is streaming through the high window in the supper room and striking the edge of the cluttered table. There is a lightness about this morning that transcends my earlier meetings with Monty.

'You can only do what you think is right, Issie.'

'Yes. I've cancelled the appointment Esme made for me at the adoption agency. I know I don't want that for my child, but I'm frightened, Monty.'

'It's only natural. You're about to bring a little one into the world who will be entirely dependent on you.'

'It's not the only reason. I have no idea how I'm going to manage financially, but that has become a secondary concern to keeping my baby. Oh, I'm not as strong and fearless as I pretend to be. Underneath I'm like jelly. But as you say, one day at a time.'

Monty understands the true implications of what I'm about to embark upon. He doesn't jolly me along with platitudes or tell me God will show the way. No, he says it's going to be a heavy load and I need to plan and find ways to get the most support I can. Monty's a thinker. He understands a lot about life. In fact, he rarely mentions his Christian beliefs; instead he places his belief in people's own ability to find solutions for themselves.

'Issie, not all decisions in life are the right ones and at times we have to find the courage to believe in ourselves.'

I know when he talks like this it's not just about me.

'Sounds like you're talking as much about yourself as me today?'

'Have another custard cream.' He hands me the plate. We laugh.

'Have you sorted out the accounts yet?' I ask. The table is just as strewn with papers as when we first met.

'Not entirely, there are a few tricky bits.'

'Perhaps I can help you sort it. After all, I've done some bookkeeping.'

'Would you, Issie?'

We shuffle closer to the table and Monty shows me the problem he's having with the church accounts.

'You just need some better systems.'

We sort the papers and I show Monty how to set up a simple creditors ledger and how to record payments as they are made. He's quick to learn and in no time we have the problem sorted. It feels good to be able to help him in this practical way.

'I do have something to tell you, Issie.' He pushes his chair back and turns to face me. 'I'm being transferred to Manchester.'

'But you've only been here a few months. When are you going?'

'In two weeks.'

'So soon?'

'My bishop is doing a favour for the Bishop of Manchester. He has asked me to assist an elderly vicar who's been there for about thirty years. He's been ill for several months and isn't managing so well.'

'And do you want to go, Monty?'

'I'll be sorry to go but I have no choice. We serve where we are needed.'

'You're needed here.'

A wry smile flickers across his face.

'You don't like some of this church stuff, do you, Issie?'

'I'm not sure, but I think you're more than just a cog in a big wheel. You're doing a fine job here. You've just started to get things sorted, the congregation is increasing and then they whisk you away? It doesn't make sense. And what about you and your sense of fulfillment?'

'Some things we just have to accept. I'm sure you understand.'

We talk for a long time as the afternoon light slowly changes its hue through the windows. Monty shrugs his shoulders; it's obvious he doesn't want to leave, but it's clear he's going to take it on the chin. There will be no complaining by him.

'It's Manchester's gain, Bermondsey's loss,' I say as I prepare to go.

'I will miss our talks, Issie. Especially the way you challenge traditional conventions, those that other people just accept, me included sometimes.'

'And we'll both miss the biscuits.' We laugh and the awkwardness disappears.

Chapter Thirty-Nine

Issie

It's dark outside as I fumble for the switch on the lamp next to my bed. My watch says two forty-five. For the past week I've had the sensation of tightening across my stomach. Esme told me it's normal, just the body getting ready for the big event.

'You'll know when it's the real thing, Issie.'

The floor is cold underfoot and I pull my coat around my shoulders. The painful tightening comes again, and then it eases. There's a throbbing in my back and I'm not sure what to do next. The special delivery pack that Esme brought last week sits next to the wicker pram, which is squashed tight against the wall.

'Just to be prepared ahead of time,' she said as she carried the large bundle up the stairs and into my room. 'All we need for the birth is in this pack.'

The sensation is there again, building and tightening, worse than before. I yelp as I shuffle across the room. Then the pain subsides. Ring Esme, someone needs to ring Esme. On the landing, I tap on Jack's door as another contraction begins. When Jack opens his door, he sees me doubled over and panting.

'My God, Issie.'

'The baby's coming, Jack,' I say as the pain eases. 'Ring Esme.'

Jack rakes his fingers through his hair, snatches the notebook containing Esme's phone number out of my hand and dives back into his room. He comes out pulling up trousers over his pyjamas.

'Come on, back to your room. I'll let Nancy know and I'll be gone. I've told Nancy we need a bloody phone connected!'

'Just go, Jack. I need Esme – hurry.'

The front door closes with a bang as I ease myself back on the bed. Then voices on the stairs.

'You all right, luv?' Nancy pokes her head around the door. Victor calls from the bottom of the stairs, 'I'll put the kettle on, Nance.'

'The baby's coming, Nancy.'

Before she can say anything, the pain of another contraction hits. To my surprise, Nancy steps slowly toward me. She doesn't want to be here; neither do I. She's standing beside me in her dressing gown with missing buttons and her hair a knotted mess. Her hands wringing and twisting in front of her.

'They say if you breathe slow, Issie ...'

Nancy pats my hand. She's looking at my stomach as if it has alien qualities, and I suspect she's praying for Esme to get here quick. So am I. The contractions are really pounding now and my waters must have broken. I can feel my nightdress wet beneath me. Nancy continues to pat my hand and rub my shoulder. She starts to hum *All things bright and beautiful* ... but the shake in her voice is too much.

The front door downstairs opens and Jack bursts into the bedroom moments later. He's puffing; he has obviously run all the way back from the phone booth in Huckle Street, three blocks away.

'Esme's on her way.'

There's a moment of relief before another contraction mounts. Jack's looking at me and Nancy is looking at Jack. They are thinking about who's going to stay with me until Esme arrives. Then Jack turns to Nancy.

'How about you go down, help Victor make the tea and wait for Esme. She might need extra hot water, so you could get the big boiler on.'

'Right, that's a good idea,' she says, already out the door.

Jack takes a deep breath. I'm glad he's there. I know he will look after me until Esme arrives. The contractions are getting faster and stronger – my hair is soaked with perspiration. Jack grabs towels from the linen cupboard in the hallway and wipes my forehead. Time vanishes. There is just me and pain. Where is Esme? Panic is kicking in when I hear her voice on the stairs. I didn't even hear the door. Jack lets out a sigh of relief; we were both worried she wasn't going to make it.

'Well, well, Issie. A week earlier than we expected,' says Esme as she hurries through the door. She nods to Jack and reaches for the pack and swiftly pulls out a waterproof sheet.

'I'm Jack, one of the lodgers here. I'll be around if you need anything.'

'Hello, I'm Esme.'

She tries to move the chair closer to the end of the bed.

'Here, let me.' Jack lifts it for her, then throws me a 'you'll be fine' look as he leaves. Esme comes to my side.

'Nice to be around a man who can hold his nerve.' She smiles at me. 'Let's have a look and see how far off this little one is.'

Esme runs her hand over my tight stomach and tells me she's going to look down below. She prods and pokes and tells me I'm fully dilated.

'This bub's in a hurry, Issie.'

Esme adjusts the sheet beneath me in between contractions and arranges items from the maternity pack on the chair. I pant in small breaths as each pain surges and my low guttural groans permeate the small room. I'm lost in what seems like a sea of motion. The waves of pain roll within my body; my body doesn't feel like mine anymore. The pain rises to a crescendo before a little cascade of relief, just enough time to take a few breaths before another assault. Esme is beside me, looking calm but serious.

'I'm going to move to the foot of the bed, Issie. Your baby will be born soon. Listen to me and follow my instructions.' She arranges sheets and towels and is rubbing my leg. 'Doing well, Issie. Just keep breathing, slow.'

'Esme, help me, I can't do this.'

'Yes, you can. I'm here with you. When the next pain comes, I want you to push, but wait for me to tell you.'

I want to be somewhere else, not here, not helpless like this.

'Help me, Esme ...'

'Almost there, Issie. Okay. Ready. Push.' Quick glimpses – the top of Esme's head bending over me at the foot of the bed, the cane pram across the room, my towel hanging on the hook behind the door… She calls again, louder this time. 'One more push and that should do it. Wait … wait … now.'

A scream escapes me as I push with all the strength I have left. Suddenly, I feel the baby leave my body in a slippery rush. Esme holds up a squirming, ruddy newborn covered in blood and vernix. She's grinning and rubbing the baby's back.

'Well done, Issie. You have a beautiful daughter.'

'A daughter. I have a daughter?' As I ease myself up again on my elbows, her cries fill the room.

'Good lungs too,' says Esme with a smile that crinkles the sides of her eyes. 'We'll just wait for the afterbirth and then we'll be in the pink.'

***

Two hours later, I'm resting on the pillows plumped up by Esme. I'm washed, tidied and my little girl is a warm bundle in my arms. There's a strange sense of being in another place. Has this really happened to me? Esme says it was a quick birth and I might feel a little bit of shock and disbelief, but it will pass, she assures me.

There are voices in the hallway, the door creaks and three heads appear around it. Jack, Nancy and Victor look to Esme for permission to enter. She nods to them, and they quietly tiptoe into the already congested room. Nancy comes over to the bed first, wringing her hands in the way she has taken to lately. Then she pats my head, in a maternal way that I'll always be grateful for, before shifting her eyes to the baby.

'She already has a mind of her own, coming in the middle of the night,' says Nancy. Her gaze is fixed on the baby. She's nodding to herself; a hint of tears is visible in her eyes. She tells Victor to take a peep at the little one that caused them to have such a sleepless night. Victor is coy but comes closer. He places his hand on Nancy's arm and peers over her shoulder.

'Your daughter's one of us now, Issie Mac. Born in Bermondsey,' says Victor, breaking into a wide smile.

'Come on,' says Nancy, taking his hand. 'We'll make another pot of tea for Issie and Esme.'

They pad out in their slippers and Jack is left leaning on the doorframe.

'Well done. A daughter, and if she's anything like her mother, she'll be one of the best.'

'Thanks, Jack, I'm so grateful.'

Jack comes closer to the bed.

'She's got a full head of hair already, Issie.'

Esme is watching him as he gently strokes the bundle in my arm.

'Have a hold of her, Jack. After all, if it hadn't been for you tonight, I would have been in a real pickle.'

'I'll second that,' says Esme as she takes the baby from me and hands her to Jack. He's hesitant at first, but gently wraps his large hands around the tightly bound bundle.

'You did a mighty job, Esme. We were relieved to hear you walk through the door,' says Jack.

'Just part of a night's work.' Esme smiles at Jack and his face lights up like a beacon.

'And her name, Issie. What do we call this little one?' says Jack, directing his attention back to me.

'Lilybeth. Her name is Lilybeth.'

'Welcome to the world, Lilybeth.' Together, Jack and Esme peer into the face of my newborn daughter.

Despite the euphoria and relief of finally giving birth, I don't miss the look that passes between them as Jack returns the baby to my arms.

Chapter Forty

Issie

Lilybeth Neva McMillan arrived safely yesterday. Both well, will write soon. Issie.

I ask Jack to send the telegram to Neva on his way to work. Later in the day, I write a quick letter to Monty and ask Nancy to post it when she goes to the grocer shop,

Dear Monty,

I have a daughter called Lilybeth. She arrived yesterday and I now know I could never part with her. We are both well and my friends at Ester House have been wonderful. I wouldn't be managing without them.

I'll always be grateful you helped me make the biggest decision in my life. Wish you were still around the corner at St Mary's.

I will write a longer letter soon.

Your friend, Issie

Lilybeth is sleeping beside me as I turn my full attention to writing the letter I've been dreading. She stretches and makes a funny little sound; this tiny little person makes me smile and gives me courage.

Dear Mother and Father ...

I falter. Where do I even begin?

CHAPTER FORTY-ONE

KNILL

It's a bleak August day and a southerly blows a bitter chill as Knill arrives home. He collects several letters from the mailbox beside the wrought iron gate and hurries along the path, fumbling the key in the front door lock. He drops the mail on the polished hallway stand and takes off his coat. It's only then he sees Isabella's handwriting on one of the letters.

He checks his watch. It will be another hour until Lily returns home from the office. He goes to the lounge room and drops into one of the thickly padded chairs. He knows he should wait until Lily gets home, but his urge to read his daughter's letter is too strong. They have been waiting weeks for news.

The past year and a half have taken a toll on their lives. Isabella leaving the way she did, then not being in contact for months, left them shattered. It might have forced them to see Isabella as an adult and not just their adored daughter, and she, like everyone else, has the right to live her own life. But the way she left? Their grief at times feels endless.

Knill flicks the switch on the standard lamp and opens the long-awaited letter. The thin paper is shaking in unison with his hands. He begins to read, then slowly leans forward.

Dear Mother and Father,

I know you will be waiting for my letter. I've been thinking of you both and missing you, especially over the last few weeks. You will soon understand the reasons for this.

I'm not proud of leaving home in the manner I did. I'm sorry for the anxiety it must have brought you. You may have guessed by now that Alexander Sadler and I were in a relationship in Oxford. I met him during my second year at university and he asked me to go to England with him.

Going into all the details right now has little purpose. Our relationship was anything but happy. His appointment at the university was also problematic and it resulted in him leaving Oxford suddenly and without telling me.

When Alexander returned to Australia, unknown to him I was carrying his child. Two days ago, I gave birth to a beautiful baby girl. Her name is Lilybeth Neva McMillan. She is healthy and well and I've decided to bring her up on my own although I am still to work out what to do next.

I know my actions and current circumstances will hurt you. I'm sorry for all the worry and distress I've caused but I am managing and will work out a way forward.

With love, Isabella

His hand rises to his face. *A beautiful baby girl ... Lilybeth ... bring her up on my own.* He reads the words over and over. Two days ago. The letter is dated twenty-fourth of July. Lilybeth must have been born on the twenty-second of July. She's two weeks old. The late-afternoon light is fading and, other than the glow of the lamp beside him, the room is darkening. A noise startles him from his thoughts – it's Lily opening the front door.

'Why haven't you drawn the curtains, Knill?'

'There's been a letter.'

Lily drops her briefcase at her feet and moves toward his outstretched hand. She takes the letter and sits on the edge of a sofa under the lamp. She is still wearing her cerise winter coat and its matching scarf. Knill turns on the light switch by the door. The room brightens but nothing changes. The silence is foreboding.

Lily doesn't move a muscle in her body. Her eyes are fixed on the letter. Twice, she reads the contents, then she folds the paper neatly and returns it to its envelope. She straightens her back and stands.

'We have to talk about this, Lily.'

'What is there to talk about? She clearly doesn't need us anymore.'

'Isabella has a daughter. We have a granddaughter.'

'In England, and need I point out to you, Knill, our granddaughter is illegitimate.'

Knill takes her hand and makes her sit with him on the couch. Tears well in his eyes.

'And do you view me the same way, Lily?'

'What do you mean?'

'You know I was also born illegitimate.'

'Knill, this is nothing like your situation. You were adopted out and …'

'But I was still born outside wedlock and my mother has carried the shame and guilt forever. People looked down on her and her own family rejected her. Covering it up with adoption made no difference to her – or me, for that matter.' Knill shifts uneasily as Lily reaches for his arm; he pulls away.

'Knill, this is not the same. And if you ask me, your mother doesn't act as if she's poorly done by. This is our daughter, who should have known better. She had a good family and everything she wanted, her life was ahead of her, and she does this? How dare she bring a child, our grandchild, into the world in such a manner.'

The room is silent except for the immutable ticking of the mantel clock. Knill doesn't look at Lily; he slowly rubs his hands together, his breathing deep but controlled. Eventually he turns to her.

'I won't have you speak of Isabella like that, Lily. She is our daughter; a mistake's been made, but I'm damned if she's to pay for this for the rest of her life. I'm as shocked and upset as you, but ostracising her is not going to happen. Isabella will need us. She has no family in England, no one to fall back on, no money. How will she manage to raise her child? A child she named after you, Lily.'

Lily's face tightens and Knill sighs inwardly.

They sit in the elegant lounge room with embossed crimson drapes and matching cushions, their grand piano gleaming in the corner; family photos in gold frames are proudly displayed on top.

'It seems as if she is very capable of living her life without us, Knill. And why would she wait until the child is born before telling us? And the child's father is a married man!'

'Perhaps she was worried about our reaction, Lily. And given yours, maybe she had good reason to be.' Knill takes his wife's hand again, tries to let the compassion he feels for his daughter flow to her mother.

'I'm pleased my dear father is not here to learn about this. All the hard work he did to ensure I had a good future and now ...'

'Lily, I understand your hurt, but this isn't about us, despite our concern – it's about Isabella and her child.'

Lily pulls her hand from his. 'I'm not just hurt, Knill. I'm devastated.'

Chapter Forty-Two

Issie

I try not to think about Alexander. Having a baby alone has taught me some valuable lessons, like not focusing on the things I can't change. Even the terrible times in Oxford have started to fade. The process of writing to Mother and Father was difficult; it has been the hardest part of all. Oh, how I struggled with telling them about the birth of Lilybeth. My angst was around not being sure how they would respond. Will they be happy or angry or somewhere in between? I haven't written to Nan Eliza. I know she will understand, but she's in China, so contacting her until she returns to Australia is out of the question. I'm delaying writing to Aunt Hattie. I know I must, but something stops me.

***

It's been raining all day and Lilybeth has been grumpy, wanting to be held, not settling well. Nancy and Victor have been to an appointment with his doctor and arrive back with kippers for our tea. They are muttering about the price of them, how they used to be able to get twice as many for half the price, when a knock at the front door ends the fish talk. I open the door to a ginger-haired telegram boy standing on one leg, his arm leaning on the door frame.

'Telegram for Isabella McMillan.'

'Yes, I'm Isabella, thank you.' I reach out and take the envelope before he scuttles down the steps, picks up his bike off the footpath and pedals away.

The telegram is from Mother and Father. It must mean they have received my letter. I'm dreading this, but simultaneously desperate to hear from them. I don't want to open it in front of Nancy and Victor. Tearing open the fine envelope, my hands shake as I unfold the telegram.

Isabella, what do you need? I can send a money order for you and the baby to come home to Australia. Love, Father.

Chapter Forty-Three

Knill and Lily

The doorbell rings as Knill and Lily are having breakfast. Since Isabella's letter earlier in the week, Lily has refused to discuss anything to do with her daughter. Knill is giving her time. He knows her well, her need to internalise issues, more so when she's hurt, and how she then processes things in her own way before she's willing to talk. There have been periods of struggle in their marriage, especially in the early years when Knill found Lily's way of dealing with difficulty unnecessarily selfish. Lily's stubbornness is one of the qualities that makes her the successful lawyer and businesswoman she is today. Still, he wishes his wife could be less intense.

On the doorstep stands a young boy in a heavy brown raincoat, dripping water. 'Telegram for Mr and Mrs McMillan, sir.'

Knill takes the envelope and thanks the shivering delivery lad, who retrieves his bike from the fence, then pedals madly back down the street in the heavy rain.

Knill opens the telegram as he walks back to the breakfast room.

> *Hattie McKenzie died suddenly last night. 7.30pm. Massive stroke. Sorry for the bad news. Rev. Dyson, Methodist Minister. Maryborough.*

The room blurs around Knill as Lily asks, 'What is it?'
'It's Hattie. She's dead.'

Lily is instantly on her feet and Knill is aware of her gently taking the telegram out of his hand, but he doesn't move. Knill and Lily had visited Hattie in Maryborough a month ago. She hadn't been well lately but there was nothing indicating anything too serious. Knill sits down slowly. Hattie's only ten years older than him, the daughter of his adoptive mother. He searched for Hattie after he found his own biological parents all those years ago. She's been part of the family for so long and now she's gone.

'Knill, are you all right?'

Lily is beside him, her hand on the sleeve of his woollen jumper; it's one Hattie knitted for him several years ago.

'What? Yes, I just can't believe it. So sudden.'

Chapter Forty-Four

Issie

'Why don't we take the little one for a walk, Issie.' Nancy and Victor are trying not to look too eager.

'I'm not sure, yes, maybe.' Lilybeth hasn't been out of my sight since she arrived four weeks ago. 'After her morning feed and only for a short walk.'

'Just down to the shops and back, Issie. Fresh air's good for babies, so they say. Not that we know much about babies, but we can learn.' They giggle together at the kitchen sink. They have a renewed love of life these days.

Lilybeth is in her pram, wrapped in her beautiful white shawl knitted in a fancy shell pattern. According to Nancy, it is a difficult pattern. I know she didn't knit it herself, but it appeared a few days after Lilybeth's birth. Did she have it tucked away from an earlier dream? It's not a discussion Nancy wants to have.

'Just half an hour,' I say.

Nancy pushes the pram down the hall, just clearing the bike, the coats, the stacked boxes and shoes. Victor is already at the door, holding it open and ready to help with the steps. They push the pram along the narrow footpath. Every few doors they stop as one of the neighbours leans over their gate to peer into the pram. I can hear Nancy skiting about what 'a good little love she is'.

By myself, the house feels empty and I'm restless. It's the first time I've been alone since coming here. Hugging a cup of tea in my hands, I wander from room to room. I've become fond of this place, its hotchpotch bits of furniture sitting haphazardly along the hallway and in the adjoining rooms. Nothing gets thrown out at Ester

House, just moved or tucked around corners. I'm back to helping with the house cleaning, but today my enthusiasm wanes. Thoughts about our future constantly intrude. And I don't know what to do. I'm not sure about going home to Australia as Father suggested in his telegram. It would mean being reliant on Mother and Father and, other than Father's few words, I haven't heard from them since my letter telling them about Lilybeth. I can't stay here too much longer. My money will run out in a month or so.

I've become attached to Nancy, Victor and Jack and even Nessa and Janet. At times they are crazy but most of all they are genuine. They live an uncomplicated life that I've learned to appreciate. They've taken me under their wing and pulled me through. I feel heartfelt loyalty to them, especially now given the unexpected interest and joy they've shown in having little Lilybeth in the house. It's going to be a big wrench to leave here, and returning home is also part of the problem.

A knock at the front door.

'Telegram for Isabella McMillan.'

I retrieve it from the same ginger-haired lad and take it to the back room.

Sad news. Aunt Hattie died yesterday. A Stroke. Mother and I will attend the funeral tomorrow. Love to you and the little one. We will write soon. Father

I let the telegram slide to the table. My eyes are dry, the memories thick.

Aunt Hattie baking trays of patty cakes when she came to stay, letting me help her ice them when they were cool enough. Kneeling on a stool in the kitchen watching her make coconut ice, those pink and white sugary squares of coconut. The snowballs she brought with her. Father and I loved Aunt Hattie's snowballs. Soft and delicious inside and covered with fine chocolate and coconut on the outside. They never lasted long into the visit. And of course, it wasn't the food, but the love. Every flake of coconut represented a little piece of her happiness. The joy she felt when

Father had found her and knowing she had a new family to love and to be loved by her.

I can't believe Aunt Hattie is dead. This will be so hard for Father. I should be there.

I check the clock several times before the front door squeaks open and I hear Victor telling Nancy to let him do it. With the pram in front, Victor arrives in the kitchen with the broadest of smiles on his face.

'She's a hit with the neighbours, this little one of yours, everyone wants to ...'

'What's happened, luv?' says Nancy.

'It's my Aunt Hattie. Oh Nancy, what am I doing here?'

'Come on, Issie. We'll have a cuppa with you. It's not good to be sad all on your own.' Nancy puts her arm around my shoulders and it's then the tears begin to flow.

Chapter Forty-Five

Knill and Lily

The winter sun shines brightly on the red-brick Methodist church on the day of Hattie's funeral. The pews brimming with her fellow parishioners, her gardening friends and others from the community. Knill gives the eulogy. He talks about Hattie's adoption by the McKenzie family and her dedication to their care as they grew older. Also, about her productive life, the garden she tended, the knitting, sewing and baking for others, and how he, Lily and their daughter Isabella loved her dearly.

Lily watches him. She can see the moment when a pang of longing for Isabella comes over him – the break in his voice as he says her name and the hurt of not mentioning Lilybeth.

Despite being a cold day, the sun warms them through the windscreen as they leave Maryborough. Lily somehow feels different when they pass through Talbot's winding main street with its bluestone gutters and age-weary shopfronts. She has been thinking a lot about Hattie these past few days. Hattie who never married or had children but carved out a life replete with purpose and happiness. Hattie's death has shaken something loose, remembering how fragile life is. She is still unable to stop the hurt of Isabella's leaving. Slinking away without telling a soul until she was safe from scrutiny or objection. But life is a good teacher and Lily has come to a position of acceptance of Isabella's actions. This is not to say for one moment she's happy with Isabella's situation. Indeed, she is not. But deep down where her true emotions hide, she knows that Isabella can't be happy either.

'It was a good service, Knill,' she says eventually. 'Your eulogy was heartfelt. Hattie would have been so grateful. She cherished you like a brother.'

'In a funny way we were like brother and sister, given her mother adopted me and brought me up.'

Lily leans back in her seat and closes her eyes.

They drive in silence, holding the emotion of the day, both the sadness because Hattie is dead and the warmth of the generous acknowledgement by those who knew her.

Over the years, Knill has danced to the familiar tune of disharmony that existed between Lily and Isabella. Honouring Lily and her well-formed views on life, as well as being willing to accept Isabella's sometimes challenging ideas and opinions, has been difficult. While he loves and adores both his wife and his daughter, there have been many times when he wished they would just accept each other's differences. Right now, he's relieved the tension between them has eased a little. He thanks Hattie for it. They are halfway home when Lily turns to him.

'Ah, life is complicated, Knill.'

'It doesn't have to be.'

'When has our world not been complicated?'

He smiles, remembering how they met.

'What are you leading up to, Lily?'

'Isabella's financial situation has just changed.'

Knill takes his eyes off the road for a moment.

'What?'

'Have you forgotten, Isabella is a beneficiary in Hattie's will? And Hattie appointed me to administer it?'

'Yes, but I can't see what ...'

'Don't you see, Knill? Now that Isabella has money of her own, she's less likely to return to Australia.' There is a break in Lily's voice as the shadow of Isabella and Lilybeth falls over them.

Chapter Forty-Six

Issie

Since Lilybeth made her appearance in the world, already she is the centre of attention at Ester House. Nancy and Victor have taken to her as if she's their own grandchild and Jack is taking on the role of uncle. Janet and Nessa have given her tiny rattles and little squeaky toys. Neva sent a baby card and a pink matinee jacket with tiny white buttons. She's coming to Bermondsey to meet little Lilybeth Neva in the next couple of months. Monty sent a book of nursery rhymes along with a letter. It sounds like his time in Manchester is anything but what he'd hoped for.

Lilybeth is a placid baby through the day, she feeds well and sleeps. At night she's testy and I worry she's going to wake the household as I pace my room and sometimes the hallway with her, patting her back and trying to get her back to sleep. When at last she drifts off, I gently ease her back into her pram but then her eyes spring open and it starts all over again. Eventually she settles and we both catch a few hours before she's awake for her morning feed. Despite my sleepless nights, I'm besotted by Lilybeth, her turned-up nose, chubby little cheeks, the deepest of blue eyes, and her thick brown hair. It's only been a few weeks and I can't imagine being without her, ever. In odd moments of sleep deprivation, I ask myself if this is real. I have a baby. I have Lilybeth.

Jack is the happiest I've seen him since I came to Ester House. Yesterday, when I had Lilybeth in her pram in the kitchen, he started singing to her. *How much is that doggie in the window, the one with the waggly tail …*

He caught me watching and grinned coyly. 'They say it's a good habit, singing and talking to babies.'

'Well, Lilybeth thinks it is. You're so good to us, Jack ...' I stopped as I thought of his own little boy, gone forever.

'She's a bonnie little thing, one to be proud of, Issie.'

I sit down beside him at the table. 'What are you still doing at home, so late in the morning, Jack?'

'I've got an interview for a new job at Peek Freans, a foreman's position in the factory. Since the war, biscuit sales have skyrocketed. They have been advertising for new workers and I thought I might as well throw my hat in the ring. Better money and conditions.'

'That's great news, Jack.'

'There's something else to tell you, Issie.' He shifts in his seat. 'I've been seeing Esme. We've been out together a few times.'

'Esme, my midwife? Ha, I'm not at all surprised. You two were making eyes at each other the night Lilybeth was born.'

We both laugh and I think about what a brave person Jack really is. He lives in the shadow of tragedy and yet he's always jovial and positive for everyone else. He deserves to have some happiness in life.

'You don't mind, then?'

'Of course not, Jack. Why should I mind? Esme is wonderful.'

'I thought you might have – it doesn't matter.'

Lilybeth makes a funny little face, then waves her tiny hands in the air. I could watch her for hours, but instead I turn to Jack.

'You've been so good to me and Lilybeth. I will always remember you as one of the people who pulled me through the toughest time in my life. I'm thrilled that you and Esme have a special friendship. I only hope it can be more than a friendship.'

'Let's not hurry things, Issie. One day at a time.'

'One date at a time, don't you mean?'

CHAPTER FORTY-SEVEN

ISSIE

Esme is coming for afternoon tea. Much to the amusement of Nancy and Victor, as soon as our Sunday roast lunch is cleared, Jack whips up a scone mixture, cuts them into shapes and carefully places them on a tray in the oven.

'Where'd you learn to cook like that, Jack?' says Victor, watching intently.

'My grandmother taught me.' Jack produces plum and strawberry jam bought at Sainsbury's especially for the occasion, then begins to beat the cream.

'No end to your talents, Jack,' says Nancy, who has arrived back with her hair combed and lipstick glowing.

'It was a treat we looked forward to every Sunday. We were poor, but our grandma had cream from our cow and picked fruit in her small orchard and we always had *teddies* in the field. Everything we had was home-made or grown in Redruth. Not like now when we go to the shops for everything.'

'When is our guest of honour arriving?' says Victor.

'About three.'

Lilybeth is in my arms. Sometimes it's an effort to have her all to myself. They all want to hold her, to gabble baby talk and sing nursery songs with her. She's a social baby and moves easily from one person to the next.

When Esme arrives, she's wearing an emerald-green dress with a flared skirt with a thin matching belt pulled tight around her small waist. She has a fluffy cream bolero over her shoulders. Today her hair is loose around her face, different to her usual ponytail. Jack is smiling at her and speaking in hushed tones as he brings her into the room. Esme and Jack have been spending a lot of time together this last little while. They've discovered they have many things in common, a love of dancing being one; they've spent many a night at Brockley's dance hall.

Nancy fusses over the teacups and Victor tries to help but gets chastised for getting in the way.

'You look lovely, Esme,' I say as she lifts Lilybeth out of my arms. Lilybeth peers curiously at Esme's face.

'I think she remembers me,' says Esme.

'Well, she should; you were the first person she saw.'

'I hear she's the princess of the house.'

'And already loves the attention.'

Esme hands Lilybeth back to me and Nancy pours the tea. As she does, Jack coughs nervously then takes Esme's hand.

'Before we have our tea, we have an announcement to make.'

We wait for the expected.

'Esme and I are engaged.'

We cheer and clap as Jack and Esme look at each other, coyly and sweetly. Jack holds his hand up for silence. 'There's something we want to ask you all.' Jack's face is flushed as he puts his arm around Esme's narrow waist.

'I've been offered a foreman's job at Peek Freans. It's better money, which means after we marry, we'll rent our own place. Esme and I want a quiet wedding here in Bermondsey. We want you all to be part of it and, if it's not too much inconvenience, we would love to have the wedding party here.'

'What grand news,' says Nancy. 'Of course the wedding party will be here.'

Jack looks relieved and happy, and we clap again, which frightens Lilybeth, who cries. Jack leans over and takes her from me, jiggles her for a moment before handing her to Nancy whose hands are already reaching for her. Esme can't stop smiling. I pour the tea and we all talk at once, wanting to know everything about the new job and where they will live.

'This is the best news yet,' I say as Esme gives me a hug.

'And thank you, Issie. If it hadn't been for you, Jack and I would never have met.'

'And when is the wedding to be?'

Esme and Jack look at each other and smile.

'We would like to get married on Christmas Eve.'

Chapter Forty-Eight

Issie

Nancy and Victor are fussing about the house and helping me sort out the tiny spare room at the top of the stairs in readiness for Neva's visit tomorrow. By the look of the dust and cobwebs covering the boxes and old pieces of furniture, the room hasn't been used for many years.

We shift some of the old boxes to a large cupboard in the hallway and make up the single bed with Nancy's best sheets and cover it with a pink chenille bedspread that mysteriously appeared after one of Nancy's trips downstairs. Nancy has also found a tiny table, with a wobbly leg, and a bed lamp with a yellow silk shade. It just squeezes into the space between the bed and the wall.

'Looks grand. Don't you think, Issie?'

'Grand it is, Nancy. Now it's time for our cuppa, and I can hear Lilybeth stirring.'

At the mention of Lilybeth, Nancy rushes to check on the smallest member of the household. The soft sound of Nancy singing to her as I bring the cleaning mops and bucket downstairs is now a regular occurrence at Ester House.

***

Neva is welcomed by Nancy and Victor like the long-lost relative she is. They fuss over her and talk about old times. Neva's visit is the highlight of the week, not just for Nancy and Victor, but also for me. She's the only person who knows what happened to me before I arrived on the doorstep of Ester House, the only person who fully understands. Our chance to talk comes later in the first evening. Victor and Nancy have gone to the front room to watch television. Visitor or not, they never miss their favourite shows. Lilybeth is sleeping in her pram.

'It's such a different feeling around here, Isabella,' says Neva as we get cosy in the kitchen.

'You might as well call me Issie, Neva. I'm known as nothing else here. The locals shorten everyone's name, and I've come to like being called Issie. I'm not the old Isabella now. That is for sure.'

Neva's watching me with her head on the side. It is comforting to have my dear friend in Bermondsey.

'Issie it is then. Yes, they change everyone's name to suit themselves.' She chuckles and looks around. 'This place is on the improve and the two of them seem happier than I've ever seen them.'

'Since Victor had his heart attack, there's been such a change in them both. And the way they've taken to Lilybeth, they really are enjoying having a baby around the house. I'm so relieved.'

'They have hearts of gold, but they were in a rut. You and your Lilybeth have changed all of that.'

We make more tea and I rock Lilybeth in her pram. Evening is the only time, except for her wakeful nights, when she doesn't settle quickly. And she's getting used to having a steady flow of people who are only too happy to rock her pram and sing to her.

'She's a beautiful baby, Isa ... Issie. When I got your telegram, then your letter a few weeks after Lilybeth was born, it made me realise how fortunate you are. Having a child alters everything – you know you have someone else in the world who relies on you. It won't always be the way, though. When you're old, you can rely on her.'

Neva looks pensive as she watches Lilybeth lose her fight against sleep. She never wanted to have children of her own. She'd told me this several times.

'I guess I'm lucky in some ways,' I say. 'I only wish ...'
'If wishes were horses, beggars would ride.'

We laugh as it's not the first time Neva has thrown this old saying into our conversations.

'Being a mother obviously suits you, Issie. You look so different now.'

'You saw me at my lowest and most desperate. And without you I'm not sure what would have happened, Neva. I'm not sure I could have left him.'

'And then the rotter left you anyway.'

'It was as if I had blinkers on. I've thought it through many times. Why I didn't see it clearly at the time. You certainly did. Why was I foolish enough to think it was possible for him to change after what he did to me?'

'It was a mystery to me, Issie.'

'It's been a wake-up call. Me and my perfect family and perfect life. Well, I sure messed up! Anyway, Neva, the blinkers are well and truly off. What do they say? Once bitten, twice shy.'

We laugh, but awkwardly. We both know how serious the situation was. Lilybeth is asleep now and it's just the two of us sitting at the table in the cluttered kitchen with the comforting rhythm of the mantel clock in the background. Neva is more talkative than she was in Iffley. She tells me about Mr James and his recent outbursts.

'One morning he had Margaret in tears. He's been particularly short-tempered and irritable lately. Anyway, Margaret decided to look for another job. She leaves in a week to work as a receptionist with a firm of lawyers in Oxford.'

'Good for her.'

'And talking of lawyers, I have a contact for you if you want a job in London.'

'A job? Here?'

I stop rocking the pram and stare at Neva, who has a self-satisfied smile on her face.

'Yes, Issie. What are you going to live on otherwise?'

'I've been leaning toward sending a telegram to Father and asking for money to travel home. He has offered to help. But you know, Neva, I'm so settled here and I don't really like the idea of leaving Ester House. But I also know I can't rely on the goodness of Nancy and Victor for much longer.'

'Well, perhaps you have a choice now.'

'What's this job about?'

'Remember I told you about the new assistant, Harold Broome? His brother is a partner in a firm of solicitors in Oxford and London. Poor Harold is the black sheep of the family – he's certainly the least accomplished anyway.' Neva is animated and smiling in a way that's new for her.

'Neva.' My face lights up. 'You're not trying to tell me that you and Harold ...'

'No.' Neva laughs. 'Never. But one morning, poor Harold tripped on a gutter on the way to work. He arrived in such a state we called an ambulance. As it turned out he had a broken ankle. Later in the day, his brother Lachlan rang to thank me for looking after Harold, then asked if he could come and collect Harold's briefcase. Anyway, one thing led to another. He bought me a drink at Stephan's down near the river and gave me a ride home.'

'And ...'

'If you must know, we've been seeing each other ever since.' Neva has uncrossed her legs and is swinging her feet in front of her. Her shoes are new and the latest style.

'Seriously?'

'I can't believe it myself. He's older than me by ten years and he's never married. But he's the first man who's ever made any impression on me. Before Lachlan, men weren't really worth bothering about.'

'I'm speechless, Neva.'

'Anyway, the real information for you is: he has a vacancy for a legal clerk here in London, in his Knightsbridge office. I've already put in a good word for you. His partner, Thomas Clarke, can interview you next week.'

'Vacancy in Knightsbridge. Next week.'

My heart lifts. I am lighter than air. I lean across to hug Neva, the woman who keeps coming to my rescue.

CHAPTER FORTY-NINE

LILY

Lily has promised Knill she will write to Isabella. She knows he expects her to somehow find it within herself to forgive, or at least accept, Isabella's circumstances. Lily's internal conflict wavers between concern and love for her daughter and what she has done to herself and to Lilybeth by having her outside wedlock. It's going to be a long and difficult road ahead for them, but she wants the road to be at home, with her and Knill, not on the other side of the world. She starts yet another letter, never quite finding the right words. It's not in her nature to be so indecisive. It's also not in her nature to tolerate situations that take her outside her comfort zone.

Dear Isabella,

We received your letter and understand how upsetting it must have been to hear the news of your Aunt Hattie's passing. Her death also came as a shock to us and we still struggle to accept she's gone. However, the funeral was a wonderful tribute to her. And Hattie would have appreciated the kind words said about her, especially the heartfelt eulogy given by your father.

It would not be truthful if I were to say that Father and I are not troubled by your circumstances. We were particularly saddened to think you were so far away on your own when your baby arrived.

Maybe you chose it that way. Either way, having a child is an enormous responsibility and whilst we instinctively know you will be a wonderful mother, it is not easy being a parent alone. I'm guessing, this is one of the reasons you didn't tell us until now.

We are concerned about your financial position and we would welcome you home at any time and support you. I'm sure if you return home there are ways to overcome the uncomfortable issues with your situation. A simple story of a husband who died in England and a name other than McMillan will satisfy unwanted curiosity.

Isabella, please consider coming home soon.

Write soon and send us news of Lilybeth.

Much love

Mother and Father

Lily checks the letter one last time, then seals the envelope before she has time to question her words again. And yet she is uneasy. Will Isabella come home? Will she allow them to see their granddaughter and watch her grow? Lily has no influence over Isabella anymore. In fact, Isabella has proved she can do without them.

Chapter Fifty

Issie

Mother's letter arrives two weeks after my interview with Clarke and Broome. I read it with mixed emotions and wonder if Father had seen it before it was posted. Jack, finding me in the kitchen when he gets home from work, hears me out as usual.

'Mother wants me home on her terms. Suggesting I pretend to be a widow and to use another name.'

'She wants the best for you, Issie. After all, many parents would suggest the same thing.'

'She's ashamed of me, Jack.'

'Only because the views of others make her that way.'

'You have a point, I suppose. But it's typical of my mother. Father would never have suggested I change my name and lie about a dead husband.'

'But Issie, you've been pretending to be Mrs McMillan whose husband is working in Scotland.'

I find myself returning his smile. He's right. So why is it okay for me to invent a husband, but then take offence when Mother suggests a similar thing.

'I think you have me there.'

'Your parents sound like good people. They probably just want you home. Chin up, Issie.'

***

I accept the job with Clarke and Broome only when Nancy and Victor offer to look after Lilybeth while I'm working. Leaving her on the first day turns out to be the most challenging part of going back to work. For the past weeks Lilybeth has been weaned to a bottle, which she is happy to take from any of us. Nancy and Victor are thriving with their new responsibility of caring for her; I suspect they're keen to get me out of the house so they are fully in charge of their little Lilybeth. Although I've had second thoughts about taking the job at Clarke and Broome, Nancy and Victor are not at all concerned.

'She'll be right as ninepence, off you go now, Issie Mac,' says Victor as I hesitate at the door.

It's true, Lilybeth is happy and thriving, but why do I feel like I am abandoning her as I leave?

***

Knightsbridge is nothing like Bermondsey. In Australia we would call it well-to-do or posh. The area has almost fully recovered from the ravages of war and is home to many wealthy families and thriving businesses. It's well known for Hill House, the elite preparatory school attended by the young Prince of Wales. One morning, sitting on the upper deck of a bus on my way to work, I saw a distinguished black car pull up at the school entrance and people crowding around it to take photos. Two men moved the onlookers away in a firm and serious manner – the prince's bodyguards I've since learned. The small prince, flanked on both sides by these men, stepped out of the car, his head down, and climbed the three steps to the door. The cameras clicked from a distance and I wondered what it must be like for a small child to have people watching his every move.

Clarke and Broome occupy the ground floor of a narrow glass-fronted building on Sloane Street. Upstairs is home to a small accounting practice and the office of a flamboyant man in his forties who, with an air of urgency, rushes in and out the front door several times a day. Peggy, our secretary, is quick to tell me he's a freelance journalist and writer, who once asked her out on a date. She knows all about the comings and goings of everyone who works in the building. Peggy also has an intense interest in fashion and often has a magazine tucked under the large appointment book on the desk for when the phones become quiet. She wears glamorous dresses with narrow waistlines and flared skirts. With perfectly painted red fingernails, Peggy does all the typing for the office. She guards her green Remington typewriter with absolute proprietary and exerts significant power in the office by insisting the letters for typing are placed in a wire basket with a note containing the date and time of placement. She refuses to type out of sequence except for the senior partners, Thomas and Lachlan, and even then does so with reluctance.

The practice is as fashionable as Peggy. Chairs of tan woven upholstery atop skinny legs. A sleek low table with magazines neatly stacked to one end. Bright abstract paintings hang on the walls. Peggy sits throne-like behind a glass screen close to the entrance. Beyond her private domain, a number of offices spider out. I have my own office – a large desk topped with wire trays filled with bundles of files, a yellow oversized desk lamp and a leather chair that swivels and adjusts by flicking a handle at the side. On the first day, seeing the files stacked high on my desk was enough to make me wish I were back mopping the floors at Ester House.

But Thomas Clarke and Lachlan Broome are easy to work for and I'm soon enjoying the world of legal practice again. They expect a high standard and the volume of work is unrelenting, but they treat everyone in a collegial, friendly way. By the second week, I'm making notes for Mother and the practice back in Melbourne. The modern office systems and procedures used at Clarke and Broome are impressive, whereas Mother is still using the same age-old methods used by my grandfather.

'It's getting easier, isn't it, luv,' says Nancy at the end of the second week.

Lilybeth is asleep, the teapot has been refilled and I'm almost too tired to climb the stairs. I give Nancy a smile, but I have a sense that combining work with looking after Lilybeth is about to get a whole lot harder.

Chapter Fifty-One

Issie

Lilybeth is growing fast. She's a happy baby, smiling joyfully at everyone. Nancy and Victor dote on her and spend all their spare time peering into the pram and lifting her out when she as much as whimpers. Victor has taken to singing nursery songs to her, encouraging Nancy to join in. Watching their beaming faces one morning, as they giggled and entertained Lilybeth, made me sad to think they'd never had the opportunity to be parents themselves, never watched their child grow and develop. They have so much to give.

Leaving my daughter in the care of others is still difficult and the guilt washes over me each day when I go to work. But there is no choice, for now. I must earn a wage to support us both. Or is there? Is it just delaying the inevitable? Is it unfair on Lilybeth not to let her grow up with her grandparents and them with her? Seeing Nancy and Victor so besotted by Lilybeth highlights what Mother and Father are missing.

***

One morning, Peggy passes on a message from Thomas Clarke: he wants to see me. My mind races and by the time I'm knocking on his door, I expect I'm about to be sacked.

'Sit down, Issie.' Thomas flashes his reassuring smile and sits behind his pristine desk. 'There's no need to look so concerned.'

I sit down on the chair opposite him.

'I've been thinking about your future here with us.'

Here it comes, he's going to dismiss me.

'Have you given any thought to your future in law?'

'Is there a problem, Thomas?'

'On the contrary, Issie. I'm wondering if you intend to finish your law degree. It would be such a waste if you never get to practise as a lawyer.'

'That would be difficult. You know I have a child, and I need to work. Studying is something I can't afford right now. I can only work as a law clerk.'

I'm not sure where this is going but he doesn't seem unhappy. He's smiling and relaxed. He shifts from his desk to stand closer to the window, gazing out for a moment.

'In the short time you have been with us, your proficiency, especially in the area of complex contract law, has impressed us, and the office is, well, let's say, because of your contribution we are much more productive. Issie, I think your talents are wasted as a clerk. Would you consider resuming your studies in law?'

'Well, as I've –'

Thomas holds up his hands to silence me. 'No, wait, before you answer, let's see how it could work. What if you were to attend university two days of the week and work here three days?'

He waits for my response. There's a long silence as I piece my thoughts together and search for words to explain why his plan is impossible.

'I would love to complete my degree and complete articles, but I need work full time to earn enough for Lilybeth and myself to live on. I am so grateful for your offer of support, but I'm afraid it's out of the question right now.'

'If we were to pay you a higher hourly wage for three days and pay your university fees, would you consider it?'

My head is spinning at the enormity of Thomas Clarke's proposal. Can I manage to work, look after Lilybeth and study? I have no idea about which university I would study at or where to start. He's waiting for a response.

'I'm not sure.'

'Issie, you only need to agree. We can arrange a place for you at Kings College.'

Chapter Fifty-Two

Issie

Christmas Eve and snow falls outside our window. Lilybeth's new clothes arrived in a parcel from Mother and Father a week ago, just in time for Jack and Esme's wedding. She's five months old now and squirms with delight as I pull cream socks and soft satin shoes over her chubby feet. The pink smocked dress, with tiny, embroidered rosebuds on the collar, and lacey cardigan with little pearl buttons match her rosy cheeks. She looks a picture with her curly hair framing her cherub face.

The guilt surfaces when I think of them, not having met their granddaughter and living so far away in Melbourne. Mother, it seems, has at last resigned herself to us staying in London while I finish my degree. When they heard about my plan to study, they were reassured and happy to know I'm thinking of my future. Father wants to come to England for a visit, but still Mother resists, saying the firm must be kept running by someone. She can be single-minded at times, usually when she's hurt. She doesn't realise that Father is the person bearing the consequences of her stubbornness. But I'm the last person who should pass judgement on her, or anyone else for that matter.

For days the house has been in a state of chaos and excitement. Nancy and Victor, assisted by a couple of helpers, have rearranged the house in readiness for the wedding breakfast. The hallway has been cleared, floors polished and a new hallway runner has appeared. Ester House has been reinvented.

Snow is falling steadily now. Dashing across the footpath to our taxis without our clothes getting covered will be a small miracle. I wrap Lilybeth's shawl over my arm as I make my way slowly down the stairs in my new patent leather stilettos. Lilybeth giggles and squirms in my arms. Jack and Esme's wedding was a good reason to buy a new dress and shoes. But my biggest extravagance was the purchase of a new swing coat, bright green with large black buttons and a trim of astrakhan on the collar. After wearing my old coat for so long, it feels like the most luxurious piece of clothing I've ever worn.

Jack's standing in the hallway in his new suit. He looks handsome, with apple blossom in his lapel and his hair sharply parted and slicked to the side.

'Look at you on your wedding day! I've never seen a more handsome groom.'

'Issie, is that really you under that amazing coat?'

We both laugh but he's fidgety and his voice isn't as steady as normal. Lilybeth puts her little hands out to him. He tickles her tummy and kisses the top of her head.

'Where are the others?' I ask.

'Nancy's fussing over Victor's tie.'

Footsteps on the stairs announce the arrival of Nessa and Janet. Nessa is wearing an aqua checked coat with large pockets edged with white fur and white gloves. Janet is in brilliant red with black gloves and handbag. Both have new hairstyles piled high – beehives, they tell me later. Nancy arrives in the hall barely recognisable. Her hair has been done at Rosie's Salon, her face is glowing and her new pale-blue coat and matching hat has transformed her. The door of the front room springs open and Victor walks out in a navy striped suit, probably from his own wedding day, a white shirt, and the brightest red tie I've ever seen. We all stop to stare at him, including Jack.

'You always looked grand in a bag of fruit, Victor,' says Nancy with a smile as wide as the door. 'Might marry you all over again!' They both roar with hearty laughter.

'The taxicabs are here,' calls Nessa.

Jack, Lilybeth and I share the first and the others climb into the one behind.

It's a small wedding at St Mary Magdalen's. Esme looks a picture in a gown of white organza with a lace bodice and fitted sleeves. It's finished with tiny pearl buttons running down the back from the neckline to a fitted waistline, with a sash of satin-edged lace tied in a plump bow. Her hair is pulled back in an elegant French roll and she's wearing a short tulle veil trimmed with fine lace. She carries a delicate bouquet made from lily-of-the-valley.

The strained voice of the elderly Anglican priest echoes through the chilly church as he reads the wedding vows. It should be Monty officiating. It's been six months since he left for Manchester. But nothing can dampen the happiness of the day. The two newlyweds walk hand in hand out of the church into the cold winter afternoon to a shower of confetti. Esme's mother and father cannot stop smiling with joy. A photographer gathers the wedding guests on the steps of the church and encourages a group smile. After a few more photographs, floating confetti and amid calls of congratulations, the bride and groom are ushered into the bridal car as the rest of us wait for taxicabs. Lilybeth is sleeping in my arms as we climb aboard.

We set off for the short ride to Ester House. For the first time in over a year an unfamiliar calm has settled over me. Is this what it is to belong? The streets are dotted with people, laden with shopping and parcels, making their way home for Christmas celebrations. Festive wreaths in greens and reds are pinned to gates and front doors. Christmas lights sparkle like fairy dust. On one corner a group of carollers are singing 'Joy to the World'. Snowflakes fall gently on their shoulders as the late-afternoon light slowly closes in.

The back room has been cleared of all furniture except for chairs lined up along the walls and the large table in the middle. Nancy and Victor have been working for weeks to make Jack's wedding reception a lively and fun celebration he and Esme will never forget. Esme's mother has been coming over for days, laden with extra plates, cutlery and wedding decorations. The table is covered with two large, embroidered tablecloths, relics from the past belonging to Nancy's grandmother. They had yellowed in the cupboard but after several soakings in Bluo they were fit for a wedding. The wedding cake, made by the unofficial family cake maker, Esme's

Aunt Maudie, takes pride of place in the centre of the table. It's a secret family recipe, only shared with those cunning enough to shower enough compliments on the cook. The cake is decorated in almond icing smoothed to perfection with finely piped icing forming a lattice pattern across the top and sides. Small yellow roses are spotted around the base. The customary small statue of a bride and groom sits on top of the cake.

Fancy gold serviettes have been folded and fanned out on the table, plates and cutlery splayed out behind. Nancy's Queen Anne dinner set forms a beautiful sea of floral at the end of the table, including a magnificent arrangement of pink and white liliums in Nancy's mother's crystal vase. Among the excited chatter, Nancy and the mother of the bride proudly carry tiered plates of salmon, cucumber and cress sandwiches. Also, curried devilled eggs, which I'd never had before but are a 'must have' at special functions, according to Nancy. Plates of scones, with raspberry, blackberry and apricot jam topped with whipped cream, are a mouth-watering display. And lastly, in a glow of satisfaction, Nancy carries in two large Victoria sponges perched high on her best cake stands. She places one at each end of the table. Victor is in charge of drinks. He has arranged stout, beer and punch on a narrow table in a corner of the room.

'Time for the speeches,' calls Nancy as Esme's nervous brother steps forward.

'Ladies and gentlemen, we are excited to be gathered here today to toast the health and happiness of Mr and Mrs Jack Tremayne. Please raise your glasses!'

We are all waving our glasses in the air and calling good wishes to Jack and Esme when Victor tugs at my sleeve.

'Issie, there's someone asking for you at the front door,' he says, nodding over his shoulder.

'For me?'

Lilybeth is asleep in her pram just a few feet away. I tiptoe past her into the passageway. The front door is ajar. I swing it open and the freezing winter chill of the night gushes in. Standing on the steps is a woman wearing a ruby-red ankle-length coat and a matching hat perched at an angle. A dusting of snow on her shoulders is almost indistinguishable from her steely white hair. As she turns to face me, my breath quickens.

'Nan Eliza! What ... what on earth are you doing here?'

CHAPTER FIFTY-THREE

ISSIE

Nan Eliza plans to spend a couple of weeks in London – she's booked into The Tower Bridge Hotel, about half a mile from Ester House – before sailing to Australia. Nancy invited her to come for Christmas lunch, but she declined, saying she needed to rest on Christmas Day. She will join us on Boxing Day instead.

Nancy and Victor have been in a state of excitement for weeks, first the wedding and then Christmas Day. They've made such a fuss because it's Lilybeth's first Christmas. They've decorated a small fir tree, delivered by one of Victor's friends from the Marygold pub, and placed gifts wrapped in glossy Christmas paper for her under the tree: a large nursery rhyme book, a hand-knitted mouse and crawling overalls. For me, a tartan umbrella.

'You'll need a smart umbrella now, given you're going to be a lawyer soon.'

'I love it and thank you, but not so fast with the lawyer talk.'

I present Victor with a new flat cap; his old one has started to fray at the edges. And for Nancy, a new purse with a silver clip and a shopping bag to replace the one with tape around the broken handle she's used for years.

We have the house to ourselves, just the four of us. Janet and Nessa have gone to spend the day with relatives and, of course, Jack and Esme are on their honeymoon. Nancy and Victor are tired but happy after the wedding celebrations. It was a beautiful party and a way of thanking Jack for all he's done for them over the years.

'He's been here eight years; he's like one of the family. We'll miss our Jack, but we're real pleased he found Esme, the best trouble and strife a man could have.'

'We'll all miss Jack,' I say.

Nancy nods in agreement.

'Anyway –' Victor gives Lilybeth's foot a little squeeze – 'enough of that. Where are those records?'

Christmas carols sung by a Welsh choir accompany us as we feast on wedding leftovers, plum pudding and custard.

'Can't have Christmas lunch without plum pudding,' says Nancy, cutting another thick slice for Victor and herself.

'In Australia on Christmas Day, even if the temperature reaches a hundred degrees, we always had plum pudding, Father insisted on it. I'm not sure Mother could see any sense in it, but she always agreed.'

'A hundred degrees, blimey!' Victor pours more custard into his bowl.

All morning I've been thinking of Mother and Father without Aunt Hattie and Nan Eliza, alone on Christmas Day. Is it sadness, or is it guilt?

***

Nancy and Victor are up early fussing around the house. The liliums in the crystal vase from the wedding appear on the kitchen table and bright cushions are placed on the chairs. Victor is out the front sweeping the steps and shaking the mat.

'Hope your nan doesn't expect us to be too fancy, Issie,' says Nancy.

'You'll like Nan Eliza, Nancy. She's a bit like you – straightforward, calls a spade a spade.'

As predicted, Nancy and Victor warm at once to Nan Eliza, and she to them. After a pleasant lunch, Nan Eliza and Nancy chat over the rattling dishes in the sink, oblivious to anyone else in the room.

'And you lived in China all those years?'

'The years passed quicker than you would think, and I was fully occupied with helping out at the orphanages.'

'I've never travelled outside Bermondsey.'

'I guess we stay where we're happy.'

'And you were happy to go to China?'

'Ah … I'm not sure I knew at the time, I just took a chance. I think wandering must be a family thing.'

Nancy pauses with a tea towel in her hand. 'You and your travels, and now Issie.'

'We certainly have a knack for complicating our lives.'

I let the conversation wash over me.

'Issie's a good girl. Given us something to live for, her and little Lilybeth. We were in a rut until she came to Ester House. Nothing had changed for years.'

'You've been good to Isabella, looking after her like she was one of your own. She would have been all alone without you and the others at Ester House.'

'She's given us as much as we gave her.'

'You know she might go home sometime, Nancy.'

Nancy briskly stirs the soap suds in the sink, rattling the cups. Her back straightens.

'It doesn't pay to think too far ahead. We stick with what's happening now. Nothing wrong with taking joy when it's in front of you.'

Lilybeth's eyelids flicker shut to the rhythm of the rocking pram. Victor is sitting at the kitchen table, gazing at her. Not once has he crept out for a cigarette.

CHAPTER FIFTY-FOUR

ISSIE

Nan Eliza invites me to her hotel for a quiet chat, 'just between us'. She orders a pot of tea in the foyer of her hotel. We sit on the lovely brocade settee in a nook by the front window, overlooking a small, manicured garden. She has visited Ester House several times and we have taken brisk walks to the park with Lilybeth rugged up in her pram. Nan Eliza loves Lilybeth and her face lights up when the baby smiles at her. It's as if meeting Lilybeth has touched a part of her she's kept hidden, maybe even from herself.

Nan Eliza has always been the steadying influence in my life. She is straight to the point and never frightened to say what needs to be said. Her unusual life has given her insight into people and circumstances that most of us will never encounter. Having a child so young – my own father – and being forced by her parents to relinquish him has toughened her and broadened her understanding of life's difficulties. She never judges and that alone makes her different to so many other people her age.

However, I know there's a difficult conversation ahead of us. She will want to know why I left Australia the way I did and it's still something I haven't reconciled at all.

The tea arrives and Nan Eliza pours it as I reach for a shortbread biscuit.

'London appears to agree with you, Isabella,' Nan Eliza says as she places the teapot back on the table.

I am happier. My life is full and busy ensuring Lilybeth is well looked after, managing my work and study, doing my bit at Ester House. My Christmas here couldn't have been any more different than last year, in Edinburgh with Alexander.

'Yes, but I still have mixed emotions about living here.'

'You've made good friends, Isabella. And a life for yourself.'

'I've been lucky. If it hadn't been for Neva, Nancy and Victor, Jack, and Esme, I'm not sure what would have happened.'

'Maybe it's not luck. Maybe it had something to do with you.'

'What do you mean?'

'Isabella, you are more than capable of running your own life. You've proved it.'

'Made a mess of it, more like.'

'Depends how you view it. You have a beautiful child back at Ester House. Quite an accomplishment, I would say.'

'Of course, I adore Lilybeth, but –'

'But nothing. Are you going to tell me about her father?'

Shifting in my chair, I place my cup and saucer on the table. The mood of our conversation has changed. It's time for serious talk. Her gentle tone tells me that Nan Eliza knows things went horribly wrong. Should I be explaining to my grandmother what happened to me? Telling her what Mother and Father don't know?

'Looking back, I was stupid and naïve to have left Australia in the first place, especially without talking to Mother and Father. It's because they would have talked me out of it and I … I needed to get away, to be myself. I wasn't special but I was made to think I was. I was suffocating in their good intentions.'

'So, you stood up for yourself?'

'What?'

'You needed to change your circumstances, so you decided to leave. Seems to me you stood up for yourself.'

'No, I ran away. How was I standing up for myself? Acting like a spoilt child and a coward.'

'Needless to say, you acted. It might have been difficult but that's another story.'

'A disaster of a story, I'm afraid.'

There is stillness in the hotel foyer accentuating the traffic noise outside. As I fight back tears, I give her the bones of the story, leaving out the parts I'm too humiliated to speak about. Nan Eliza doesn't interrupt me as I explain how I found myself at Ester House with Nancy and Victor.

'And does Alexander know he has a daughter?'

'No.'

'And you don't intend to tell him?'

'I don't intend to ever see him again. He has no right to know about Lilybeth, no right at all.'

Before Nan Eliza has a chance to reply, the concierge comes quickly to her side.

'Mrs O'Dare. There's a telephone call for you. The gentleman says it's urgent.'

Nan Eliza goes to the foyer desk and takes the telephone. An expression of concern crosses her face. I'm immediately on my feet and beside her. Is it Lilybeth?

'There's been an accident. Nancy's been hit by a car. It sounds serious.'

'Lilybeth, is she …?'

'She's fine. Jack and Esme are there. We should go now. I'll come with you to look after Lilybeth. I'll get us a cab.'

In Tolley Street, a few neighbours are gathered near the front of Ester House. I push past them and the door flings open. Jack ushers me and Nan Eliza in. His face is ashen. In the back room, Victor's face is buried in his hands. Esme comforts him. The room is cold, bereft.

'It's not good news, Issie,' Jack says.

'Which hospital is Nancy in? Where's Lilybeth?'

'Lilybeth is asleep upstairs. Esme just checked on her. They took Nancy to Guy's and St Thomas.'

'Shouldn't Victor be there with her?'

'Issie …' Jack's voice cracks. 'Nancy died about an hour ago.'

Chapter Fifty-Five

Issie

We farewell Nancy on a Tuesday. She liked Tuesdays. Not the start, the middle, or the end of the week, just Tuesday. It's only a couple of weeks since we were here at St Mary Magdalen celebrating Jack and Esme's wedding.

The narrow church pews are packed with people from Bermondsey and beyond. The organ plays mournfully and it's freezing inside the church. Nancy disliked the cold weather and complained every day during winter, yet here we are saying goodbye in the depths of winter. I can't help but think she deserved a warm sunny day for her final departure.

In the church, a sea of faces from the neighbourhood wait for the service to begin. In their overcoats, scarves and hats, they gather. Old Shirl is a couple of rows back, wearing a dark-grey coat and scarf. She's craning her neck to see who else is there. The women from Manze's huddle together in one pew and neighbours from Tolley Street look for spaces to squeeze into in the packed church. Many of the women, handbags in the crook of their arms, are clutching handkerchiefs to their faces.

When he was told of Nancy's death, Victor refused to believe it. Dutifully, Jack rugged him up in warm clothes and took him to Guy's and St Thomas hospital to see Nancy. Since then, he has been in a state of shock and unable to think or contribute to our conversations, even about the funeral. He's hardly eaten and smokes one cigarette after another in his chair in the front room. The day after Nancy died, he barely moved until Jack insisted he come out to the dining table and eat something. Jack and Esme took charge of the funeral arrangements and slept in

Jack's old room. Neva arrived yesterday and is staying in the spare room. Nan Eliza has been coming to Ester House in the mornings to help look after Lilybeth.

As the organ stops, the elderly minister who replaced Monty and married Jack and Esme, takes his place at the pulpit. In the front row, Jack and Esme sit on Victor's left and Neva, Lachlan and I are on the right. Nessa and Janet are squashed next to each other in the row behind us, defiantly flamboyant, determined to send Nancy off in style despite their puffed, reddened eyes. Nancy's coffin is stark in front of us but for a wreath of large white lilies, sprigs of holly and daphne. She loved daphne.

Neva and Jack have prepared a eulogy on behalf of Victor and us all at Ester House. As Jack takes his place at the lectern, a hush falls over the mourners.

'Today we are here to bid farewell to a person you all knew well. Nancy was born in 1898, she grew up and lived in Bermondsey all her life and it was where she met the love of her life, Victor. They married forty years ago.'

Jack takes a deep breath and looks to Victor, who is dabbing his eyes with a white handkerchief.

'Nancy has been many things to many people over the years. She was kind, honest and down to earth. She was no fool, she summed up people well, but was never one to judge. Many of you will be aware of her generosity during the war years when she supported several Bermondsey families when they fell on hard times. Nancy often came to the aid of women who, through no fault of their own, were short of food or had trouble paying their rent. She always insisted they tell no one, but everyone was aware of Nancy's many acts of kindness. To many of us here, she gave us hope and security in the simple routine she offered at Ester House. Some of us, me included, had times when life got on top of us, when grief shadowed our days, but Nancy was there with a cuppa and a joke and always a kind word or two. Victor will miss his Nancy and this community will mourn the loss of a good Bermondsey women who will never be replaced.'

We stand as Nancy's coffin is moved toward the aisle for her final farewell. Jack and Esme help Victor to his feet. He is sobbing as they follow the coffin. We file behind them. The organ starts up again with a hymn Nancy loved, 'All Things Bright and Beautiful'. She often hummed it when she was going about her daily chores in the kitchen and while she was cooking, and, of course, she often sang it to Lilybeth.

Nothing will be the same at Ester House now. The many things Nancy did each day, the reassuring pats on my arm when I left Lilybeth each morning, the welcome call from the kitchen when any one of us arrived home from work, the kind but direct advice, the grumbling over Victor making a mess, the little bits of gossip, the loving fussing over Lilybeth and the endless cups of tea. It's all changed now, for Victor, for everyone.

CHAPTER FIFTY-SIX

ISSIE

It's been three weeks since Nancy's funeral and Ester House is cold and bereft. It's quiet, miserably quiet. Victor spends most of his days in the front room, only brightening when his friend Paddy arrives with a bottle of stout. The two of them smoke and drink in the front room, something Nancy would never have approved of, and talk about the old days at the tannery. Paddy tries to persuade Victor to go down to the Marygold, but Victor says he's not ready for other company yet. Victor relies on Paddy's visits; they seem to take his mind off the massive hole that's been created by Nancy's passing.

Jack and Esme are staying on at Ester House until Victor gets back on his feet. Janet and Nessa are already grumbling about who will get meals, who will clean, who will do all the things Nancy did. Victor pays little attention to their concerns. Even his favourite Lilybeth barely draws a smile from him these days. When he first saw her after Nancy's funeral, he cried and turned away. He is cocoon like in his grief.

Neva and Lachlan plan to marry in the spring and are looking for a house to live in. They have also come up with a plan to put to Victor. They would like to buy Ester House, make some improvements, and then put in a caretaker to manage the daily tasks. Victor will be able to live here for as long as he wishes, but the financial burden of running the property and dealing with the boarders will not be his responsibility. It will also mean he has no financial worries coming into old age.

'He needs more time to get used to things, so we'll wait for a while before putting the plan to him,' says Neva. 'Grief does funny things to people.' She cuddles Lilybeth closer to her. 'And now there's something else I have to ask you, Issie.'

'Just ask. It's usually me asking you for something.'

'Will you be my bridesmaid at my marriage to Lachlan?'

'The best news yet. Yes, wild horses couldn't stop me.'

***

Nan Eliza has also decided to stay for another month before going back to Australia and each morning she comes to Ester House to look after Lilybeth while I go to work. My fortunate situation will not last much longer. She summons me for a talk one afternoon after work.

We are sitting in Nancy's kitchen, which has taken on a forlorn appearance these past few weeks. It's difficult to be here without expecting Nancy to come down the passageway humming away and then to announce she's putting the kettle on. Her apron still hangs on the back of the door and I've washed and placed her favourite teacup on the mantelpiece. But it won't be used. Her shopping bag, the one I gave her for Christmas, sits on the nearby bench. She had it with her the day she had the accident, when she was knocked down by the lorry delivering furniture to a nearby store. Someone picked up her bag from the side of the road.

Nan Eliza has saved the day for us all, minding Lilybeth and keeping the house running by employing a woman for a couple of hours each day to do light house-keeping, shopping and cooking.

'There is something we should discuss, Isabella.'

This is the moment when she asks me my plans. I have no options. With Nancy gone, I have no one to care for Lilybeth. She was *the* person who allowed me to stay in London. I totally trusted and relied on her.

'Yes, I guess there are a few decisions to make.'

'What are you thinking, Isabella?'

'My thinking is simple. I can't remain studying and working without having reliable care for Lilybeth. I have no choice but to return home.'

'Is that what you want, Isabella?'

'No. I want to stay, finish my degree, and stand on my own two feet. But I need to look after Lilybeth and I simply can't afford a nanny. Nancy in all her generosity allowed me to work and know Lilybeth was safe and happy. It was a gift I can never repay.'

The emotion rises in my throat when I think of Nancy and Victor with my little girl, all their love for her. How silly they looked as they danced around the back room, singing nursery rhymes and pulling funny faces to make Lilybeth giggle. How much joy she brought them. Oh Nancy, oh Victor.

Nan Eliza places her cup on the table and looks out the window. It is already dark. These winter nights come down so quickly. We all need spring to arrive, especially Victor. I'm lost in my thoughts when Nan Eliza turns back to me.

'There might be another way, Isabella, for you to stay here and finish your studies.'

'Don't you think I haven't considered –'

Nan Eliza hushes me. 'I was under the impression you have an inheritance from your Aunt Hattie.'

'It would mean asking Mother to release the money to me. I have caused them enough grief. They'll be expecting me to return home now. It would be a cruel blow to them if I remain in England. They have forgiven me once; I'm not sure they have it in them to do it again.'

'The money is rightfully yours and with it you could hire a nanny and finish your studies, if that's what you want.'

'Yes, but –'

'Isabella, you're not a child anymore. Stay here or return home, but do it for the right reasons – your reasons, not because of guilt or to make your parents happy.'

Nan Eliza's words envelop me along with the night. She gathers her things and squeezes my hand as she leaves.

Return for the right reasons ... stay for the right reasons. What are the right reasons?

PART THREE

Australia

1962

CHAPTER FIFTY-SEVEN

ISSIE

'When will we see Grandma and Grandpa?'

'Soon, Lilybeth. A few more minutes.'

'But they won't know me. They may not even believe I'm Lilybeth.'

'Oh, Lilybeth, of course they will know you. They have your photo and they've been waiting for a long time to meet you.'

The queue at the immigration and customs area at Melbourne Airport stretches ahead of us as we wait to have our passports stamped. The plane journey has been long and we're both tired and in need of sleep. Lilybeth pouts as she wriggles from foot to foot and fiddles with her hair and pulls on the pink ribbon until it unravels. Lilybeth's looking forward to meeting her grandparents, but she was uncertain about leaving London; after all, it's all she knows. She will miss Clara, her nanny for the past five years, her little friends at nursery school in Knightsbridge and especially Poppy Victor. We'll both miss Neva and Lachlan, Esme, Jack and their newborn daughter, Connie. Emotional farewells, finalising travel arrangements and packing, all the time hoping I was making the right decision. My worry about Victor is eased only because Neva and Lachlan live just ten minutes from Ester House. They did buy the property, which eased Victor's burden, and they keep a keen eye on him. But his health is poor; he's never fully recovered after Nancy's death. And now I'm taking Lilybeth away as well.

He was quiet when I told him we were leaving. He'd been pushing Lilybeth on the swings at the park where we went each Saturday after lunch. He missed two or three swings as he took in the news, refusing to let me see how devastated he was.

'Poppy Victor,' Lilybeth shouted. 'I'm slowing down.'

'Come with us, Victor,' I said. 'Please.'

He resumed pushing Lilybeth.

'I'm too old, Issie.' He brushed his eyes. 'Well past travelling to foreign places, no matter how much I'll miss the two of you.'

'Oh, Victor.'

Lilybeth keeps saying she'll visit Poppy Victor, but she's too young to understand the tyranny of distance.

I had to return. Mother has been diagnosed with a heart condition and is no longer able to travel. I could not keep Lilybeth away forever. They have a right to get to know their only granddaughter. But arriving home after six years away is surreal and disconcerting. My life has been in England, my friends are there and I'm a different person now. Nothing like the naïve Isabella who left all those years ago. Waiting in line with a fidgety child, I can only trust in my decision to return home.

The doors open and I see them immediately in the front row behind the rope barricade. Father is scanning the faces of the arriving passengers; he looks no different except his grey hair is thinning. Mother's hair is silver and pulled back more harshly than I ever remember. I bend down to Lilybeth.

'There they are, Lilybeth. Your grandma and grandpa.'

Time stands still as they hurry toward us. Lilybeth pulls back, suddenly shy, and hot tears run down my face as Father hugs me like he's never going to let me go. Mother does the same, squashing the bunch of crimson and pink roses she's carrying. She's crying softly. Lilybeth clutches the back of my slacks, hiding. Her eyes darting from me to Mother and Father. Father kneels and gently takes Lilybeth's hands in his.

'Hello, Lilybeth. I'm your grandpa and I've waited so long to meet you.'

I touch Father's shoulder; he is shaking.

Mother dabs her eyes with a lace handkerchief before crouching to speak to her granddaughter.

'Lilybeth, I'm Grandma. I'm so happy you're here. I have something special for you.' She produces a beautiful rag doll with shiny golden-brown hair, dressed in a pink frilly dress with shoes to match. Lilybeth's eyes light up; the tension and built-up emotion lifts for us all. Mother and Father straighten and wipe their tear-stained faces. Lilybeth gently strokes the rag doll's face.

'Thank you, Grandma. Does she have a name?'

'Not yet, Lilybeth; you can choose her name.' Mother takes her hand. Lilybeth looks to me for approval, then moves off tentatively with her grandmother. Father and I focus on our luggage trolley as we follow them down the long arrival hall.

'This means so much to us, Isabella.'

'We need to get out of here before we all start blubbering again.' I give him a watery smile. 'Come on, Father.'

'Lilybeth's delightful and we've missed you more than you can imagine,' says Father.

'She's been so excited about coming to Australia and looking forward to meeting her grandpa and grandma. It is all she's talked about for weeks.'

Father rests his free hand on my arm, and for a moment the pain of the last years is replaced by something else.

'Let's talk more when we get home and you two have had some sleep.' Father's shoulders relax and he looks lighter. 'We have plenty of time now. All the time in the world.'

Chapter Fifty-Eight

Issie

The city is bustling. Trams surge and slow with a metallic clang. Throngs of people gather at crossings waiting for the lights to turn. This is not the Melbourne I remember. The city has changed. It's faster, denser and with a loud intensity more akin to London.

Closer to home, things are different and yet the same. The familiar scent in the clear air, the bright sun as it strikes the ground like paint on a new wall, a solid stripe. It is mid-January and already my clothes are too heavy for the heat. The sky is sea blue and vast above us and I realise I haven't noticed the sky in a conscious way in six whole years. In London, most of the sensory stimulation is in your direct vision: people, buildings, trains, and buses. I can't recall the London sky.

When we step out of the car, a slow exhaustion descends over me. Father unloads and carries our luggage into the hall. Lilybeth has suddenly found an abundance of energy and is exploring the house with Mother, her excited chatter echoing along the hallway.

'And this room is where your mummy slept, but it's yours now,' Mother says as they arrive at the door to my old room.

'Can I put my clothes in here?'

'Yes, and tomorrow we can ...'

Mother turns when she notices me behind her.

'We've changed things around, Isabella. Lilybeth can have your old room and we've set up one of the guest rooms across the hall for you. It's bigger.'

My old room has been painted and there are new curtains to match. The old shelves have disappeared; a white cupboard filled with children's books and dolls' furniture now stands against the wall. Lilybeth is bouncing joyfully on the new rosebud bedspread.

'Look, Mummy, it's all pink, my favourite colour.'

'It certainly is pink! You should thank Grandma for making it so beautiful for you.'

'Thank you, Grandma. It's the best room in the whole world.'

We laugh and the awkward moment passes. Mother is delighted that Lilybeth is overjoyed with her new room and I'm too tired to think any more of it. In the space of an hour, she's taken to her grandmother with an extraordinary enthusiasm.

Father watches from the passageway. His smile tells me everything. Seeing Mother and Father so elated affirms my decision to return home. Yes, it's the right thing for them and Lilybeth.

There's a moment of elation, then a wave of loss. Grief and sadness for what I left behind in England. My job with Lachlan and Thomas. Their support. Thanks to them I have my law degree; without them, I would still be clerking. And Neva ... I miss her already, the hurried sandwiches in our lunch hours, shopping for her and Lachlan's new apartment. We went through so much together. What happened to me in Oxford, her falling in love but all the while feeling ambivalent about moving to London. And Victor, my biggest worry and wrench of all.

There are challenges ahead. What worries me the most is working in the practice with Mother. It will take some negotiating and quite a bit of diplomacy. I'm no longer her young, inexperienced daughter, and I have no intention of returning to an arrangement that is anything other than collegial and equal.

***

Lilybeth and I sleep long and spend the days quietly adjusting to the summer heat. Lilybeth is the happiest I've seen her and is revelling in her grandparents' attention. Often my mind wanders back to winter London. What time of the day is it? Has Victor taken his medication? Here, I feel like a visitor, returning to something I knew long ago but unable to step back into. I don't know how to. And, if I'm honest, I don't know if I want to. Will it be the same? How could it be?

When we've been back a few days, Mother announces she's arranged lunch on Sunday. Nan Eliza will be here and she has also asked Danny.

'He's looking forward to seeing you both, Isabella,' she says as she checks her shopping list. 'I don't know how the practice would have survived these past few years without him.'

***

Sunday morning is busy in the kitchen. In true Mother fashion she has everything under control and doesn't want help. I find Father and Lilybeth in the backyard happily floating a plastic boat in the little fishpond. Lilybeth's hair is tangled and falling in her eyes. As she tosses her head to flick the unruly locks from her face, I gasp. For a split second I see Alexander. Then, as quickly as it came, the resemblance falls away. She is delighted with the toy boat Grandpa found for her in the garden shed.

'Mummy, it floats just like a real boat.'

Nan Eliza arrives in a spotted navy sun dress and matching jacket, her silver hair as stylish as ever. Her back is now slightly stooped as she makes her way down the hall and her steps are not quite as brisk. But the strength in her voice reveals that she's still a force to be reckoned with.

'Welcome home, Isabella. You're looking splendid.' She embraces me for a long moment. 'Now, where is our little monkey? There she is. Lilybeth, come see your Great Nan.'

Lilybeth kisses her and Nan Eliza strokes Lilybeth's long curly hair.

'The first golden-haired child in the family,' says Nan Eliza.

'Mummy says it's honey brown, not golden,' says Lilybeth.

'Well, honey brown it is.'

Before another word is spoken, the doorbell rings and Mother greets Danny. Soon he is by my side. Lovely, gentle Danny. I hug him and immediately it's as if I haven't been away. He's clutching a bunch of delicate cream carnations; we've almost squashed them in our homecoming hug. We laugh, the way we did all those years ago when Mother was in a flap at the office and we'd make bets about how long it would take for her to come out of the office again with more instructions.

'It's wonderful to see you again, Isabella.'

'And you too, Danny. Come and meet Lilybeth.'

Lilybeth is standing beside Mother, who gently nudges her to step forward.

Danny retrieves a small bag he's brought with him, then bends down to her height.

'Hello, Lilybeth. Hope you like rabbits.'

Danny passes Lilybeth the bag and she peeps in with caution.

'It won't bite, I promise you,' says Danny with a gentle laugh.

Lilybeth pulls out a soft, fluffy bunny with floppy ears. She gives a squeal of delight, clasping the toy to her chest.

'Does Uncle Danny deserve a thank you?'

'Thanks for the bunny, Uncle Danny.'

'You'd better watch he doesn't hop around the house when everyone's asleep,' says Danny.

Lilybeth makes a funny face at him, then Mother ushers us into the dining room for lunch. The room is alive with chatter and a joyful sense of homecoming. Mother and Father are happy to have us all together and Nan Eliza is sporting one of her contented looks. Danny is relaxed and handsome in his crisp sports shirt and dark slacks. I can't stop glancing at him. It's the same Danny, my dear friend from long ago. But six years have given him more confidence, more self-assurance. It's clear

Mother and Father respect him and even defer to him. Lilybeth is chatting excitedly and asking which seat she can sit in.

'Next to me,' Father tells her. 'But there is something we have to do before we sit down for lunch. We have a special toast to propose.'

He pulls out a bottle of champagne from the ice bucket on the sideboard and pops the cork, which momentarily startles Lilybeth. Father pours the champagne and hands a delicate flute to each of us. Lilybeth gets lemonade in a frosted green glass.

'This is a toast to welcome home Isabella and our beautiful granddaughter, Lilybeth. May there be happy times ahead for us all.'

Father's eyes glisten and I feel my own throat constrict as I watch him, so happy and proud. My guilt rises. Guilt at depriving them of my presence for six years and then missing Lilybeth's babyhood and guilt that I didn't meet their expectations.

'To Isabella and Lilybeth,' says Danny, cheerfully raising his glass.

'For our fortune at having two special people with us again,' says Nan Eliza.

Mother steps forward and the room goes quiet. She's smiling as she graciously holds her long-stemmed glass in front of her.

'Thank you, Isabella. Thank you for making our family whole again. And welcome, Lilybeth. Already our lives are full of renewed purpose.'

Mother raises her glass and smiles at her granddaughter across the room. Lilybeth blushes at the attention and squirms closer to my legs. Danny is watching me; Father and Nan Eliza have gone silent. I'm about to respond when Mother speaks again.

'We should eat,' she says.

'Not before I have a chance to say something,' I say and put my hands on Lilybeth's shoulders. 'Lilybeth and I are happy to be here, in Melbourne. Family's important and so are friends. We've been our own little team for quite a while now, so coming back to the family might take some adjusting. Already, we feel loved and welcome, we can't thank you enough for being here for us through thick and thin. Now let's sit down and eat; I'm starving.'

***

After lunch, we gather in the lounge room. Aunt Hattie is on my mind; she would normally be here for family gatherings and her absence is noticeable today. Lilybeth is playing on the floor with her new rabbit while Nan Eliza compliments Mother about lunch: roast lamb with mint sauce and beautifully baked vegetables. 'It was delicious,' says Nan Eliza and asks where she got her pavlova recipe. Mother referred to the dessert as a frivolous sugary extravagance, but of course the pavlova was made to perfection. Apparently, it's become one of Father's favourites.

'Is it time for a tune or two on the piano?' says Father.

Lilybeth looks up and claps. 'Yes, yes, Grandma play for us.'

Mother pulls a face and I think she is going to refuse when she turns to Knill and says, 'I will play if Grandpa accompanies me.'

With a gracious smile he stands and puts his hand out to help Mother up. A gentle smile passes between them and they know exactly what to do next. Seated at the piano, Mother turns to us.

'Many years ago when we were young, so young, we played together for the first time on a ship headed for China.' She turns back to Father. 'Do you remember what we played that evening, Knill?'

'How could I ever forget? We were both nervous and had no sheet music, but somehow the notes flowed. Tchaikovsky's "Piano Concerto No.1". It was the start of our life together and I'll always remember it. And the passengers cheered for the tall Australian lad and the petite Chinese girl who just happened to be pianists.'

'Let's see how well we remember it.'

Mother and Father are looking at each other fondly as the rest of us sit in silence. Tears well up, but they don't fall. Mother and Father are too happy for the moment of sadness and emotion to bloom. They warm up, laugh briefly and then, as if they are on the ship again, begin playing. At first the notes are quiet, soft, and then they find their rhythm and the true beauty of Tchaikovsky's arrangement fills the room.

Their shoulders touch and they move as one. Lilybeth is spellbound as she sits beside me, clutching her floppy-eared rabbit. Nan Eliza has her head back and eyes closed. Emotion fills the room. Danny smiles kindly at me as I struggle to hold back tears. I've never seen my parents this way before.

I imagine them on the journey from Australia to China and see a different couple. Not my parents but two young people of different backgrounds and cultures bonded together by circumstance and their love of music. When their piece comes to an end, Father places his arm around Mother's shoulders.

Chapter Fifty-Nine

Issie

The adjustment to hot February weather hasn't affected Lilybeth at all. She's delighted by the park, the swimming pool and playing outdoors. Mother and Father have given us everything we've needed and it's obvious they love having us under their roof. I am grateful to my parents for all they are doing, for their generosity and especially for their joyous welcoming of Lilybeth into their lives. But at the same time, I have a foreboding sense they want it to be like this forever. But it can't be. However, for now, I'm taking one day at a time, including starting work with Mother. And, if I'm to be honest, it fills me with trepidation.

*****

The aura of the office with its musty tang is the first thing I notice as I step in through the front door. This familiarity is curiously comforting; it transports me back to my earlier years as a child and then a young woman. In fact, nothing has changed at all. The furniture, the blinds and the wall hangings belonging to my late grandfather are all still here in the same place. Danny now works in one of the large offices next to Mother's. At the front desk, Lucy and Audrey Rodgers, the new legal secretary, are stationed. There is a modern chair looking terribly out of place among the remnants of grandfather's original office furniture. I smile to myself as I remember the old chairs with their wobbly arms and well-worn leather upholstery. I loved climbing on them as a small child and making them spin. I make a mental note to ask Danny about the new furniture; there's bound to be a story attached.

Danny arrives beside me.

'A big day, Isabella. For you and for us,' he says.

'Isabella!' Lucy is on her feet, hugging me and laughing. 'I can't believe it's you – you look so different. I missed you so, so much.'

'I missed you more.' I squeeze her hand. 'And you got married!'

'Two years ago. I can't wait for you to meet him.' Lucy nods toward Audrey, who is sitting at her desk waiting to be introduced.

'This is Audrey,' Danny says, grinning at her. 'She's the organised one around here.'

'Hello, Audrey.' I step closer and hold out my hand. She seems taken aback but shakes my hand nevertheless. 'Mother and Danny sing your praises.'

'Pleased to meet you, Isabella.' Her voice is cool. 'I'm sure they exaggerate.'

She sits back in the new chair and continues working. Danny nods at me and we move toward Mother's office. Hmm, so perhaps Audrey isn't happy to see me. No doubt I'll have to work hard to earn my stripes with her. Things may look just the same, but a lot has happened here since I left. I can't wait to have a good talk with Danny, alone.

Mother wants to discuss my transition back into the firm. It's her way of holding onto the reins, controlling how the firm will continue; after all, she has spent a good part of her life running her late father's business. She doesn't want her wayward daughter returning with fancy ideas and making changes. It's understandable and I have empathy for her situation, but I'm determined to stand up for myself from the beginning. If I'm to be here in my own right, some things will have to change, maybe not immediately but unquestionably the practice needs an overhaul.

'I've written out some points for discussion,' Mother says as Danny and I sit down opposite her. 'We should start with the hours of work for us all, and responsibilities.'

Mother would like to reduce her time in the practice, and she's asked if she and Father can care for Lilybeth at home while I work. I've agreed to the arrangements but have also booked Lilybeth into kindergarten for three half days a week. I'm counting on Danny taking more senior responsibilities in the practice to give me a few months to familiarise myself.

'I assume Danny and I will be full-time, Mother.'

Danny nods in agreement.

'As do I,' Mother says. She glances at the papers in front of her, then raises her eyes before she speaks. 'Daniel, I would like to offer you a partnership in the firm.'

Danny straightens as if he's been prodded sharply in the back. He goes to say something but Mother hushes him and continues.

'I know this may be a surprise to you, Daniel, and perhaps you too, Isabella,' she says, nodding at me before returning her gaze to Danny. 'But without your work and the considerable efforts you have made these last years, I would not have been able to carry on.'

Danny glances at me, his face serious; he's been taken totally off guard.

'I'm surprised and honoured by your offer, Lily. But I'm wondering if this is a conversation for you and Isabella. After all, I'm not family.'

Mother has a way of throwing important matters into a conversation and expecting others to respond on the hop. She would have thought this through in detail and discussed it with Father. So, in her mind she's clear and comfortable with the proposal. It's Mother's style; she doesn't take anyone, except Father, on board in her process until she's made up her mind, she then expects others to agree. But it's Danny. I smile. 'Danny, I fully support Mother's offer. It's well earned.'

Mother looks relieved. Why wouldn't I support her idea? It's a sound proposition, and if the truth is to be known, we need Danny more than he needs us.

'If you are willing to accept the offer, I'll draw up the details and start to get the paperwork ready. And when the time is right, Isabella, you will take over my role and become a joint partner with Daniel.'

Danny glances at me again before accepting Mother's offer of a full partnership with Sing, McMillan and Associates. We talk about how we will divide the work and the role Mother will play in the meantime. Mother naturally wants to be involved but is resigned to working only two days a week. Her health is an issue and her newly formed relationship with Lilybeth has been a big factor in her decision to hand over many of her responsibilities to Danny and eventually, me. I have never seen her so soft and considerate of others before. However, I suspect she's not going to allow me to become a full partner until she's convinced I'm up to it. I can't blame her. Mother has never been one to take chances. I've let her down before and she's not going to let it happen again.

'Now,' Mother says, 'there's no time like the present to get started. I'll leave you to it. Knill and I are taking Lilybeth to the zoo.'

Danny is looking at me, but I can't return his gaze. It is barely ten o'clock. With her back straight, her hair perfect, Mother is out the door. Danny and I are left alone, both of us speechless. She has been true to her word to step away from full-time practice.

CHAPTER SIXTY

ISSIE

The June winter hovers over us as Danny and I walk to the tiny café across the street from the office. We come here each week on a Monday morning with our minds fresh after the weekend. It's our chance to discuss any pressing business issues without interruptions.

I love Mondays. Feeling recovered and rejuvenated by the break from work the weekends bring. The traffic slows, businesses close and a quiet descends across neighbourhoods. There are, of course, football matches, which Danny loves. He's a loyal South Melbourne supporter and has already convinced Lilybeth to barrack for them as well. Lilybeth has even asked Mother to teach her to knit so that she can make a scarf in red and white club colours.

'It's my reward for all the hard work we do during the week, Isabella,' Danny says whenever I tease him about his footy addiction.

Shivering, we remove our coats and hang them on the backs of the chairs at our favourite red Laminex table near the window. Danny drinks his coffee black and I always have tea, made strong in the pot. Mario, the café owner, waves from behind the counter and within a couple of minutes our tea and coffee arrive. It's drizzling outside; the door to Sing, McMillan and Associates is shut tight during winter days. Being able to see the office from here, keeping an eye on who comes and goes, is a bonus. When we started our café trips on Monday mornings, Audrey made it clear she disapproved.

'What if a client arrives early for an appointment?'

'Tell them we will be there on time for the appointment,' I say, and she tuts.

'We're just over the road.' Danny smiles at me.

Audrey purses her lips as she turns back to her typewriter.

'There is another solution, Audrey,' says Danny. 'We can close for thirty minutes, and you and Lucy can come to the café as well.'

'Don't be ridiculous.' The keystrokes on Audrey's typewriter quicken.

The business is thriving. We are receiving new referrals weekly and our fee revenue has increased. Mother has stuck to her two days a week in the office and loves taking care of Lilybeth with Father. Danny and I are both somewhat surprised she's been true to her word and stayed in the background. Audrey makes an extra effort to help Mother with her work when she's here. Her uncompromising allegiance to Mother can be less than helpful when I introduce small changes. When Danny suggests the same changes, Audrey complies, although sometimes reluctantly.

Danny and I have worked well together these past few months and share an understanding that our office practices must be improved to meet current professional standards. This is our current goal. We inform Mother before we make any major changes and usually, she agrees. It's Audrey who digs her heels in and Mother won't have a word said against her, or to her, for that matter.

'It's working well, Isabella.'

I look up from my tea as Danny stirs sugar in his coffee.

'Please call me Issie. I was so used to it in England.'

'Issie suits you.'

'Thank you. You mean the two of us are working well together?'

'I meant the new arrangements in the office. And yes ... yes, of course we work well together, we always did, Isa ... Issie.'

'We had some funny times back then, Danny.'

'Remember when we lost a file I'd been updating? We searched everywhere before working up the courage to tell your mother.'

Both of us are already laughing.

'You'd taken it with you when you sneaked out the back to have a cigarette, put it on the bench just inside the door and forgot about it. Someone put newspapers on top of it.'

'When I confessed to losing the file, your mother laughed and told us she'd been wondering when we were going confess. She'd found it among the newspapers and had it on her desk all the time.'

'And the day poor old Mrs Madigan came in and wanted to buy carrots and potatoes. She came back three times and each time Mother insisted I make her another cup of tea. Eventually, you took her home and alerted her family to her daytime wanderings.'

'You know, Issie, after you left nothing seemed funny anymore. No laughter, just quiet days and hard work.'

'I sure know how to upset the applecart,' I say, trying to lighten the mood again.

'There's something you don't know.'

'There are many things I don't know, Danny.'

'Seriously. Just a few days before you ... well, before you cleared out to England, I was going to ask you out on a date.'

Mario is grinding coffee beans behind the counter. Two more customers arrive; the cold draught from the open door hits my legs before it closes. Danny is waiting for my response, head on the side, crooked tie, crooked smile. He raises one eyebrow and reaches across the table for my hand.

'I might regret telling you that. Don't worry, I'm not going to hold you to it, Issie.'

'You were going to ask me out on a ...'

'But you were distracted, so distracted back then. Now I understand why.'

There is a silence between us, his hand is still on mine, it's warm and I feel a tingle of emotion stir within me. Since Alexander, I have not contemplated a relationship or even considered another man in my life. Bringing Lilybeth into the world, working and studying has fully occupied me. And now, out of the blue, here's Danny with his gentle, kind eyes sitting across from me, simply looking at me. I've known Danny for so long and I adore him like a brother, but suddenly this doesn't feel like brotherly love.

Chapter Sixty-One

Issie

Dear Neva,

So much has happened since last I wrote. The practice continues to thrive, new clients and referrals come in daily. We are thinking we might employ another solicitor to take some of the pressure from us but will wait another month or so to see if the current flow of work continues. Danny is the backbone of this place. I can't imagine what I would possibly do without him. He is so calm and when I hesitate or question myself, he is quick to reassure me.

Mother has surprised us all by relinquishing control. She still does a small amount of work but she's no longer running the business like she used to. Her main interest is Lilybeth and since Father has retired, he has joined her with gusto. Neva, I never would have believed my family could be so besotted by my little girl who is, by the way, thriving and learning so many new things. Her piano playing needs some practice but she is already mastering the basics.

Danny and I have become quite close and have been spending a good deal of time together away from work. He's fun to be with and we laugh at each other's jokes. He's the kindest man I've ever met. Sorry, I'm going on a bit, Neva, but I never saw it coming. Sometimes, I feel breathless when I think of all that's happened in the past.

How are you, my dear Neva, how are you really? Are you happy in London and when can I convince you and Lachlan to come out to Australia for a visit? Is Victor still managing? He sometimes writes but his letters are brief and I get a sense of false cheer. Poor Victor, he was never meant to be without his Nancy.

Write soon, my friend. I miss our times together, talking and working out what to do next. You do realise, Neva, our friendship has been built around sorting out the next tricky dilemma lurking just around the corner. The difficulties were mostly mine and fortunately for me, you always seemed to have an answer. Hopefully, those times are behind us and our friendship can exist without this constant need of mine. Though you, my friend, are the best problem solver I know.

Sending my love to you and Lachlan.

Your dearest friend,

Issie

With the envelope sealed and half an hour to spare before my next client, I decide to go for a walk, breathe in some fresh air, and post the letter myself. Normally I would drop the letter in the office tray for posting the next day. I tell Audrey I'll be back in fifteen minutes. She nods above the staccato tapping on her typewriter and gives me one of her questioning looks.

The air outside is crisp as I pull the door closed behind me. A light breeze blows against my forehead and the sun catches the edge of the stately buildings in Collins Street. I have a sense of wellbeing. This is the first time since I've returned home that I feel in touch with my surroundings. As if I might belong again. I walk up the steps to the G.P.O., buy an airmail stamp, attach it and drop the letter in the overseas mailbox at the front.

It's from the top of the steps that I catch a glimpse of him. He's hurriedly moving down the steps before turning the corner into Elizabeth Street. I'm momentarily frozen to the spot; my mouth feels dry. I run to the corner, but he's vanished. Was it really Alexander? Or was it my mind playing tricks? The old familiar feelings return: my stomach churns, I'm alert, jittery, watchful.

Back at work, I scoot past Audrey to my office and close the door. It must have been someone else. Why would it be Alexander? I have to settle; a new client is due any minute.

CHAPTER SIXTY-TWO

LILY

Lily sits opposite her daughter in the old tearooms they used to visit when Isabella was a child. Sugar bowls, spoons and white scallop-edged serviettes are clustered together in the middle of the polished tables. Nothing has changed in all the years Lily has been coming here. The fine lacey café curtains throw a filtered light onto their table near the window. Fancy English plates hang below the picture rails; Lily wonders if anyone ever climbs up to dust them.

'I'd forgotten about this little place, Mother.'

'Father and I often take afternoon tea here. It has stayed the same despite changing hands a couple of times and they still make a good pot of tea.'

Lily places her handbag beside the chair and folds her hands loosely on the table. Isabella examines the room for a long moment before returning her gaze. Lily can sense the awkwardness of the situation and she's unsure how her daughter will respond to the conversation she wants to have with her.

'So, what's this about, Mother?'

'You have become very direct, Isabella.' The waitress arrives and they sit back quietly while she places the teapot and the delicate cups and saucers in front of them.

'I'll be back with the cakes.'

'Mother, I know there's something you want to discuss in private, otherwise we could have talked at home.'

'We rarely get to talk between ourselves and some matters need to be discussed away from little ears.'

'She doesn't miss much, does she?'

They both laugh. Lily feels the tension ease.

'Lilybeth's curious and full of questions, much like another young girl I once knew.'

The young woman returns with two plates: a neenish tart for Lily and a slice of Victoria sponge for Isabella. Lily sips her tea and places the cup back down on the delicate saucer.

'I've been thinking about Lilybeth's name, and yours as well,' Lily says.

'What about our name?'

'Your Father and I have been thinking you might want to consider using Lilybeth's father's name for her. It would –'

'It would what? Pretend she has a father and I have a husband?' Issie pushes her sponge cake aside.

'Yes, given you put it that way. It will make it easier for her at school, Isabella.'

Lily feels a tremor in her own hands and sees the same shakiness in her daughter's. She is so quick to anger.

'Her name is McMillan, same as mine, same as yours.'

'Why do you always have to be so stubborn? I just want to talk about Lilybeth's future. You know we want the best for her and –'

'Is it for Lilybeth or for you, Mother?'

'Isabella, please.' Lily picks up her cake fork before quickly replacing it beside the plate. Her face is serious as she draws her shoulders up. 'There are times in life when conforming makes it easier for everyone concerned.'

Through the lace curtains, the afternoon light is fading and the quaint room has turned gloomy. Lily has often tried to convince Isabella that she and Knill love her and Lilybeth. They would do anything for them. But Isabella's stubbornness and independence spring to the fore whenever a suggestion is put forward. Lily suddenly decides to give up on the topic.

'It was just a thought. Let's not talk about it again.'

'You have to stop doing this, Mother.'

'Stop doing what?'

'Stop interfering to make things more comfortable for you.'

'Absolutely ridiculous, Isabella. It's not about me, or your father. It's –'

'It's my business. I am not going to use Alexander's name. I didn't then and I won't now. Have you any idea how difficult it's been for me these last six years? Sure, I did the wrong thing. I left without telling you and Father and I'll always be sorry for that. It was a huge mistake. Alexander wasn't who I thought he was. But, Mother, you and Father's constant attention stifled me. I didn't know how to make my own decisions because you had my life planned out for me. But now, I am my own person. I'm an adult, Mother. I learnt the hard way. There will be no name changes for the sake of conformity.'

Lily is white in the face as she fiddles in her tapestry handbag for her purse.

'Your father said it was a bad idea to raise this with you. He was right.'

'Oh, Mother. Can't you just accept things the way they are?'

'Yes, I've just said I won't raise it again. You've made yourself perfectly clear. You're strong-willed like your grandmother. She's stubborn and never easily persuaded.'

'That is the funniest thing I've ever heard you say, Mother. You of all people calling Nan Eliza stubborn!'

Lily rises, her handbag firmly on her arm. The din of crockery on trays as the waitresses clear the tables around them fills the silence that has fallen between them. Issie follows her dignified mother to the door, leaving behind their unfinished afternoon tea.

Chapter Sixty-Three

Knill

Knill has spent the afternoon cleaning the fishpond with enthusiastic help from Lilybeth. As the shadows lengthen across the garden, he's aware Lily will soon be arriving home. Knill was uneasy about her plan to speak to Isabella about Lilybeth's name and tried his best to dissuade her, 'I'm not sure it's of such high importance.'

But Lily, being Lily, was determined to have the discussion.

As he thinks of his loving wife on a mission to do what she believes is wise and sensible, he's acutely aware of how much Lily likes to get her own way. Knill's also aware their daughter is no longer likely to agree with her mother's suggestions. He sighs when he thinks of treading a middle path between two strong women; he wants life to be less challenging and he thought Lily did too. Perhaps, just perhaps, this time Lily will have to back down.

To his surprise, Lily is in reasonable spirits when she arrives home. She has cake for Lilybeth and pours two glasses of sherry.

'Before you ask, no, she didn't agree. Stubborn as your mother, I told her.'

Knill doesn't respond to the quip about his mother, but a restrained smile creeps to his face as they sit on the bench under the peppercorn tree. Lilybeth has the little sailing boat on the pond and is busy pushing it from one side to the other.

'Was it an amiable discussion?'

'Of course. I have come to admire our headstrong daughter, Knill. Today I realised Isabella has a strength of character that I've not recognised before. She has a voice of her own and she is going to live her life the way she wants.

'I wasn't happy, mind you. She dismissed my suggestion outright.'

Lily sips her sherry and Knill watches his granddaughter. The breeze is cool as he thinks of the past years and adjusting their lives to Isabella's absence. They had to learn and learn they did. Not quickly, not easily, but life went on. Still, the emptiness they felt is not far from the surface. He can see Lily in her office, carrying on with stoic dignity because she thought it was the right and the only thing to do. But that was then, and this is now. Dare he think life might now bring calmer waters?

Chapter Sixty-Four

Issie

Mother hasn't mentioned our tearoom discussion again and Father hasn't said a word about it. Each day, after kindergarten, they take Lilybeth to the park. She loves the swings and they spend many happy hours pushing the roundabout, catching her as she lands at the bottom of the slide and watching her play on the small monkey bar. Lilybeth is nimble and can't wait to climb the big bars.

'You'll be able to when you're a schoolgirl.'

'But I really could do it now, Grandpa. For practice.'

'Some things we have to be patient about, Lilybeth.'

'Can you push me higher on the swing, please?'

Father laughs at her request but secretly admires her stamina and grit. He says she is like me at the same age, but perhaps a bit more determined. Mother is teaching Lilybeth to play piano and Father is teaching her the violin. Next year she has been promised formal lessons with a music teacher. Lilybeth is eager for all new challenges and I've come to realise the benefits of returning to Australia. I would never have been able to work and provide the same opportunities for her in London. My only concern is she's being given too much attention. After all, I know only too well how that can end up.

***

Every Friday afternoon, Mother and Father bring Lilybeth into the office for afternoon tea to mark the end of the week. We often have lamingtons with cream and cupcakes with coloured icing from Mother's favourite cake shop in East Melbourne. Lilybeth gets to choose hers first, always chocolate. The men have a beer. I would love one too, but Mother has an aversion to women drinking beer. So, Lucy, Audrey, Mother, and I have tea or a lemonade shandy. Lilybeth has Fanta, a new orange soft drink bought by Danny at Mario's café.

Today, we're running late for afternoon tea. Danny, Mother and I are in my office discussing a particularly complex case. Father is fixing a door handle in the bathroom and Audrey is filing the last of the week's documents into the old grey filing cabinet behind the counter. Lucy is in the kitchen making the tea. In the waiting room, Lilybeth is lying on the floor singing to herself as she concentrates on her colouring book. Her pencils are spread out in an arc on the floor in order of colour; Lilybeth loves order and applies it whenever she can.

It's almost four o'clock when the three of us come out of my office. Audrey covers her typewriter and we head for the tearoom. Mother calls to Father and Lilybeth as we go. A couple of minutes later, Father arrives, pleased with himself.

'It's as right as rain again, a broken screw. Think I might have missed my calling as a handyman.' He laughs and sits down at the table.

'Where's Lilybeth?' I say.

'In the waiting room,' says Lucy.

I call out to her. There's no answer and I assume she's playing hide and seek with us. Her book and pencils are still on the floor. For a minute I play along, calling to her, telling her she's missing the cakes and soft drink, usually guaranteed to get her moving. Still no answer. I check my office, Danny's office, behind the counter near Audrey's desk, then the tearoom. Still no Lilybeth.

'She must be somewhere,' Father says, getting to his feet and following me out of the tearoom. I've looked everywhere; she must be here.

'Lilybeth, come out now.'

Danny and Mother are behind us now and looking in all the obvious places. I check the front door. It's unlocked.

'Audrey, did you lock the door?'

'No. Lucy locked it before she went to the kitchen.'

'But it's unlocked.'

'I definitely locked it and left the key in the lock as usual,' calls Lucy, coming out of the tearoom, looking worried.

'Lilybeth,' calls Father, his voice stern.

We check again in all the offices and the back door leading to the small courtyard, calling Lilybeth's name. I run to the steps outside the front door. She's not there, or on the street. Half expecting the others to have found her, I hurry back in.

'She's not here,' says Danny, running to meet me.

A tightening in my chest tells me something is wrong, very wrong. We search behind the counter again and Audrey checks the stationery cupboard. Father and Mother are out the front door. I follow them. We call from the steps.

A man is walking by. 'Have you seen a little girl, wearing a blue check dress? She has curly hair, a white hair ribbon?' He shakes his head. Further along the footpath now, still calling to Lilybeth, and people begin to stare. I can hear Father asking a young couple if they've seen a small child on her own. Danny is suddenly by my side. He tells me Audrey is ringing the police. When the police are mentioned, my legs begin to tremble.

'She must be somewhere close by, Danny. She can't have just disappeared.'

He puts his arm around me.

'LILYBETH, LILYBETH!'

CHAPTER SIXTY-FIVE

ISSIE

It's five o'clock. Over an hour has passed but it seems an eternity. We pace the waiting room, checking again the spaces she could be hiding in. We've exhausted ourselves running up and down the street, believing we'll catch a glimpse of her any minute, wandering along, probably frightened and realising she's lost, but there's no sign of her. People passing by try to help when they realise a child is missing. Thankfully the police finally arrive. They park across the footpath and come swiftly up the steps. I'm relieved they're here, but as time goes on, it becomes clear they're not getting anywhere either.

I move to the front door, resisting the urge to again run out into the early-evening shadows. Danny, who's been out with Father searching the streets, comes to my side.

The office is taken over by the police; they set themselves up at the front counter next to Audrey's desk. They have officers on foot patrolling the area, they tell us.

'Could she have left with someone?' the police sergeant asks. He has just called the station to check in, which he's been doing every fifteen minutes. He doesn't want to voice his concern, but if she'd just wandered off and become lost, she would have been found by now. They are trying not to alarm us, but their obvious concern does just that.

'And you say she was in the waiting area and the front door was locked?'

'I locked the door before I went to the kitchen,' says Lucy, starting to get teary. 'I really did lock it.'

Father goes to her and puts his arm around her shoulders.

'Is it difficult to unlock from inside? What I mean is, could the child have unlocked it herself?'

'It's possible. She's clever enough to work out how to, but there was no reason. She never looks to go anywhere on her own and she loves Friday cakes ...' Father's voice trails off.

'Would she have unlocked it to let someone in, maybe if they called out or knocked loudly?'

'Maybe. The key was still in the lock. We don't take the key out until we all leave the building,' says Danny.

Mother is sitting in the waiting room, her face pale. Danny moves to my side and rubs my back.

'We'll find her, Issie,' Danny says. 'A kid can't just disappear.'

'But she has ...'

In the bathroom, I vomit into the toilet. When the nausea passes, I lean back on the wall and try to make myself stand upright. I can't do this; falling to pieces isn't an option right now. I've been in difficult situations before and managed. Stay strong; I must stay strong for her.

Where is she? Why haven't the police found her? I throw water on my face and dry it off. A tight unsettling sensation rises in my chest. I try to slow down my breathing, but it continues to come out in rapid gasps. My pulse is pounding, racing. Then, Danny calls to me. His voice sounds distant as I move toward him.

'Please find her, Danny. I just want her back. Will someone please just find her?'

He puts his arm around my shoulders. I lean against the firmness of his chest and for a few seconds, take comfort from someone in control.

Four more policemen and a single policewoman arrive. Outside the entrance, several newspaper reporters are milling around. Pedestrians linger on the footpath and watch as the police come and go. The police are telling us not to talk to anyone at this stage, referring to the press. Father and Mother are both distraught and thankfully Danny's taken on the role of spokesperson. He talks to the police, their heads close and voices low. A doctor arrives and is allowed access. Father has expressed concern about Mother's heart condition, although she insists she's fine, but she's shaking uncontrollably. Father helps her to the front office as the doctor, bag in hand, follows.

My mouth is dry, and a bitter taste lingers but I can't swallow the water that Lucy pushes into my hand. Lucy's eyes are rimmed red from crying. She's picked up Lilybeth's colouring book and pencils and placed them on the reception desk.

'I just want her back. She's out there somewhere and it's getting dark. Someone has to find her.' Gulping back loud sobs, I try to keep some sense of calm but there is no calm left in me. This is the worst moment of my life. My child is missing, she's gone, we can't find her, and I can't bear it, I can't. Danny has me by the shoulders and gently pulls me up from my slumped position.

'Breathe, breathe slowly, Issie.'

Danny and Audrey steady me against the wall as a wet towel hits my brow.

'What are they saying now, Danny?'

'They want to know if anyone has made threats against the law firm or if anyone has tried to blackmail the family.'

'No, of course not ... oh Danny.'

Then a flash of the man on the steps of the post office. But it couldn't be him. Why would Alexander be here? He doesn't know about Lilybeth, unless ...

'What is it, Issie?' Tell me.'

'I'm probably confused. There is something but it's probably not ...'

'What is it you're not saying, Issie?'

I tell Danny about the man on the steps. He knows nothing about Lilybeth's father and this wasn't how I wanted to tell him about my time in Oxford. Instantly alarmed, Danny relays the story to the police.

***

It's a little after seven o'clock. Full-dark. All the lights are on and the streetlamps glow on the footpath. A shout from a young policeman stationed at the front door has everyone on their feet.

'Someone's found her,' he calls. Camera flashes light the evening as the photographers and reporters surge from the steps to the footpath. Danny and I follow. He has my arm, but I loosen from his grip and start running, running, towards Lilybeth, a small figure hand in hand with a woman in a red coat. The woman is grabbed roughly by two policemen before I reach them and one of the policeman scoops Lilybeth up into his arms. Lilybeth is protesting, telling them not to hurt the lady. A crowd of onlookers swell around as I lift Lilybeth from the arms of the officer. Her eyes are wide and she's looking scared, her little arms lock around my neck. She buries her face in my shoulder as we head back along the footpath.

'Mummy, Mummy, you didn't come.'

'Come where, Lilybeth? We've been so worried. Where have you been?

Lilybeth is crying now as I shield her from onlookers and the flashing lights. Her pale face soaked with tears. In place of my confident, alert, curious Lilybeth is a scared child.

'You ... you didn't come.'

'It's all fine, Lilybeth. Let's get you back inside.'

Danny has his arm around us and is shielding us from the crowd. The police close ranks around us and we are ushered up the steps. I stumble through the door with Danny holding us firmly. The office is still full of police. Mother is crying and Father is rubbing his hands across his brow. Both Audrey and Lucy look wretched.

Lilybeth starts to sob again; I stroke her hair as she clings to me.

'The man ... the man said you would come, Mummy.'

Chapter Sixty-Six

Issie

Lilybeth sleeps in my bed but she's restless and calls out in her sleep. My eyes refuse to close. I'm not sure I sleep at all. When she finally wakes, it's as if the events of the day before hadn't happened.

'Where are Grandma and Grandpa?' She yawns and throws her legs over the side of the bed. 'I want to go to the park.'

'Not just yet, Lilybeth.'

'After breakfast?'

'Oh, Lilybeth, you were so tired last night, let's just have a rest this morning. And we have to have a little talk later.'

'You mean about going to the park with the man?'

'Yes, darling. Did you unlock the door at Mummy's work?'

'Yes, I saw the man through the window and then he knocked at the door. The man said he was my daddy, and you were coming to have lemonade with us. But you didn't come.'

'Lilybeth, you must never go anywhere with someone you don't know. We were worried about you.'

'Is he my daddy?'

'No. You don't have a daddy.'

'I just have Grandpa and Uncle Danny?'

'Yes, Lilybeth.'

'But the man, the daddy man, said we could go back to the park when you came. The park has big swings and the man let me go on them, but I hurt my knee on the climbing bars.'

Lilybeth peers down at her scuffed knee and rubs it.

'What happened when I didn't come, Lilybeth?'

'I already told you, Mummy. We went to the hotel to wait for you. I had four biscuits, and he gave me a box of Smarties. The man had beer, like Grandpa and Uncle Danny. Then I wanted to go to the toilet and he asked the nice lady if she would take me.'

'And did she?'

'Yes, but when we came back, the daddy man was gone, and the lady and her friend kept asking me what his name was.'

The police pieced together the events of Lilybeth's disappearance with the help of a few people who had seen them at the Market Square Park and the woman who brought her back from the ladies' lounge at the Market Hotel. While in the park, they surmised, Alexander became aware the police were searching the area for Lilybeth and he panicked. He took her to the hotel across the road and sometime later asked a woman in the lounge to take Lilybeth to the toilet, wrote a hurried note with the address of where to take her and then left.

'The man was sad, Mummy.'

'How do you know, darling?'

'He was crying and wiped his eyes on his sleeve.'

'Did he say anything else to you, Lilybeth? Were you frightened?'

'No, he was a nice man. He kept crying though. Why did he cry, Mummy?'

'He must have been sad about something, but nothing for you to worry about. I want you to promise me, darling, you will never, ever, go with anyone you don't know. Do you promise?'

'I promise. Can we go to the park now?'

***

The police arrive in the afternoon and ask a few more questions of Lilybeth. When she is finished answering in her small voice, Danny says, 'Lilybeth, I bet you could beat me in a race from the clothesline to the pond,' and they leave us to talk to the police. Mother and Father have both aged ten years overnight. Mother seems particularly shaky; Father hasn't left her side.

'We've issued a warrant for Sadler,' the policeman says. 'We'll find him.'

Luckily, I'd kept Helen's letter when she tried to contact Alexander in Oxford. The police had managed to track her down in Sydney overnight but she hadn't seen him for three months, they tell us. Not since he came to visit the boys. On that occasion he'd been drinking, and she'd refused to let Michael and Duncan leave the house with him. The police tell us to take extra precautions but are of the view he may have returned to New South Wales. The woman in the maroon coat was able to give the police a good description of him and they also have a photo of Alexander from his days at the University of Melbourne. A man answering his description was seen boarding the early train to Sydney this morning. The New South Wales police have been alerted and they'll be waiting for the train at the other end. In only a few short hours, this might all be over. Several newspapers are running the story, but as promised, Lilybeth's name and many of the circumstances were withheld.

Danny and Lilybeth come back in when the police have gone; Father brings out the checkerboard to play a game with Lilybeth. I take Father's place next to Mother and she turns to hug me. We embrace for much longer than usual and I feel something dissolving between us. Does she understand now why I would never want Lilybeth to take her father's surname?

How did Alexander know I was back in Australia? How did he know I had a child and then conclude he was her father? I think of him following me from Sing, McMillan and Associates to my parents' home, lurking there. There's no other way he could have seen Lilybeth. And it wouldn't have been difficult to conclude

Lilybeth was his when he caught a glimpse of her. She is the right age and, even more convincingly, she resembles him. Her golden-brown hair is in tangles across her face, and the confident, happy way she carries herself. When Lilybeth beams her love of life and her easy disposition for all to enjoy, I recognise Alexander in her. The Alexander he sometimes was. The person he wanted to be. Lilybeth has inherited the good and clever parts of Alexander. The task ahead is to nurture her and ensure she stays balanced and measured, unlike her father who couldn't hold all parts of his personality together.

Lilybeth has the right to know the truth about her father; it's not fair to continue the charade. But it's not the right time now – yesterday's events have taken too much out of us. And I'm not sure how to tell her that the man she went to the park with is really her father.

Chapter Sixty-Seven

Issie

The New South Wales police didn't find Alexander when the train pulled into Central Station. A month later, we are still vigilant. Mother and Father are hyperalert when they're with Lilybeth, especially outside the home, and they both go with her everywhere. The kindergarten teachers have been told about Alexander and no one except Mother, Father, or myself is allowed to collect her. Danny has also drawn up legal papers prohibiting Alexander from coming near us at the practice or home.

Lilybeth's abduction has made me realise how much I depend on Danny. His strength has carried me through. He has kept us all on an even keel – running the office, showing concern for Mother and Father and reassuring Lilybeth she has nothing to be afraid of. The old feelings of guilt and shame are back. I feel so bad for what Mother and Father went through. I set it in motion six years ago and I blame myself for everything.

Lilybeth herself shows no real signs of having been affected by what happened except she sometimes asks me to stay home from work and play with her. I've been collecting her after kindergarten a couple of times a week and taking her to the park.

Some days I relive the awful moment of realising Lilybeth was missing. On days like this, I busy myself and wait for the trembling and panic to dissipate. To my surprise, it's Audrey who notices when this happens. She brings me a cup of tea and, without saying anything, fusses about me. I marvel at the change in our relationship since the afternoon Lilybeth was lost. Audrey, for reasons I haven't quite worked out, has accepted me at last and gives me the support she lavished on Mother in the past. Maybe seeing my vulnerability at the time changed her view of me. I'm just thankful something good came from that terrible day.

***

The practice is getting busier and we have advertised for another solicitor. We are interviewing three applicants for the position: a woman and two men. All are young but each has some experience.

Lucy brings the mail to my desk and I flick through. There's a letter from Esme and Jack among them.

Dear Issie,

Hoping you and Lilybeth are happy in Melbourne. We still miss the two of you so very much.

A piece of news for you, Father Monty is back as the Priest at St Mary Magdalen's. He's popular in the neighbourhood and has been to visit Victor a few times. Victor enjoys his visits and Monty asks after you and Lilybeth.

Victor's much the same. We visit him once a week. He's lucky to have his group of mates at the local and luckier still with Neva keeping him or-ganised. Ester House is much quieter these days. The new Housekeeper, Pearl Devlin, keeps the house spick and span and is a wonderful cook according to Victor. No new boarders except for a stray black cat with ginger ears and a woeful meow. Victor has taken the poor creature in and is very fond of him.

Our Connie is growing like a mushroom and we both continue to be besotted by our little miracle. To think we were told our chances of having children were minimal. Jack and I thank our lucky stars each day for our precious baby girl. And not only do we have her, but another miracle has taken place, I'm pregnant again. It's an exciting and busy time, our little house is going to be overflowing. I know you will be pleased for us, and we wanted you to be one of the first to know.

Love to our little Lilybeth, tell her we miss her very much.

Love from

Esme, Jack and Connie.

I'm crying by the end of the letter. I'm missing being part of their lives, especially on special occasions like the birth of a new baby.

I miss Lachlan and Thomas with their tough no-nonsense approach to their work, their fair and tangible support of me through my studies and through my transition to becoming a qualified lawyer. And then there's Victor. When we left, I worried if he would cope on his own without us. Well, he seems to be doing well enough. I miss Neva and her honest, pithy way of getting me back on track when I doubt myself. Neva, Esme, and Jack knew me better than anyone and they saw me through the dark and difficult times.

It's times like this when I still yearn for my dear friends. It feels like so long ago since I lived in their world. So much has happened since my return home, but I also notice the ache for my former life in London has faded a little.

Chapter Sixty-Eight

Issie

Lucy taps on my door. 'There's a woman in the waiting room asking to see you.'

'She doesn't have an appointment?' I look at the stack of client files and groan at the thought of fitting anyone else in.

'She says it's personal but she can wait.' Lucy raises her eyebrows. 'She insists on seeing you, Isabella.'

'Well then.' I follow Lucy to the waiting room.

The woman is attractive and wearing a paisley dress with matching orange shoes and bag. Her fair hair cut in a chic style, flicking gently around her face. When she sees me, she rises quickly and nods a reserved acknowledgement. Back in my office, she sits uneasily on the edge of her chair.

'Sorry, I don't know your name and I haven't introduced myself. I'm Isabella McMillan.'

'I know who you are, Isabella. Thank you for seeing me at short notice. I should have made an appointment but ... there is something you should know, something that's just happened.'

'And your name is?'

She looks directly at me. 'I'm Helen – Helen Sadler.'

I push back against the spine of my chair; the silence in the room swallows me. This woman often occupied my thoughts in England. What was it like to be left to raise two children alone? Was she still in love with Alexander? Did she hold me responsible for the demise of her marriage? And was she also a victim of her husband's erratic behaviour? His aggression?

And now, the two of us with a legacy of choosing or being chosen by a man who changed our lives sit silent, staring at each other across a desk.

She edges back in her seat with what seems to be relief. Her face calmer now, giving me time to recompose myself after her unexpected arrival.

'I'm sorry, I wasn't expecting ...'

'No, of course not. I should have introduced myself to your receptionist, but I was so intent on seeing you and didn't want to be turned away. You see, I'm only in Melbourne for two days.'

'I don't know what to say, I'm –'

'Please, you need to hear me out. I'm not here to place any blame on you. My marriage to Alexander is long finished. It was a shock when he left for England without telling us but ...'

'Without telling you ... I didn't know ... He said ...'

'Alexander rarely told the truth, Isabella. You must have discovered that.'

'Yes, I did but ...'

My knees are shaking under the desk and suddenly I'm reliving my time in Oxford. I'd assumed those times were in the past. But here it is, the wrongs of the past in my face. I breathe slowly to remain calm. Helen is still and waiting for me to respond; my shame looms over me. I was the one who had an affair with her husband, the one who ran off to England with him. Ruined her marriage, deprived her children of a father. And yet, she calmly sits across my desk waiting for me to recover from the shock of meeting her.

'I don't know what to say to you.'

'There is nothing you have to say, Isabella. I came because the police contacted me about Alexander kidnapping your daughter.'

Kidnapping. I quiver at the impact of the word.

'Helen, I haven't seen Alexander since he left me in difficult circumstances in Oxford. I still don't know how he discovered I'd had a child.'

'He would have come snooping around, looking for you. And he would have worked it out. Don't forget, Isabella, he was a man who was able to use his cleverness in cunning ways. Ways that always ended in disaster.'

'I suppose I thought he wouldn't want to find me again. After all, he left Oxford without leaving any message. He just fled back here. He left as if I had never existed.'

Helen half-smiles, fiddles with the looped earring on her left ear and sighs.

'Alexander was never capable of being responsible for his actions, Isabella. At his best he could impress anyone. But it was all veneer. Something happened to him as a kid. It seemed to haunt him and perhaps it never allowed him to be the person he wanted to be.'

'Do you know what it was?'

'Something to do with his father's death. But your guess, my guess, who knows? We never talked about his childhood. Even at family gatherings, his mother and brothers were careful not to push too hard, but there's no point talking about it now.'

'Has he contacted you, Helen?'

'I had a phone call this morning from the police. They found Alexander yesterday.'

Helen voice is suddenly low; she looks away.

'He's been arrested?'

'They found him at Coney's old farm at Miles Creek. Alexander's dead, Isabella. He killed himself.'

Chapter Sixty-Nine

Issie

Dear Neva,

He's dead.

I can hardly write, my hands are shaking so hard. He was found near his childhood home yesterday. The police say he committed suicide.

On hearing this it took me back to the days in Oxford when his mood oscillated between being cheerful to one of intense outrage without warning. I used to worry he might do something terrible to himself. I thought I was over the Oxford days, Neva, but here I sit huddled and immobilised just like the old days. I can't stop crying and yet, I don't know why I'm weeping so. I loved him once or was certainly besotted by him.

I'm sad he never knew his daughter. But, to snatch her from us in the manner he did was just unforgivable. So why am I so shocked and confused by his death? He died for me six years ago, Neva, but I'm so wretched and upset.

Here I go again, pouring out my troubles to you.

I will write again soon, Neva. When I can think straight, and my hands stop shaking.

Love from your dearest friend

Issie.

CHAPTER SEVENTY

ISSIE

It's midday when the outskirts of Miles Creek appear. Dilapidated wire fences with crooked timber posts around mostly empty paddocks. An outline of skeletal trees in the distance. A landscape starved of water and care. When I told my parents I was going to visit Alexander's mother, Father insisted he go with me. Danny also offered to come. But in the end, I won out and set off alone in Father's prized dark-blue Wolseley. Both Danny and Father were concerned about the distance, and they were right. The drive from Melbourne to Miles Creek seemed never-ending but it was something I had to do on my own.

Now Alexander is gone, the urge to understand more about him has intensified. After all, he was Lilybeth's father, and as much as I'd like it to be, the fact can't be erased, despite once thinking it could. There will be a time when she wants to and is entitled to know more about her father and that's my responsibility. Helen's words keep playing on my mind, *something* happened to him as a kid. What was it?

Turning off the highway takes me onto a dusty gravel road with weatherboard farmhouses dotted here and there. Empty sheds and weathered farm equipment lie idle. Sheep graze on what little feed the paddocks have to offer. Closer to the town, the sun bounces off the rusted iron rooftops. A hotchpotch of shops, many with drooping verandas, line the main street. A once-imposing double-storey McIvor Hotel has clearly seen better days.

Miles Creek reminds me of other country towns I visited as a kid. Shops in one long street with smaller streets off each side. But this town has another element to it

– an eeriness, a lack of activity, almost a ghost town. A local man leaves the butcher shop, stops at the sight of a strange car and stares. The front of the newsagency is strewn with faded posters advertising the *Sydney Morning Herald* and the *Australian Woman's Weekly*. I could go in to ask for directions, but thinking it can't be too hard to find, I drive on, looking for Wiley Street.

The palms of my hands are sweating. What if she refuses to speak with me? After all, she hasn't replied to my letter telling her I would like to visit. Past the shops, the weatherboard houses show signs of age and little care. Several properties appear vacant with long grass up to the fence. Then a sign, Wiley Street, faded but readable.

An old man looks up from his seat on his veranda as I turn into the street. He watches, his chin jutted out, as I slow the Wolseley to a crawl. A few doors down, a rusted letter box with a hand-painted fifty-six appears.

The timber house was once white. The windows have been patched at some stage and painted brown. Bricks line the edge of the garden path and small shrubs are planted across in front of the veranda, evidence of an earlier attempt to create a garden. But it hasn't been tended recently.

Mother's words are ringing in my ears: 'Isabella, are you sure there's anything to be gained by going?'

The lace curtains twitch in the front window as I step onto the veranda. A single terracotta pot, holding a large geranium, sits beside the faded brown door and a worn mat sits askew. There is no doorbell, so I tap on the door. It's silent all around, in the street and on the veranda. The old man is now leaning on his gate, watching. There's movement inside and slowly the door creaks open a few inches. A dog barks loudly from somewhere close by in the street.

'Mrs Sadler, I'm Isabella McMillan. I wrote to you a couple of weeks ago.'

'Mm ... thought you'd come sometime.' Her face is blank. 'Suppose you'd better come in, then.'

She beckons me to follow her down the passageway. The blinds are drawn and the place is dark as she ushers me into the kitchen. She motions for me to sit down at the table.

She mutters something about making tea and moves to the stove where she opens the small door of the stove, takes two lumps of wood from the painted hearth and pushes them in. She stokes the fire sharply and then closes the door with a bang. She slides the kettle across the stovetop and collects cups and saucers from the pine dresser in the corner. Eventually, when the ritual is over, she sits heavily on the chair facing me and folds her hands in front of her. Her grey hair is pinned back with long bobby pins; her faded apron covers a fawn knitted cardigan that's seen better days. Her tartan skirt flows almost to the floor; the pleats, probably once sharp and defined, are now slack and misshapen. She's a woman who's had more than her share of hardship.

'What is it you want?' she says in a voice with a hint of annoyance.

'I'm not sure, but I thought it only right to speak with you, given –'

'Given he had an affair with you!'

Her eyes, the same eyes as Alexander's and not unlike Lilybeth's, watch me across the table.

'I'm sorry for Alexander's passing, Mrs Sadler. Can we talk about him? After all, my daughter is Alexander's daughter. She's your ... your granddaughter.'

She says nothing. The kettle is bubbling. She gets to her feet to tend to it. She is unhurried in her movements and the silence is close to unbearable. After what seems like an eternity, she comes back to the table with a metal teapot. She pours two cups of strong tea, pushes the milk jug and sugar bowl toward me and then sighs.

'You should never have gone away with him. He was married.'

'You're right. I did the wrong thing by going to England with Alexander. What we both did was wrong.'

'But taking the little girl was unforgivable. I'm sorry.'

'You don't have to be sorry on his behalf, Mrs Sadler.'

For the first time, she looks at me directly. Her faded eyes reflect weariness with the whole business. 'Alexander did a terrible thing but ... he's gone now.'

Pulling a large handkerchief from her apron, she lowers her head. Her quiet sobbing spills across the kitchen. I try to take her hand, but she refuses it. There is no comforting her; she is a woman who distances herself from physical support and she seems barely able to accept kind words. Eventually, she wipes her eyes and blows her nose before poking the large handkerchief back in her apron pocket.

She now looks everywhere but at me. In my own shame, I recognise hers. This woman has known proud moments. Alexander went to university and graduated with honours, completed his doctorate and went on to become an academic, his marriage to Helen and the arrival of the two little boys. There were times of joy and pride, I'm sure, and perhaps other occasions I don't know about. But not anymore; there is no joy left in her life.

It's unclear how much Mrs Sadler knows about what transpired between Alexander and Helen. Or Alexander and me. She barely had contact with Alexander when we were in Oxford. When the police contacted her, she said she hadn't heard from him for over a year, then had to withstand the shock of the police looking for him when he took Lilybeth. And then his death.

'Alexander's death must have been a shock for you and the family.'

She nods.

'I think you should talk to his brothers.' She picks up a pencil and scribbles an address on the back of an envelope.

'Martin lives in Sydney, but Hugh lives just around the corner. He'll be more helpful to you than me. I just can't talk about Alexander anymore. Not to anyone.'

'I didn't know Hugh lived in Miles Creek. Thank you. I'll leave you in peace. But I have something for you, if you would like it.'

I take the photo from my bag and pass it across the table. She looks at it silently. The muscles in her face twitch and her hands shake slightly as she gazes intently at Lilybeth's smiling face with her golden-brown curls and dark-blue eyes.

'Those eyes ... they're his eyes. Just promise me one thing. Don't let her make the mistakes her father made.'

She then places the photograph face down on the table and the visit is over.

CHAPTER SEVENTY-ONE

ISSIE

The dog's barking again, its shrill protest at the presence of a stranger in the neighbourhood. The old man is back on his veranda seat, still watching.

I find Hugh two streets away at the address given to me by Mrs Sadler. When he opens the door, the likeness to Alexander is disarming. He has the same curly hair, but he's taller and wears glasses.

'I'm Isabella McMillan. Your mother told me where I could find you.' Hugh glances past me into the street where Father's car is parked. 'I lived with Alexander in England ...' I'm not sure he knows who I am.

'And you've spoken to my mother?' His voice is identical to Alexander's.

'Yes, she sent me here.'

Hugh stands in the door frame, rubbing his neck. It's difficult to read his expression, but he says, 'Come in, Isabella.'

He ushers me into the front room, which is furnished with a Jacobean oak lounge suite with velvet cushions and a muted floral carpet square atop grey linoleum. An Australian landscape painting hangs above the timber mantelpiece above the blackened fireplace. The mantelpiece is bare except for a small family photo – two adults, two boys and a baby. A black and white cat is curled up on one of the chairs and stretches as Hugh indicates for me to sit in the other.

'I was in Oxford with Alexander.'

'I know who you are. I just wasn't expecting you.'

'I wrote to your mother.'

'She never mentioned it. Thought we'd be the last people you'd want anything to do with.'

'You could think the same about me.'

'Blaming others won't help. Alexander was his own worst enemy.'

Both of us are uneasy, both unsure of where this conversation might lead. Hearing Alexander's voice again is … difficult. Do I really have the right to ask anything of Hugh? But I'm here now. And he seems kind. Decent.

'He was the father of my child. I need to understand more about him, what he was like growing up.'

Hugh's face grimaces. 'I gave up trying to understand Alexander a long time ago. We should've tried harder. He was in bigger trouble than we'd imagined. Wasn't keeping his life together at all.'

'And when he was younger?'

'He was the clever one, always going to make something of himself.'

Hugh shifts nervously and stretches his legs in front of him. Next door, someone begins chopping wood.

'I'm sorry, I know this must be hard.'

'No harder than it's always been. We didn't have a good family life. Mum tried her best, but the Old Man was a shocker. Martin and I were older than Alexander by six and seven years. Left this place as soon as we had jobs to go to. It meant Mum and Alexander had to cope with the Old Man's craziness by themselves.' Hugh's face reddens. 'We always felt bad about that, especially given the circumstances. Anyway …'

'What circumstances?'

'So, he never told you about it?'

'About?'

'He always avoided it. Can't say I blame him.'

'I'm not following you.'

Hugh averts his eyes to the painting above the fireplace.

'Guess there's no harm in telling you now, but it was a no-go area for all of Alexander's life. No one dared speak of it.'

'Something happened to him?'

'Yes, but before ... sure you want to know all this?'

'Want to know? Perhaps not. But I think I should know. After all, he was the father of my daughter.'

Hugh scratches his ear, leans back in the sofa.

'The Old Man left Mum for another woman, someone he'd met at the pub. She wasn't the first, he was always at it. But this time he left Miles Creek and us. He went to Sydney with his new girlfriend.' Hugh lets out a loud sigh. 'Can't say we missed him, except money was tight and Mum had to get a job as a housekeeper at the pub to make ends meet. If it hadn't been for Paddy O'Connell, it would have been a rough time for us.'

'Who's Paddy O'Connell?'

'Our neighbour across the road.' Hugh points to the front window. 'He was a bachelor and lived with his older sister. About Mum's age and a great bloke. We loved him, and, as it turned out, so did Mum. Anyway, to cut a long story short, Mum and Paddy, well, they became involved with each other ... sorry, I haven't talked about this for a long time.'

Hugh's face contorts and he blinks back more tears before wiping his hand across his face.

'I'm sorry I'm making you relive this.'

'It's all right. You see, Paddy was a good bloke, an Irishman. He looked after us and Mum, we were happy, probably for the first time ever. We felt safe when Paddy was around.' A long stare at the painting followed.

'A year after the Old Man left, Mum was pregnant with Alexander. They were happy but I suppose it was difficult – they weren't married, and people talk.'

'Yes, I know a bit about how awful people can be.'

'Then a terrible thing happened. Paddy was killed in a logging accident out at the timber mill where he worked.'

Outside the rhythmic thud of chopping wood continues. A truck brakes somewhere in the distance.

'I'm so sorry, Hugh.'

'We were brought home from school and Mum was, well, Mum was in total shock. She just sat at the kitchen table and stared into nothing. The following week Alexander was born. But good old Paddy, he left Mum a small nest egg to get us over the first few months. When it was gone the future wasn't looking good. Mum was an absolute mess and withdrew from the community. We had no choice, we had to go to school. And then the worst thing happened. One day after school, we found the Old Man sitting at the kitchen table having a cup of tea with Mum. The rest is history: he moved back in and after a short time he resumed his crazy ways. He ignored Alexander unless it was to abuse him. Mum retreated into her shell and life limped on.'

'Did Alexander know his father was Paddy O'Connell?'

'Not until he was about twelve or thirteen – there had been nasty comments and teasing at school and Alexander confronted Mum, who finally told him the truth.'

'How did he take it?'

'Strangely enough, he said nothing. And from then on, he set about doing well at school. But the Old Man never let up on him. He had a rotten time, Isabella. So did Mum. I just wish Martin and I hadn't left them to fend for themselves.'

'We all make decisions we later regret.'

'Yep, spilt milk and all, but you drew the short straw with Alexander. He was a good little kid, sunny smile, couldn't help it with Paddy's blood in him. But the Old Man twisted anything good away.'

'At least I have Lilybeth.'

A smile flickers across Hugh's face for the first time.

'Just dawned on me. Your daughter's my niece.'

'Yes.'

'Martin and I never married, no kids. Our only relatives are Mum and Alexander's boys.'

'When she's old enough, I'll tell Lilybeth the truth about her father.'

'I'd like to meet her sometime. Helen's promised Mum she'll bring the boys to visit in a few months.'

Hugh is deep in his thoughts when I interrupt.

'There is something else I'd like to ask. Helen mentioned about Alexander and his father's death.'

Hugh straightens his back against the couch.

'You're not one to mince words, are you?'

'Sorry, if you don't want to talk …'

'You might as well know. Can't hurt now.'

The cat stretches and jumps down and rubs its back against my legs as it passes. It wanders across to Hugh, jumps up and curls against his thigh. He strokes the cat as he begins to talk.

'The Old Man was always out shooting – liked to go spotlighting at night for rabbits in the paddocks.' Hugh exhales, pauses, then takes a long breath. 'Well, anyway, one night when Alexander was about fourteen, the Old Man insisted he go out in the ute with him. Alexander arced up and Mum tried to stand up for him, but no-one refused our bloody father. He was a nasty bugger, especially when he'd been drinking, as was the case on the night he died.'

I'm lost in my thoughts, thinking about Alexander as a young kid being bullied by a person who should have loved him. Alexander's words echo in my head, when in Oxford he told me that Harrington-Jones was 'like my bloody father'. The light has faded in the room and outside the afternoon shadows have started to lengthen. The wood chopping has stopped and the mood in the neat lounge room has changed.

'If it's too upsetting …'

'We rarely talk about it … maybe we should have.' Hugh leans forward again. 'What happened that night was this – after dark Alexander and the Old Man set out for Coney's old farm, a few miles out of town. He and Coney were drinking mates and often went out shooting together. Coney was too sick to go out that night, but the Old Man insisted he and Alexander go anyway. Ned Coney later told the police that Alexander and his father again argued about going but as usual the Old Man got his way and they drove the ute down to the creek in the end paddock. About an hour later Alexander arrived back at Coney's place in a terrible state, crying and distressed. He told Coney his father was injured in the back of the ute down in the paddock. Coney called the ambulance but there wasn't anything anyone could do. Hours later the police took Alexander home and told Mum there had been an accident – the gun went off and the Old Man was dead.'

Hugh sighs. The cat stretches.

'Did Alexander ever talk about it to you or Martin?'

'Not much. He just kept saying the Old Man left his gun cocked and somehow it went off, the bullet went through his chest. The police agreed it was an accident.'

Hugh now looks uncomfortable and shifts in his seat. The cat moves from his side.

'And did you ever think ...?'

'No-one really knows what happened. Over the years we've wondered if there was more to it. It's a terrible thing to say but, to be honest, we were all relieved.'

Hugh's gaze is fixed on the window. Out of the corner of my eye I can see the lower branch of a flowering gum waving in the front yard, brushing the tip of the tin veranda.

'And what happened after?'

'Life was calmer than before, but still not happy. Mum was full of nerves and didn't go out much – thought the locals were gossiping about her and Alexander. She never really recovered from all the bad years. By then she had no friends and refused all offers of help and support made by her neighbours and the people in town. She basically hid in the house. But Alexander was bright: he finished high school and won a scholarship to university. Martin and I were both working in Sydney at the time and Alexander stayed with us for a year or two when he was studying. To support himself he worked in the early hours of the morning for the *Sydney Morning Herald* on their delivery vans. He was tough, Isabella. Always one to stand up for the rights of the workers. If he didn't like the way they were treated, he made sure it was known to management. But looking back, we recognise how he must have carried his anger just under the surface. Hated injustice and often thought he was being bullied when we couldn't see it. But despite that, we all thought he was doing well. He met Helen in his undergraduate years and married her when he started studying for his doctorate.'

'He must have been focused enough to get through his studies.'

'He was always able to achieve what he wanted. It wasn't until their son Michael was born that the real trouble began. He started drinking and behaving just like the Old Man. He had affairs with other women but somehow managed to hold down good lecturing positions. Helen told us it was like living with two different people. One was good and capable. The other, well ... Helen left several times and took Michael and Duncan to her parents outside Sydney. She was worried for the boys; they were witnessing too much.'

'And the see-saw behaviour continued!'

'Yes. I think you know the rest of the story, Isabella. They moved to Melbourne, but nothing changed. He promised Helen countless times he'd stop drinking but never did. The last straw for Helen was when he disappeared without telling her. And you know about that! And now ... now he's gone.' Hugh takes a handkerchief out of his pocket and dabs his nose before wiping his eyes.

I can hardly look at him.

'I shouldn't have gone to England with Alexander. He was married, but I was in love with him. I thought we had a future together. There are no excuses, Hugh. I also did the wrong thing.'

'No one blames you, Isabella. If it hadn't been you, it would have been someone else.'

Hugh's a good man, straightforward and honest.

'And you came back to Miles Creek, Hugh?'

'Only last year. I have a part-time job with the local timber mill. Mum wasn't doing well and with Alexander's death ... well, someone has to be here for her.'

***

When I leave Hugh's house, it's with a sense of connection, even if it is tentative, with Alexander's family. I would like to see him again. I would like Lilybeth to meet her uncle someday. And then there are her half-brothers Michael and Duncan, but that's for the future.

Chapter Seventy-Two

Issie

The cyclone wire cemetery gate squeaks as it swings open. The stillness broken, a flock of cockatoos in the tall gums nearby screech and surge skyward. The dirt path to the right leads to a tap on the corner, as described by Hugh. He offered to show me the way, but this is between Alexander and me. Four graves to the right, no headstone – only a metal stake that displays his name, A. Sadler, in red paint.

The sun is setting on the scorched earth of Alexander's grave; the ground surrounding it is parched and bare. The heaped grave still bears the now long-dead flowers from his burial weeks before. A covey of eastern rosellas glide past and alight in a small grevillea as I discard the dead flowers in a rubbish drum near the tap. The few sprigs of the scarlet bottle brush I placed on the grave look stark and alone in comparison. In the long shadow of the sun, I crouch beside Alexander's resting place, my thoughts vacillating between sadness and anger as I grapple to find the last words I need to express to him.

'I now realise how little we knew each other, Alexander. And yet we travelled to England together. We were attracted to each other, I'll give you that much, but we were so blind. Sailing away from the parts of our lives because they weren't right, hoping being somewhere else would magically resolve our discontent. It was wrong, what we did. I made a foolish choice, but you did so much more – you deceived Helen and your little boys. I know you were burdened but on one level you also knew what you were doing. No amount of sorrow or torment or anger in our past lives can excuse hurting others and yet, Alexander, that's what you did.'

A breeze touches my face, bringing with it an eerie sense of calm. I turn to him again.

'I heard about your father – your stepfather. A dreadful man without a soul. I also heard about your real father, Paddy O'Connell; he sounded like a good man. I wish you'd known him, Alexander; it was a tragedy you didn't. I don't know what happened that awful night at Coney's farm, but whatever happened, you weren't to blame. At least, no one blames you, Alexander; you were only a kid.'

As I whisper a final goodbye, silent tears run down my cheeks and dry into my neck. It's not exactly grief, but sadness for a tangled life, a life that could have been so different.

Chapter Seventy-Three

Issie

Mother's office was once Pa Joseph's all those years ago. After Pa Joseph died, Mother left it empty for over a year before she felt she could use it. Perhaps she thought he might appear at any moment, sit behind his large desk and all would be the same again. I couldn't understand it at the time, but I now appreciate the sentiments behind Mother's ongoing respect for her father's achievements. She allowed Pa Joseph's office to be a shrine to her father's memory, at least until she believed she had earned the privilege to sit at his desk.

The old, lacquered chairs, the faded Chinese paintings on the pale walls collecting Melbourne dust – this space holds precious memories of a man who dared to forge a life in a foreign country. Nothing has changed here except for Mother's framed university degree, which hangs next to her father's.

Danny and I glance at each other as we sit down and wait for her to reveal the reason for the meeting with her and Father.

'There's not much point in stretching this conversation out,' she says. 'I'm going to fully retire from the practice. I'm sure you've been anticipating this news.'

There's an unusual shrill edge to her laugh as she fiddles with the worn jade handle of Pa Joseph's letter opener. Her eyes rest on Father for support. Danny is quiet, waiting for me to speak first.

'Is this a bit sudden, Mother?'

'It's right for me and right for the practice. You and Daniel are running the place and are more than competent to do so. No, Isabella, it's not sudden. In fact, you have actually allowed me to make the decision.'

'How –'

'If you hadn't returned to Australia, it would have been impossible. And then there's Lilybeth. I want to spend as much time with her as possible. Children grow up so quickly.'

'And it's your health as well, Lily. Your doctor says you have to do less,' says Father.

'Yes, of course, but it's time for change as well,' she says.

Mother has never liked to talk about her own needs or how she's feeling and today is no exception. She wants to get the detail sorted without fuss.

'Mother, this is a huge decision. For you and for us ...'

The Chinese wall hanging with its faded gold fringe catches my eye. Pa Joseph once told me he brought it with him from Hiyang, his birthplace in China. It was his good luck charm, a link between East and West, a daily reminder of how respect for the past ensures opportunities in the future.

'All things change, Isabella.' A comfortable smile settles on Mother's face. She's over the fragile moment of telling us she's retiring from her life's work. And we all know Mother well – when a decision is made, she knows exactly how to execute it.

'When is this going to happen?' I ask.

'Next month. But before we work out those details, there is another matter to settle.' Father uncrosses his legs, Mother sits upright. 'It's time for you to become a full partner in the firm, Isabella. You and Daniel, joint partners.'

Danny's face has broken into a broad, delighted smile. Mother watches me, her dark eyes unblinking. Father is smiling, his beautifully groomed grey hair shimmering in the lamp light.

'I don't know what to say. It's unexpected ... I'm thrilled you want me to do this, Mother.'

'There is nothing more to say. It's your right now, Isabella. It was always intended you would take over from me. Three generations, hopefully four when it's Lilybeth's turn.'

Tears slide down my face as Danny gets up and hugs me. Father winks at me just as he did when I was a kid and in trouble with Mother. Behind her desk, Mother is still holding Pa Joseph's letter opener and Father is smiling at her. The moment is monumental for them, and me. Something important has shifted between us and the problems of the last years are truly relegated to the past.

'Let's not get ahead of ourselves. Lilybeth has her life ahead of her and may well choose another path,' I say.

'She may, but one never knows,' says Mother quietly.

Mother stands and steps from behind her desk and hands me the letter opener. It's warm in my hand and the carved handle is smooth from wear.

'This came with your grandfather from Canton. It's yours now, for good luck.'

Chapter Seventy-Four

Issie

At kindergarten, Lilybeth's friend Eloise tells her that everyone has a daddy.

'Well, yes, but not everyone knows who their father is, Lilybeth,' I say when I pick her up one afternoon.

'Eloise says my daddy must be in England because I was *borned* in England.'

'Born. Yes, you were born in England. But you don't have a daddy there.'

A look of confusion crosses Lilybeth's little face. I know this can't go on for much longer; she's smart and already she's questioning why her family is different from most of her little friends'.

But how can I tell her? What do I tell her? Danny thinks I should deal with it before she gets any older.

'It's not just telling her Alexander is her father, it's explaining she'll never be able to meet him. And how can I tell her that the "daddy man" who took her to the park and the hotel really was her daddy? It seems so cruel.'

'It's hard, but it might be harder in the future. She will soon realise you're not telling her the truth.'

'I can't tell her he's dead. I just can't.'

'No, but you can't keep denying she had a father. For now, at least, you can acknowledge this.'

***

It's a perfect Melbourne day. Still and sunny with the freshness of early morning. Lilybeth is skipping ahead as we walk the two blocks to the park. Saturday mornings have become our time, Lilybeth's and mine. Lilybeth insists on having a turn on all the swings in the park. Sometimes, others have the same idea. As she stands in line, she chats to other children and is the first to laugh at the funny antics of the kids around her. Occasionally, she glances over at me, but she shows no signs of needing me by her side. She loves the big slide that only the older children are allowed to use. I smile to myself at her look of concentration as she climbs the metal ladder to the top. She wriggles into position and when she's ready she throws her hands in the air and lets herself go. Her curly hair splays out behind her as she descends toward a perfect feet-first landing. She looks for me and throws me a grin as big as the sky.

After the swings, we buy the promised ice creams at the milk bar across from the park. Lilybeth always bargains to have a double header. 'I promise I won't spill it, Mummy.' Today I give in to her request without hesitation. She orders one scoop of chocolate and one of strawberry. I have a single vanilla.

'Let's find a seat while we eat our ice creams,' I suggest as Lilybeth marvels at the cone in her hand. We stroll back to the park with our ice creams.

'I like strawberry the best of all,' says Lilybeth as we sit on a vacant park bench. She frantically licks the edges of her cone so it doesn't drip down the front of her gingham dress.

'That's not hard to guess, Lilybeth.'

'Chocolate's my second best. Eloise likes chocolate the best.'

'Lilybeth, remember when you asked about your daddy?'

'I don't have a daddy.'

'Well, actually you do.'

Lilybeth turns to me and as she does, the chocolate ice cream drips onto the bodice of her dress. It soaks into the blue and white fabric, causing the beginning of a murky stain. There's no breeze and we've chosen a bench in the sun. My hands are perspiring, and I wish I didn't have a sodden ice cream cone in my hand. The sun now has a sting to it and Lilybeth's face is flushed.

'But you said I didn't have a daddy.' She's licking her ice cream again and swinging her legs under the seat, scuffing the tips of her shoes on the fine gravel as she does.

'Well, you don't have a daddy who lives with us.'

There's a dribble of melted strawberry ice cream sliding down Lilybeth's wrist. She quickly catches it and wriggles further back into the seat.

'Lilybeth, you did have a daddy in England.' I take a deep breath. She continues to lick her ice cream, but her legs have stopped swinging.

'In England. Where I was *borned*?'

'Born. Yes, sort of.'

'Is he still in England? Eloise says –'

'No. He met you once, here in Australia.'

'You mean the daddy man who took me to the park?'

'Yes.'

'He gave me biscuits and a box of Smarties.'

'Yes.'

She tilts her head to the side, her golden-brown curls falling to her shoulder. Her eyes are questioning. I see it clearly this time, the likeness to Alexander.

'Will I see him again?' Chocolate ice cream drips onto her gathered skirt.

'No.'

Her little face frowns for a few seconds before she wriggles in her seat and begins to swing her legs once more. She looks toward the other children lining up for their turn on the big slide.

'Mummy, after we finish our ice creams, can we go back to the swings?'

Chapter Seventy-Five

Eliza

Lily has managed Eliza's financial affairs for years and has always carried them out in a thorough and respectful manner. But now, with Lily retiring, Eliza wants Isabella to deal with the details. Besides, there are a few changes she wants to make.

'Best you come to my house, Isabella. I'm too old to be getting on the tram to come into the office.'

'Of course, I'll come to you, but what's this "getting old" talk all about?'

'One day you'll understand.'

For the last year, Eliza has been feeling less and less active; her knees constantly ache and she's not as sure-footed as she once was. She hasn't mentioned it to the family, but she has toppled over twice in the last month, luckily close enough to a chair to pull herself up again. These mishaps have made her wary. Despite a chat with old Doctor Spence who told her there's nothing wrong, she's not herself and knows it. If this is what old age is, she's not sure she cares for it.

She's dozing in the warmth of the front window when she hears the doorbell chime. For a moment she's disoriented but then remembers where she is: she's waiting for Isabella to arrive. She moves slowly into the passageway.

'What kept you, Nan Eliza? I rang three times.'

'Sorry, Isabella. I must have nodded off.'

Isabella frowns at Eliza before giving her a kiss on the cheek and stepping past her with two bulging folders.

'When did you start sleeping in the daytime? These files are heavy, Nan Eliza. Probably time to have a good sort out.'

Eliza pulls herself up to full height. 'The purpose of our meeting is not just to sort things out, but to make some significant changes. Let's get a cuppa and then we can discuss it.'

Eliza gathers cups and saucers from the sideboard as Isabella puts the kettle on.

'Are you feeling unwell?' Isabella asks her.

Eliza smiles to herself. It's always been difficult to hide anything from her granddaughter. Isabella's always had good intuition. Except when it came to Alexander.

'Not exactly, just a little tired. But Doctor Spence says there's nothing wrong with me and I suppose he should know.'

They take the tea tray and files to the dining room.

'I want some changes,' Eliza says and pours the tea. 'One of the changes I want is to hand over my late husband's charities to his younger sons in China. They are ready and responsible to carry on his legacy. I have some notes here, all the information you need.'

'But you've left instructions for when you, well, when you are no longer with us, Nan Eliza.'

'I want them to start now. Why wait until I'm dead?'

'Any reason?'

'It's time for them to take on their father's legacy. It's overdue. I also want to let go of the responsibility.'

'And the second change?' Isabella brings her cup to her lips.

'My estate. I want to leave it to three charities and to Lilybeth. It's to be divided equally between them. Here is the list of the charities.' Eliza examines her granddaughter's face, so beloved to her. 'You might ask why you are not included, Isabella, but I think you already know the reason. You have a substantial inheritance to come from your parents and it was Aunt Hattie's gift to you that allowed you to remain in England.'

Isabella reaches for Eliza's hand and presses softly. 'I have no questions about it, Nan Eliza. You've always been more than generous to me. I'm grateful to you for Lilybeth. She is a fortunate girl.'

***

Eliza remains in her seat next to the window and watches the clouds on the horizon and the day closing in. The streetlights come on, glimmering into the evening. Today, sitting with Isabella reminded her of her own days in China when she was full of energy and optimism setting up the orphanages. Eliza also recalls the years with Fong Choon and the sudden meeting with her son, Knill. She smiles when she remembers Isabella's surprise on the doorstep of Ester House in Bermondsey when she visited unannounced. And then there was the joy of meeting her great-granddaughter.

No-one in their family has escaped hardship over the years, but it's the fight for survival that's made them strong and she's grateful. Eliza also knows she's not strong anymore. She is an old woman now and her days are drawing to a close.

Chapter Seventy-Six

Issie

It's Sunday afternoon and Danny has organised a picnic basket. For once, it's just the two of us going to St Kilda beach. Lilybeth is excited to be going to Eloise's party and it certainly rates higher than a beach visit today.

Mid-afternoon, the sky is threatening with storm clouds rolling in across the bay.

'No beaches like this in England,' jokes Danny.

'Pebbles, striped deck chairs and not enough sunshine. I miss the place though, the people and the quirky way they do things. Well, quirky to me, not to them.'

'Being in England was a special time for you, Issie. Somehow, I think it was destiny that took you away. You needed to be away from here to become your true self.'

'All this talk of destiny is a bit heavy for a Sunday afternoon, Danny.' I turn to face him. 'I'm not sure I became my real self, got into a real mess, though.' We are sitting in Danny's car watching the ocean. The windows are wound down and the salty air is on my cheeks. Danny is staring across the bay and his hair is ruffled by sea breeze.

'You're a bit hard on yourself, Issie. Always have been.'

'Well, Danny, you weren't the one who ran away when the going got tough. When your mother was sick, demanded your attention and barely let you have a day to yourself. No, you stayed, did the right thing. Endured.'

Danny turns to me now. The grey of his eyes deepens as he becomes serious.

'I did think of going away after my father died, Issie. Yes, I felt an obligation to my mother, but I'm no saint. There were plenty of moments when I deeply resented her claim on my time and my life. But I had my work.'

'Where did you think of going?'

'Sydney. Even applied for a couple of jobs after you went to London, but I hoped you'd return.' A pause. Danny's gaze returns to the bay. 'I waited for you, you know.'

'But … I was gone for six years. Surely you didn't …'

'Not exactly. There were other girls. Like Carol. She lived in South Melbourne, close to the Lake Oval. She was a nurse at the Royal Melbourne Hospital, but it didn't work out. The thing going for the relationship was her two brothers; they were Swans supporters.'

The mood breaks and we laugh. I slap him on the arm, marvelling at Danny's ability to be serious and then funny at the same time. He lights up two cigarettes and hands one to me. We sit quietly now, enjoying our time. The clouds have blown over and the sun is glistening on the water. Danny stubs his Rothmans in the car ashtray.

'Isabella, can we talk, really talk about us?'

Although we've been spending constant time together, stealing time alone and generally flirting with each other, we have never talked about what is going on between us. I adore Danny and love being with him, but somehow I'm frightened to step closer – don't trust myself anymore. I stub my cigarette and turn to him.

'What do we need to talk about?'

'Maybe the past and the present.'

'You mean England?'

'I can't imagine how difficult these last years were for you. But despite the bad things that happened with Alexander, you were obviously mad about the bloke to leave with him the way you did.'

'At the time I don't think I had any idea of the risk I was taking. One thing's for sure, I'm not mad about him anymore.'

'But my point is, Isabella, he was your first real love.'

The waves lap onto the shore and small children are frolicking along the water's edge. Seagulls caw as they swoop and dive from above as Danny's words take effect. He's right, Alexander was my first love. And my first crippling step toward adulthood.

'My first disastrous love.'

'No one can replace that first heady love, and I would never try. All I have to offer is forever love, Isabella. I've always loved you, always will.'

He's holding my hand now and I'm staring at his handsome face, the square jaw line, the half-smile, and his trusting eyes waiting for my reaction. All I want to do is cry.

'Danny, you're the most beautiful person I know, my best friend, and of course I'll always love you.'

'So, marry me then, Isabella.'

'Marry you? You want to marry me? Seriously, Danny?'

'Yep, never been more serious about anything.'

'I ...'

He pulls me to him. I fit so easily into the shape of his body. My heart is beating erratically, but my body is still, perfectly relaxed; my mind is free from doubt.

'I'll marry you, Danny, if you'll marry me. Will you marry me?'

'I will, Issie McMillan.'

CHAPTER SEVENTY-SEVEN

ISSIE

The Christmas tree in the waiting room is laden with tinsel and shiny baubles. Lilybeth helped Lucy decorate it last week, the two of them singing carols and laughing together. It was a joy to watch providing you didn't catch a glimpse of Audrey's face. It's three days until Christmas. Lucy, who loves Christmas, has also decorated the office and gone a 'bit overboard', according to Audrey. Lucy then taught Lilybeth to make paper chains, which now decorate the front counter but not too close to Audrey's desk.

Mother and Father invited Audrey to spend Christmas Day with our family given she is from Sydney, but she's to have lunch with a distant aunt in Brighton. Lucy, on the other hand, needed no invitation. She's spending the day with her large family and will travel to Geelong on Christmas morning to be part of their traditional celebrations. She's been talking about it for weeks.

Danny's been working late into the evenings for the past two weeks and I've been coming in early to keep up with the last of the client instructions before we close. We are looking forward to time away from the office. We've booked a beach house in Lorne for a week's holiday. Lilybeth has new bathers and a beach towel already packed in the beach bag given to her by Nan Eliza for her birthday.

Christmas Day is to be a simple event, except nothing Mother does is simple. It will end up being a beautiful lunch with all the trimmings. Just the six of us: Mother, Father, Danny, Nan Eliza, Lilybeth and me. Mother and Father have found a new lease on life since Danny and I announced our engagement. They were ecstatic at the news, even surprising the two of us. Champagne and tears.

Lilybeth has sent several letters to Santa Claus and is beside herself with excitement.

'How will he fit a bicycle down the chimney?' she wants to know.

'You'll have to wait until Christmas Day to see if he brings you a bicycle,' I say. 'It all depends on if you've been good enough.'

'I've been good, really good. I've helped Pa and Ma in the garden, and I don't interrupt when the grown-ups are talking.'

We all laugh, because one of Lilybeth's most annoying habits is interrupting any conversation.

'We'll see on Christmas morning.'

'A bike can't fit down a chimney, can it?'

'Santa has his special ways, Lilybeth.'

***

It's Christmas Eve and we are almost finished and ready to close up for the holidays. Danny appears in the doorway, closes the door behind him and comes behind my desk. He kisses my cheek and ruffles my new hair style.

'My very own Cilla Black.'

I straighten it and we laugh. I had no idea cutting my hair would have such an impact on those around me. All my life I've had long hair, halfway down my back. Not anymore. It's now short and sleek. Lilybeth shrieked when she saw it and Mother and Father were speechless. Audrey raised her eyebrows and resumed typing, but I saw her sneaking another look as I walked away. Danny teases me but I know he approves.

'Let's have a quick smoke break,' Danny says and grabs my hand. Outside the back door, he lights up and I have a few puffs on his Rothmans. We both hide our smoking from Mother and Father and particularly Lilybeth. Audrey knows we have the occasional cigarette. She disapproves, but she can be trusted to be tight-lipped. It's something I admire about Audrey: despite her solemn views on most matters, she can be relied upon to stay quiet. When I said this to Danny, he laughed and said she has no need to say anything, her facial expressions say it for her.

Mother arrives with Lilybeth and a plate of Christmas cake and mince pies. In her basket she has Christmas presents for Audrey and Lucy.

'Where is Father?' I ask.

'He'll be here shortly. He's doing some last-minute messages,' says Mother.

Audrey and Lucy are clearing their desks and the filing cabinets are locked.

'Must be time for drinks and mince pies,' says Danny, rubbing his hands together with a look of relief.

'And time for Christmas presents for Audrey and Lucy,' says Lilybeth, who can't wait to hand over the presents she helped Mother wrap.

'Let's just wait a few minutes for Grandpa,' says Mother.

As we all move to the kitchen, the doorbell sounds. Danny goes out to let Father in.

'He's here now. Drinks can begin,' I say.

Nan Eliza appears ahead of Father.

'Nan Eliza. What a lovely surprise,' I say, and kiss her cheek. 'I didn't know you were coming.'

'Isabella, there's someone in the waiting room asking for you,' says Father.

'Now? I thought we'd locked the front door? Start the drinks – I'll be right back.' But everyone trails out after me.

In the waiting room is a woman with her head turned toward the window. She's tall and wearing a paisley shift dress above her knees. By her side is a matching green handbag.

'Can I help you?'

The others are behind me as the woman slowly turns. For a split second there's confusion and then I'm looking into the smiling face of my dearest friend, Neva.

'Aunty Neva!' Lilybeth runs past me and throws herself at Neva.

'I can't believe this. When? How? Neva, we've missed you so much!'

Chapter Seventy-Eight

Issie

Neva and I sit on the slatted seat in the garden, underneath the drooping branches of the old peppercorn tree. Mother dislikes this peppercorn tree and she and Father have been at odds over its existence for many years. Father takes the view, it's been here for decades, serving a good purpose, why disturb it now?

It's a hot day but there's a light breeze, just enough for the branches of the tree to quiver. Lilybeth has gone to the park with Father; his patience is endless when it's anything to do with his only granddaughter. Mother left earlier to collect Nan Eliza for the Boxing Day recital at St Paul's Cathedral. She'd persuaded her to go along despite Nan Eliza's protests about feeling too tired.

'The look on your face was priceless, Issie,' says Neva.

'I couldn't believe it was really you. And Lilybeth's shrieks of excitement, I've never seen her so exuberant.'

'She's doing so well, Issie. Oh, how I've missed you two.'

Neva flew into Melbourne and to keep the surprise, stayed at Nan Eliza's. The next day, Father picked up Nan Eliza and Neva and drove them to the office.

'It was the best Christmas surprise ever.'

'Lachlan insisted I come. After all, having a godchild in Australia is a good enough reason for anyone. Lachlan's brother Harold is unwell again, but Lachlan promises he'll be here for the next visit. I took some convincing to come alone, though. As you know, Issie, I've never travelled outside England before.'

'And Father, he was in on it all along?'

'Lachlan contacted your father and the two of them made the arrangements.'

'I can't believe someone didn't give the plot away. Not telling Lilybeth was a smart move.'

'She's such an amazing little girl. And she's very settled here. It seems your decision to come home to Australia was the right one for her. What about you, Issie?'

'Ha, that's taken quite a time to reconcile. You know I loved living in London, Neva. I had you, Jack and Esme, dear Victor, and my job. And you know how much I enjoyed working with Lachlan and Thomas. And being there to keep an eye on Victor was something I wanted to do. I did it for Nancy as well. She would have felt relieved to know Victor was being looked after. But being so far away from home had its difficult side as well.'

Neva fills our glasses with iced tea, though the ice has melted in the warmth of the afternoon.

'Nothing stays cold in Australia.' Neva laughs as she hands me a glass. 'So, any regrets?'

'No real regrets, Neva, but I guess there was a fear I'd lose my new self. A self I fought hard for in London. I'm not the same person who left here all those years earlier. England and all that happened there changed me. Really changed me. Coming home was a big gamble but I owed Mother and Father a chance to be grandparents and Lilybeth deserved family around her as well.' Neva stretches her legs and flicks her newly styled short hair. 'I knew I'd have to guard against losing my new self, but what I hadn't realised was, Mother and Father had also changed. And life here, as I recalled it from six years ago, had moved on, it had changed.'

'Except for one thing.' Neva pokes me in the side. 'Danny was under your nose the whole time.' Neva pretends to fan herself. 'So handsome ... so smart ...'

I poke her back; I can't keep a smile from my face.

'Danny is the best part about being home. Love must be grounded, not crazy infatuation. He's intelligent and funny, he is strong and dependable as well. I'm so fortunate and so is Lilybeth. He's the husband I never thought I would have. And the father figure that Lilybeth deserves.'

'The exact opposite to Alexander?' The breeze has picked up and a passing cloud has temporarily blocked the afternoon sun. Neva tucks her knees under her chin as she waits for me to reply.

'You haven't lost the knack of asking the hard questions.' We laugh. 'But you are right. Danny is all the things Alexander couldn't be. I don't think about Oxford so much now. But, Neva, I've promised myself I will never, ever allow myself to be in a situation like that again.'

If I'd stayed with Alexander, I think I would have eventually taken on the grief of Mrs Sadler, Alexander's mother. A life gutted of purpose and hope. Making excuses and hoping against hope he would or could change. There is still a bit of me who believes, deep down, that Alexander wasn't a bad person. In a strange way I'm pleased he saw Lilybeth. I can't talk about it to anyone, though. I keep the thought deep inside where I know it belongs.

Beside Mother's pots of pink and milky-mauve petunias, Neva and I continue to enjoy our tea. It seems so long ago when I left for England. Full of foolish anticipation about being somewhere other than home. I try not to linger on the Oxford times, but I do think often about how lucky I was to have met the people I did.

'If it hadn't been for you, Neva. Looking after me and packing me off to Bermondsey.'

Neva laughs. 'I wasn't too sure about sending you to Ester House, I have to say. Nancy and Victor had their own idiosyncrasies. It could have gone either way, but your presence seemed to provide them with a positive slant on life. You and Jack.'

A pang of affection combined with sadness floods in. All those mornings spent cleaning the house, the endless cups of tea, listening to Nancy telling stories about the people in the street, the shopkeepers, her family, and grumbling about Victor with his annoying habits. And Victor, sneaking out the back for his cigarettes, not wanting Nancy to know how many he'd smoked each day.

'They were good to me, Neva.'

'And Victor will always cherish the time he had with you and Lilybeth. And speaking of Victor, I have something for you.'

Neva comes back from the house with a parcel and places it beside me. It's a box wrapped in brown paper. As I peel back the paper and lift the lid, my heart misses a beat. It's Nancy's special crystal vase, once her mother's, the one she kept high on the shelf in the back room at Tolley Street and wouldn't let anyone touch.

'Victor was insistent you have it. He thought of sending her prized cup and saucer, but even for you he couldn't part with them. The next-precious thing was this vase. They loved you, Issie, and for a short time in their lives they had something meaningful to focus on: Issie Mac and her beautiful baby.'

We sit in the dappled shade, two friends who have shared the bad times, now enjoying the good times together. I sigh as I stretch in the wooden seat. I can't believe my luck to have Neva here beside me again. She's wearing white pedal pushers and a sleeveless guipure top bought in Oxford Street, especially for her visit to Australia. The sun is warm against my skin and for a few moments I'm back there by the River Thames in Iffley where we chatted so intently, we'd forget the time and have to run all the way back to the office. Neva's little flat, with her English teacups and tiny kitchen. My luck was high the day I met Neva.

Lilybeth's and Father's voices float toward us from the side path of the house. Lilybeth is asking Father about swimming in the ocean and whether it's different from swimming in a swimming pool. Father chuckles and begins to tell her about the waves and how to catch them. 'Don't worry, Lilybeth,' he says, 'your mum and Danny will teach you.'

'Grandpa, will I be able to swim to England?'

ACKNOWLEDGEMENTS

To my wonderful prereaders of an early version of *Issie Mac*, Denise Chapman, Fran Quigley, Jane Vanderstoel and Linda Young. Your feedback, ongoing support and friendship is invaluable.

My writing colleagues, Dr Jill Blee and Dr Karen Sparnon, thank you for your wise input along the way; it kept me going when the going got tough, as it did from time to time!

Heartfelt gratitude to the late Barbara Howard 1935-2020. Her amazing stories and recollections of London where she was a young midwife in the 1950s proved priceless to parts of this story. Our coffee shop meetings were an inspiration.

Thank you to my dear friends Rev John Minotti and Gayee Minotti who broadened my understanding of the Anglican Church's hierarchy and customs. Any errors are mine.

For Alison Arnold, my trusted and clever editor who makes all the difference; Alison, you are so appreciated.

To Dr Jason Nahrung, for your expert and professional input. Jason, you inspire and enrich my writing space.

A shout out to my 'discussion group' who contribute to my world of reading, writing and philosophical debate. To Linda, Frank, Maureen, Jen, Elisabeth and Rhonda, you people are the best.

Thanks to Sarah and Toby from The Rural Publishing Company for making *Issie Mac* happen.

For Emma Harrington, Director of M Manze Pie and Mash, Tower Bridge Road, London, thank you for your generous agreement for the use of your family historical photo on the front of my book.

To my readership of *Finding Eliza* and my extended family and friends, thanks for giving me encouragement to write *Issie Mac*. And a prod when I lingered!

Andrew and Sophie, Ben and Chimmi, the family I'm so fortunate to have.

To my husband, Kevin, who has been more than supportive with this book and who has taught me to never give up.

About the Author

Heather Whitford Roche

Heather Whitford Roche lives in Ballarat, Victoria. She is also the author of *Finding Eliza* published in 2018.

A family therapist for over thirty years, Heather is married with two adult sons. *Issie Mac* is her second novel.